Conceived the morning after VE
and educated in London. He wo
ical engineer for thirty-four yea
acknowledged UK specialist in t
missile propulsion systems. Retii
and following a period of consult
writes full time while living in a village between Bath and Bristol.

Following the success of *an unknown soldier* published in 2017, this is his second publication with SilverWood Books.

Also by Peter Morse

an unknown soldier

random consequences

random
consequences
peter morse

SilverWood

Published in 2018 by SilverWood Books

SilverWood Books Ltd
14 Small Street, Bristol, BS1 1DE, United Kingdom
www.silverwoodbooks.co.uk

Copyright © Peter Morse 2018

The right of Peter Morse to be identified as the author of this
work has been asserted in accordance with the Copyright, Designs
and Patents Act 1988 Sections 77 and 78.

All rights reserved. No part of this publication may be reproduced,
stored in a retrieval system, or transmitted in any form or by any means,
electronic, mechanical, photocopying, recording or otherwise,
without prior permission of the copyright holder.

This is a work of fiction. Names, characters, places and incidents
either are products of the author's imagination or are used fictitiously.
Any resemblance to actual events or locales or persons,
living or dead, is entirely coincidental.

ISBN 978-1-78132-782-1 (paperback)
ISBN 978-1-78132-783-8 (ebook)

British Library Cataloguing in Publication Data
A CIP catalogue record for this book is available from the British Library

Page design and typesetting by SilverWood Books
Printed on responsibly sourced paper

*In nature there are no rewards or punishments;
there are consequences.*

before

one

Doing nothing wasn't easy. Doing very little was harder, much harder. You knew where you were doing nothing.

He'd done very little for the past few days and was exhausted from the effort. Moving a leg, he felt for the floor with a foot. The wood felt unnaturally warm. Sunlight. He rolled off the sofa, walked in the direction of the kitchen and made coffee. His watch suggested the hour. Checking with the cooker confirmed it was 3pm; it was an early start, still light.

Simon turned on the radio and caught the end of the news. The world did not seem to have advanced particularly since his last occupation.

He sat, coffee in hand, and focused his eyes on the floor. It was, as he remembered, a Tuesday. Each day of the week had its own particular significance. Today was the evening to put out the rubbish and the recycling box, ready for collection the following morning. Wednesday was remembering to collect his twice-weekly milk from beyond the front door before the birds, or the weather, got to it. Other days, other trivia. It was good to have a pattern to one's life, however trite. Between mugs of coffee, he collected the post and the newspapers. His day had begun.

It had not progressed much before he caught himself staring at the far wall. It was beginning to become a habit of his, staring at walls; restful certainly, but somehow unfortunate. Simon shifted his gaze, first to the floor and then, by way of the ceiling, to another wall. This one had a window and he stared out of it. The wind had got up and it was starting to rain. The weather suited his mood. An early promise, not fulfilled.

So far, it had been an uninspiring week. That little was likely to suggest itself as an improvement began to depress him. He knew there should be more, but he lacked the motivation or the interest to stir himself beyond a casual expectation. Exploration would require an effort that he seemed to be unable to muster. After a final glance at the weather, he returned to browsing through what remained of the papers.

Simon had developed the habit of laziness. That by choice he was no longer forced to transport himself twenty-odd miles every morning to a place of permanent employment to earn a living had, in part, been disastrous. An important discipline had been removed, and not replaced. Instead of the new freedom acting as some kind of liberator, it had become the opposite. Bewildered by choice, he had become inhibited.

It was, however, a well-informed inhibition. Thorough reading of three heavy newspapers, mixed with a diet of Radio 4, saw to that. Little that was reported escaped him. But that only served to increase his feelings of isolation and inaction. Surrounded by so much that was obviously wrong he felt somehow responsible, and too conscious of his impotence to wreak any worthwhile or lasting change. It led him into long periods of introspection, the detachment varying in degree with mood. He felt both vulnerable and culpable. It was a confusing mixture, neither reactive nor proactive: suspended. An ability to care, transfixed by an inability to change.

Simon gave up his unequal struggle with the papers and returned his eyes to the window. The rain continued, disturbing the cobwebs.

A spider appeared on a web and he watched it. Life must be considerably simplified if one were an insect, he reasoned. Non-sentient organisms had four primary responses to external stimuli: fight or flee, feed or fuck, and in the case of certain spiders, fuck then feed. Human society was considered more complicated; there were many more choices. For example, should he engage it in polite conversation by enquiring of its health? Received wisdom might suggest a greater level of complexity and sophistication, but there were times when he wondered. The basics never seemed to change.

The environment was hostile, and so was most that lived within it. The veneer of civilisation was tragically thin, as was, Simon had realised, his understanding of it.

The passing months of his imposed idleness had proved salutary. Ample opportunity, ample time alone for recollection and reflection. The spirit, the harshest critic of the soul. Simon had managed to reduce what passed for a life's achievement to very little; inconsequential heaps of mostly ashes.

Major faults many, virtues few. Nothing destroyed the ego more thoroughly than inward criticism. It was rare for him to distance himself so far from the self. Crept out from within the accustomed shell, it displayed little charm. To be always honest had sometimes proved a trial to those around him. Being unable to lie to himself was hard. And having always to view from the inside out had become a constant strain. He envied those who seemed to have the knack of outside in. They appeared to have more to share, more to give.

What he could offer was always complicated by thought and doubt. Always the self, standing on the path, the leg extended to trip and then mock the effort.

On days of quiet depression he doubted his remaining energy, his ability, or even inclination, to jump. And there was no one to blame but himself. And, in the meantime, he could not grow. The potential: promised, not fulfilled.

Tuesdays, he thought ruefully, were beginning to be a disappointment. Mondays were still favoured, the recurring relief of not having to rise at some ungodly hour to go to work. But, by Tuesday, reality had begun to set in. Perhaps it was simply one of nature's laws, like never being able to fold up a piece of paper more than seven times without resorting to a vice and hammer.

The basic process was simple enough; the effective thickness of the paper doubling with each fold, the applied leverage halving. But, from his brief experiments with several sizes and weights of paper, the possible folds stayed resolutely stuck at seven. He chose not to be irritated; there was something almost reassuring about being defeated by something quite so simple.

He collected up the discarded paper and tossed it in the general direction of the bin, beginning another assault on the newspapers. His coffee had gone cold but he drank it anyway. The clouds and rain had cleared and the sun seemed to be declaring an intention of more than a passing visit. It had the makings of one of those spring evenings that people used to write songs about. He stood up and walked to the window, looking up higher into the sky, wondering what to do with the remaining day.

He leant on the windowsill, disturbing the dust. The avoidance of housework was a subject on which he'd accidentally become something of an expert. A quick vacuum every couple of months and the occasional dusting were about the extent of his efforts.

It happened that there had been several extended periods when he had lived by himself. They were not entirely by choice, but circumstance and geography had so affected, and, partly as a consequence his effort and inclination towards housework had eroded. It helped that he was relatively tidy. The natural clutter of one who dealt with things mostly on paper was collected in specific areas, care being taken to leave clear paths around most items of furniture. Similarly, waste bins and other areas of scrap were regularly emptied and serviced. A protracted effort of perhaps five minutes a week.

But the real secret he'd discovered was to avoid plain carpets: they showed everything. Unplain carpet, the merest hint of pattern or fleck would do, buried a multitude of inconsequential litter. Plain wood, faintly uneven, was almost as good.

It always amused Simon how acquaintances, when visiting the house, would invariably remark on how tidy and clean it looked. He would, naturally, demur, mutter something appropriate and reflect that his natural reaction on hearing the doorbell ring was to run up the stairs to the bathroom and pour copious amounts of bleach down the lavatory, just in case. Their problem was that they always equated an apparent tidiness with cleanliness. The house might be superficially tidy, but he could never describe it as clean. More like a pervading, but healthy, patina of filth.

He stood back and examined the marks in the dust. The Quentin

Crisp principle stated that dust ceased to thicken after about four years. Perhaps he should get a cleaning woman before he found out, a woman who does. He corrected his thought: a cleaning person.

With a final glance at the sky, Simon returned to the sofa. You could buy time, but you couldn't defeat it. He had bought time, and now he was only conscious of its passing. Time was limited and he was continuing to waste it.

The first few weeks had passed pleasantly enough. But he had soon done most of the things he had listed to do and, with those done, the others seemed unimportant. He still managed to get up most mornings, he filled his time, but it was without conviction. It passed, but he wasn't using it. Before, others had made more effective use of his time, and rewarded him for it. With time his own, there seemed to be little compensation or satisfaction, and the freedom merely confused him further.

A wealth of opportunity beckoned, but little seemed to interest him. He had allowed himself the time, the luxury to think, and the thoughts had depressed him. And once the mood was set, the little that happened around him did nothing but confirm it.

It was a dangerous thing, time. Unused it manacled the will.

Simon was getting older, visibly. Twenty-five had marked the first registered ending. A lot of things had been supposedly over at twenty-five. Youth, and with it, youthful hope. It hadn't been true: one didn't so much lose the hope, more became tired of the waiting. And the powers of rationalisation increased. Given enough time one could justify any amount of failure, inability and sloth.

Early middle age, he'd decided. The Middle Ages, that part of his old history textbook that had been preceded by the Dark Ages. A time of ferment, little known, the lowland before the scaling of the later peaks. Optimism demanded such illusion. It could be that the heights were long ago ascended; he could be on the long freewheel to the sea.

Most people who had occupied the planet had died long before reaching his age. Now, with modern medicine's ever accelerating prowess, he could live another thirty, forty years. Forty years was more than he could comfortably remember. The thought appalled him. So much future, so little past accommodated.

And while his body was ageing, it was as nothing compared to the constituents. Every atom of his body was as old as the universe, much used before his transient stewardship. Beyond his decomposition, the parts again far greater than the whole. Nothing wasted.

Getting older was something that couldn't be taught, only experienced. An ambivalent process. While some things became so much easier, others became ridiculously harder. Dependent upon the individual conceits, growing older could be either an enabling or humbling experience. Occasionally, it could be both.

It was the fate of most to spend their lives doing what they had to do whilst pretending it was what they wanted to do. Lives lived by dictated circumstance. It was a common experience and nothing, however promised, had changed it.

Simon did not have their ready excuses. There was little, almost nothing, that he had to do. His life could be, within reason, whatever he chose it to be. The ties and responsibilities had been avoided. He recognised no boundaries and there were no accidents of fate, nemeses, to restrain him. It was a position to be envied by those denied it.

But freedom brought its own, peculiar, responsibilities. An inverse growth, knowing more and more about less and less. Had he been asked at twenty to predict his views thirty years hence, he would have replied, more certain. The opposite. Ageing unravelled. Perhaps old age reaffirmed, though experience suggested otherwise. More likely reach the age where no longer cared. Drifting. Watch the colours swirl, ignore the pigmentation.

And he had no answers. The more he thought, even the questions blurred. Old slate, old chalk much rubbed, grey.

The passing months had demonstrated the truism that innocence, once lost, was not regained. Though he had managed, fleetingly, to almost remember what it was like. And, like all memories, it was tinged, colour casts and shades. The memories remained, reasonably constant. But the emphasis, the particular recalled – the touch, the smell – depended on the prevailing mood and whatever had caused the need for recollection.

Memory was selective and seductive, convenient, remembering the past in fragments then reinventing the whole, negotiating between old certainty, present faith and future hope.

Simon sat, and he listened. Sometimes…what was that aphorism? "Sometimes I sit and think, and sometimes I just sit." He sat, keeping his mind company.

It was a mind that wandered, and sometimes far from what it knew, and even further from what it thought it used to understand. On the difficult days it wandered even further, to be torn back, reluctant, to be bewildered and sickened with confusion. It called these dreams.

Sometimes he called them nightmares. And, on the really terrifying times, he called them nothing at all.

Simon sat. It was four in the morning. He'd listened to the news on World Service, struggled to relate the names of African countries changed since independence, school and empire, and rejected the programme that followed. The Open University offering was a repeated repeat. A book, unopened, lay at his feet. He sat in silence. The heating had switched off several hours before. He listened to the house, cooling around him. It was very quiet.

Counting the peripheries, there were twenty or so rooms. This he knew. And, after twenty-plus years, he knew the sounds of all of them. Peculiar, individual, reflecting their content and their size. Carpeted: a deadened, thoughtful sound. Wooden-floored, but occupied: a sharpened pitch. Empty, but for storage, echoed. The garage: hollow. Each room with its own characteristic, a singularity of voice.

He listened as they spoke to him. Making conversation.

two

Someone had once remarked that life is lived forwards, but understood backwards. Chronologically perhaps, though not if measured by events. Real life contained much lateral motion.

Simon's original intention, idly thought some years before, had been to retire at fifty. With events conspiring against that, a revised target was not to have to attend a place of salaried employment in the new century. With sufficient sacrifice, a possibility. His attainment had been a neat bisection; voluntary redundancy aged fifty-two.

Many factors contributed to Simon's decision to leave, events furnished any manner of excuses, but there was only the one real reason. Simply, he'd lost that essential emotional commitment, instead, an emotional absence. It had become a job, just like any other, done for the common reasons. A marriage in name only. Enabled financially by his mother's death, he divorced. It was a consistency throughout his life, that paramount need for the total emotional involvement. The training and the education might be scientific, logical, but the impetus, the drive, the motivation, always the emotion. The heart and the head; always led by the heart.

Employed by the same company since the age of eighteen, it was not a casual act. The easy reason – when the company decided to withdraw its business interest in his speciality, a twenty-five-year experience become expertise, dispossessed overnight – was not in itself enough. Neither was his estimate that he could, with care, just about afford to. There were more insidious reasons to suggest his time was up.

He had joined towards the end of a twenty-year expansion. In the years before, senior positions had been filled with young, eminently capable people, who then stayed in post for thirty years. They had been an eclectic mix, his bosses. The quiet family men, the egomaniacs, the driven questors, the cynical manipulators. The slowly declining failures. The soul sellers. There had been geniuses, two. And none had been without any real talent.

And all had given him, or had appeared to, the one thing he needed: freedom. The licence to do practically whatever he wished within his discipline, the little or the much, and the belief, a shared conviction in the rightness of it. It had been very spoiling. The years of taking his own decisions did not conformity make. He had long before disqualified himself from high position by refusing to accept the doctrine of collective responsibility. An inability to speak anything but the truth, however subjective, compounded.

Eventually, as his directors either died or retired, his senior support dwindled, his acceptability declined and he became unsound. A description Simon accepted as a compliment, the ultimate accolade. The old generation of thinkers had been replaced with a new breed; those with corporate-speak mentality and vision deficiency. Those that did not subscribe to the belief that some things were done because they should be, rather than they had to be. In a large organisation you worked for your friends and the few left above that retained your respect. Gradually, they were gone.

It was trust. Trust implied a hope for a future. Born into a generation of idealists, becoming slowly more cynical as each subsumed, he had, however, kept his promises. Even to himself. One was that he would never work purely for the money. And then, his mother enabled him to leave of his own choosing.

His mother's death had been sudden and mercifully quick. It was a Saturday morning: the evening and the night before had been distinctly average. A liaison with a service contract, functional without being particularly involving. He had been relieved to be going home. And then he knew.

Driving down the hill before the road that led to the house, he just knew.

He swung the car around on the drive in readiness to leave, and then let himself in. As anticipated, the red light on the answerphone was flashing. He repacked his overnight bag, enough for three or four days, adding a mixture of stationery and finally, a guide from the Consumers' Association that had lived on the bookshelves for years.

Simon was very calm, frighteningly so. He made coffee, a sandwich and had a shave and a shower. He changed his clothes. Only with everything prepared did he press the play button. He listened to the message twice. It was from his mother's local hospital. She had been admitted two hours before after being knocked down on a zebra crossing. She had a serious head injury and was very poorly. He rang the number.

The ward sister was very kind. His mother had been scanned. Heavy and extensive internal cranial bleeding. She was stable, though gradually declining. He was encouraged to arrive soon.

It was a completely uneventful journey. He broke every speed limit there was: a hundred and twenty-six miles in an hour and twenty minutes. Never had he wished to see a police patrol car on the motorway more to request an escort. He saw nothing.

He reached the hospital, was directed to her ward, paused and walked in. He did not get far. Intercepted by a nurse he was led into a side room. A doctor followed.

"My mother's dying, isn't she," said Simon flatly.

"Yes. I'm very sorry but she is, Mr Kendal."

Simon sat down as the doctor paused, embarrassed.

"Do you watch *Casualty*?"

"No," replied Simon, surprised. "Is it relevant?"

The doctor shook his head. "It's just that there's a standard assessment system that we use."

Simon nodded. "Yes, I've heard of that. It scores from one to ten doesn't it?"

"One to twenty."

"And the minimum?"

"Seven."

"And my mother?"

"Four."

Simon looked at the floor between his feet, and then at his hands. He felt utterly powerless.

"I see," he said. "So there's no hope at all then?"

"None. I'm very sorry."

Simon smiled, remembering. "Don't be," he said. "She always wanted to die quickly. Not to end up as a vegetable. I was to smother her in that case. Had to promise every Christmas. Likewise for me." He shrugged an apology while the doctor nodded. "I presume she's not in any pain?"

"None. There's very little brain activity. It's just a question of waiting for the body to stop."

"How long?" Simon thought as he asked: *That old question.*

"It could be hours. It could be days. There's no way of knowing. She has a very strong heart."

"She always did," said Simon, absently.

His mother was in a room to herself, dressed in a white nightdress, lying on her back. There was a drip connected to her arm and she had a face mask. Her breath was rasping, uneven.

He lifted the mask and kissed her. "Hello, love," he said softly. "What have they been doing to you?"

She felt very hot, but her breathing seemed to ease immediately.

The ward sister was standing behind him. "She may be able to hear you," she said quietly.

Simon nodded. "I can certainly hear her."

He asked for some water and bathed her lips and face. "Can I move her onto her side?"

They found him a pillow and he rolled her over, propping her head sideways and forwards. The recovery position.

"She always snores on her back," he said, explaining.

He sat beside her, holding her hands, talking to her. She seemed to be calm.

They left him like that for a while until someone, whom Simon took to be the almoner, joined him. She had a plastic carrier bag with his mother's clothes and her handbag. There was a battered loaf and some broken eggs, the reason for her going out that morning. She also carried a clutch of forms, partially completed.

Simon looked at them. They'd estimated her age at sixty-seven. He corrected it: eighty-three. He commented on it to his mother; her female vanity would have enjoyed that. He glanced at the rest and suggested that he dictate the answers. They would never read his writing and, at that moment, he really didn't have the patience. His mother breathed on, even in dying her presence dominating the room.

A nurse brought him some tea and he sat with his mother alone, talking for a while. Her breathing was steady now, even, quiet.

The room was on the top floor of the building, with a large window overlooking parkland. His mother lived on the other side of the park and, as a child, they had gone to that park often. To the lending library housed in the old gatehouse and stables of the old house, the formal gardens, extended now over the ruins, with its array of interlocking ponds and ornamental bridges; the grassland beyond. Here they had collected conkers, played games; she'd taught him the rudiments of cricket there, he'd ridden his first bike, flown his first model aeroplanes. Lots of childhood memories. Too many.

He stood at the window and described the view, and what he could see going on, to her. A Saturday evening, late summer sun, parents and children doing much the same sort of things as they had done. It was comforting somehow.

He could not cry; not then, not yet. He sat again beside her, stroking her hands. It was the longest he'd ever been with her when she hadn't spoken. How often before had he wished for that, just a moment's peace. And now, how much the opposite. He reached for the bowl and bathed her lips and face again.

Unable to process the fluid from the drip, his mother's body had begun to swell. Her rings and the silver bangle, now no more than wire, given to remind which was her right hand and not removed since her mother's death in 1920, had tightened viciously. With the hospital staff unable to find a functional ring-cutter at the weekend,

Simon used wire-cutters and pliers taken from the car. The gold was hard, work-hardened from the years of wear, wedding and eternity rings lapped flat together. Her fingers began to turn pink from blue.

He looked at her engagement ring, much prized, the two diamonds flashing, defiant. He knew that ring only too well. Countless panics as a child when she lost it; him searching through sink trays and plumbing traps, dustbins, the ring always found. It looked tired now, distorted, its shank cut and bent for removal.

Simon put her jewellery and her watch into a specimen bag, carefully folded it, and put it safely into a jacket pocket.

An hour passed while his mother continued to breathe unhurriedly. The sister brought him more tea, checked on his mother's condition and suggested it might be time that he got something to eat. The hospital's cafeteria was closed but his mother's flat was only minutes away, a pub at the bottom of her road. He left her telephone number, and found that of the pub from a directory. The sister promised to ring immediately if there was any significant change.

Simon parked his car outside his mother's flat and stared at the front door. He'd never liked the colour, turquoise blue, and still didn't, even though she'd chosen it and he'd painted it the summer before. The thought of going in without her seemed somehow disloyal. He would go to the Black Horse first. He walked back down the road.

The pub was beginning to fill up. He ordered a pint and stared at the evening's menu suspended at one end of the bar. He did not feel at all hungry, but it would be sensible to eat. He looked at the menu again, nine courses in all; five meat, three fish, and a token vegetarian. Nothing suggested itself. Suspecting that he was destined to eat there for some days he chose to work his way through, starting at the top. It was served and he managed to eat some of it. It was the loneliest meal of his life. After a decent interval, he walked slowly back up the hill to his mother's flat.

Simon collected his bag and her carrier bag from the boot of the car and let himself in with her keys. The flat was as it ever was, neat and clean and tidy: entirely normal. The crockery from her morning tea, washed up and stacked on the draining board. On the dining table, next to the pot plant, a note to herself he didn't comprehend. A *Radio Times*, opened to the afternoon's racing schedule, beside her chair.

There were messages on the answerphone, a new innovation bought by himself the previous spring. The Women's Institute, details of the following day's church service. A message from one of her dancing groups about a forthcoming holiday; they'd managed to get her a single room as requested. A message from the hospital to himself: no change, ring back at ten o'clock.

Simon opened the back door leading from the kitchen and sat on the top step overlooking her garden. He looked at the garden, the years of careful nurturing, the lawn freshly cut, he knew, last Thursday; she'd complained at the effort. He could smell the grass. The light began to fade but he sat there until it was completely dark. Simon cried, not for his mother, but for himself.

His mother's condition remained unchanged. The hospital suggested that he get some sleep. They did not suggest how.

He took off his boots, washed and sat on the sofa. He felt suddenly cold and put on the gas fire to take off the chill. He would sleep dressed, on the sofa, the telephone to hand. He could get there in five minutes should he be called.

The delivery of her Sunday paper woke him. He sat up, stiff, uncomfortable, momentarily confused. The news, excitedly reported across the front page, utterly irrelevant. He rang the hospital. A comfortable night, no significant change.

Simon made coffee, washed and shaved, cleaned his teeth, tried to feel normal, failed. He reached the hospital soon after ten. His mother lay much as he had left her, eyes closed, facing towards the window. Her breathing seemed more laboured, but otherwise she seemed unchanged.

He held her hands, talked to her, bathed her face, drank the tea he was brought, and talked to her some more. At one point, at a loss at what to do, he read her sections of the newspaper, pieces he knew she might read.

Sometimes, he just looked at her, watching her breathe. His mother, in death as in life, stubborn to the last.

And then she stopped. Suddenly, no warning, she stopped breathing. Her life just ended.

He kissed her, holding her head in his hands, his tears splashing on her face. It was the fourteenth of September, the date that he had first started work.

His mother had been the youngest of four children, the others being boys. She had outlived her brothers. Two of them had died some years earlier, the youngest, unmarried brother only a few months before his sister. They had been a close, private family, his mother and her brothers. He remembered the regular visits from his uncles when he had been a child; the weekly outings with one or another of them after his father had ceased to take any interest. The quiet, providing support.

The amount, how consistent and continuous that support, was not evident until Simon went through his mother's papers. Sixty years of personal, domestic activity, neatly recorded. His uncles, he found, had supported him through all those years at college. The funds that always somehow materialised when needed had all come from them. He owed them each a debt, unknowingly received, too late to repay, even by a simple thank you. And, as they had provided for him and their sister in life, so they had in death. His mother had inherited substantially from all of them, particularly the last. And, in turn, as her brothers had provided for her, so his mother had provided for her son. She had left her affairs all neat, tidy, orderly arranged, the way the family would.

Simon had found a letter, addressed to himself, in his mother's writing desk. It had been written during that part of the previous winter while she'd had a heavy cold. The letter bore the date of his birthday. He still had the card she'd sent him, posted early by a neighbour. He remembered the card: it had a fine linen finish and featured an idealistic view of a Scottish loch. That it had been produced in the USA amused him at the time and he'd wondered if she'd selected it. Now he suspected that she had; the irony would have amused her. He'd received five cards in all: his mother's, one from an ex-wife, two from ex-lovers and one late, from an old friend. All had been women.

In his mother's letter he had found a copy of the farewell speech from Polonius to his son from Hamlet that she'd copied out into his twenty-first card, a note updating several small bequests, and the name and address of her solicitor. There were several other small, neatly folded sheets of notepaper. The first contained the express wish that he should spend the money, wisely or unwisely, however he saw fit, and made particular reference to enjoying it. The final sheet was a prayer and an instruction not to grieve. Up to then Simon had not really cried. From that point, he had.

He had thought he knew her but, in retrospect, he had understood his mother far better from then. So much of her lifetime, sometimes discussed but moderated, reconciled after her death. Her life, restricted by her father who then, as his grandfather, encouraged him: gender. Her hopes, his intentions. The time, the attention and advantage given, the childhood sharing. Adolescence, youth rebellion. A twenties pause, begrudgingly, then gladly, the reconciliation. And the latter years of amused, amusing, something. An equality, but never on equal terms.

A woman of irritation. Simon, her only child, too often seen only as a child. He was past forty before she conceded that, occasionally, he knew more than she did.

Simon followed his instructions, those of his mother's letter and the legal requirements, as around him the well-practised oiled bureaucracy of death slid effortlessly into action. A recognised procedure, with a known conclusion and an almost surprising amount of particularly human generosity from complete strangers to ease. So much to do to occupy the time: first the certification, and then the solicitor's office, the vicar, the undertakers, all without exception courteous and kind. In between he used the energy of his anger, his rage, to write his address for the funeral.

He wrote as his mother's son, at night, sitting in her flat without her. He remembered so much he had forgotten, feeling her with him.

He remembered her phrases, lots of them, mostly derogatory. 'Wouldn't give you fourpence' was a favourite, applied to anything of cheap appeal. As a child he'd taken it literally – twelve pennies to the shilling, twenty shillings to the pound. It was years before he'd appreciated the derivation.

Before the Great War, fourpence was the generally accepted tariff for a 'prossie', a working girl. And there was a joke. His mother was dreadful at telling jokes; she laughed too soon and was hopeless at the timing.

A pensioner couple had fallen on hard times. The rent was due and they were desperate. The husband decided that there was only one solution: the wife would have to go on the game.

Unable to think of any alternative, reluctantly she agreed. But there would be competition, and younger. She would have to offer double time, longer hours, special services.

The next day she left at eight in the morning, returning at ten at night. She slumped in a chair as eagerly the husband counted out the money from her pockets. Thirteen shillings and fourpence: 13s 4d.

"But who gave you the fourpence?"

"They all did."

His mother always enjoyed that joke; it was perhaps her favourite, as old as the phrase.

There were over fifty people at her funeral, far more than she would ever have expected. But still, less perhaps than a whole life deserved.

Simon buried his mother, as she had wished and how she knew he would, with her brother and her parents in the family grave.

It had been his mother's practice to visit the grave, beside her beloved Thames, on Christmas Eve, the anniversary of her parents' wedding. As she'd suspected, Simon had kept up the ritual. And then there was her birthday in February, Mothering Sunday, other significant dates. He visited too often that first year. Somehow, after all the formalities were over, his grief, inexorably, increased and for the most part, unseen. It had taken him a year, and those first anniversaries – the death, the funeral – to surface consistently. It still continued.

Grief is a selfish emotion, entirely for, and about, the self. And that grief, the loss of someone truly loved, makes a hole that nothing ever fills. In time, the edges may erode, but the depth remains.

Simon still talked to his mother – not that he expected any answer, but the sharing helped. Mothers and sons: continuous connections.

three

After an interval of a few days to regain a little equilibrium, Simon presented himself at his mother's solicitor as arranged. He was intrigued to be offered a glass of sherry upon arrival. In the event, brandy might have been more appropriate. Simon learnt that he was the executor and only beneficiary of what he would learn to call his mother's estate. In accordance with his instructions, the solicitor had it arrayed for his visit. Bundles of papers, tied with red ribbon, littered the side of his desk.

The solicitor reached for the nearest and untied it. Share certificates, a collection of bonds and a few building society pass books were displayed before him. The solicitor consulted his notes.

"I took the liberty of valuing these. As of last Friday, the combined realisation value was a fraction over two hundred and thirty-six thousand pounds." Simon stared at him, then reached for the sherry. "Your mother was a careful woman, Mr Kendal." He smiled. "As I'm sure you were aware."

Simon replied that he was. The solicitor took another bundle from the desk and untied it. Simon saw that they were deeds. The solicitor continued, his style brisk but unhurried.

"There is the question of your mother's flat. Should you not wish to retain it, and I gather this was your mother's suggestion, I would advise an immediate sale. The market is approaching a peak and it would, in that case, seem a pity to miss the crest. I would further suggest that, consistent with your wishes, the property be sold with the majority of the furniture and the fittings in place. Unoccupied property rapidly loses its charm if unfurnished."

Simon nodded – there seemed no reason not to. The solicitor consulted his notes again.

"I made some preliminary enquiries this morning. The flat should realise something in the region of two hundred and eighty-five thousand after fees. That is, you understand, a working figure. It may even be a little higher." He smiled slightly. "One can never be sure these days."

Simon put down his, by now, empty glass and thanked him. The figures the solicitor had so confidently expounded were around double what he had expected. He began to stand up. The solicitor, slightly alarmed, gestured for him to stay seated. He reached for another bundle and, unbinding it, put it on the desk before him. He formed a steeple with his fingers and peered at Simon over the tips of them.

"You were not aware of your uncle's rental investment that your mother had recently inherited?" Simon shook his head. "Ah," said the solicitor, more kindly. "Let me explain."

Simon listened with an increasing sense of shock. He understood the meaning of the words, but the realisation took a little longer to sink in.

His uncle, some months before his death, had bought a Georgian house in Chiswick, West London, which he'd set about converting into flats. Simon's mother had completed the transformation.

Later that week, Simon had been to see it. A large but otherwise undistinguished house overlooking the Thames. There were seven flats in all: four small on the ground floor, two on the second and a large penthouse at the top, the upper floors with balconies. In line with his mother's instructions, premium rents were charged for the upper floors to act as a subsidy for those on the ground, the tenants for which were restricted to either firemen or nurses. Notwithstanding his mother's largesse, the net rental income comfortably exceeded that of Simon's pension.

He had not stayed long. There was no reason to. The agent appointed by his mother to act as property manager and now, in turn, adopted by Simon, described it as a most excellent investment.

Simon sat in the solicitor's office, clutching the cup of coffee a secretary had brought him when the explanations were completed. The solicitor, recognising his state of mind, gave him time to compose himself before he spoke again. When he did, his tone was gentle and considerate. After an outline of the procedures that the law required following a death, and the tax implications, he consulted another file.

"There is one final thing, Mr Kendal. As you know, your mother was knocked down by a car. I understand that the police are prosecuting the driver for drunken driving and, most probably, manslaughter. From the evidence, one may assume a conviction. Once that is secured, it will only be a matter of time, and negotiation, until there is a settlement for compensation from the driver's insurance company. Though," he added, "one would hesitate to predict a timescale."

He closed the file on his desk and began to gather together the various heaps of documents.

Having formalised the relationship between them, Simon left the office. He walked for a time. It was quite a long time. Eventually he found a pub and ordered coffee and a brandy. He sat in a quiet corner, staring into the empty grate of a fireplace. He sat there for a long time, replacing the coffee as it cooled, sipping the brandy, filling the ashtray.

His mother's assets had been considerably greater than he had ever realised. She had always been a careful woman, the husbandry of the old who had known more difficult times. Quite how careful though, he had not suspected.

In common with most sons, he supposed, he had thought he had known his mother well. Perhaps he had but, as the details of her affairs unfolded, he had begun to appreciate that his knowledge of her had been as superficial as he had always presumed her knowledge of him to be. This belated appreciation was proving salutary. A deeper understanding, bought at considerable cost. That she had not chosen to make more of her resources, had chosen instead to preserve them for him, caused him anguish.

He could not put a value on his mother's life. He couldn't even try. To inherit, at whatever the gain, was not a pleasurable thing. He'd only had the one mother, and now he had none. He was now an orphan, remembering unfulfilled promises.

The due process of probate had been accomplished in the manner that the solicitor, now his solicitor, had described at that first meeting.

The sale of his mother's flat had been completed in an almost indecent haste and, as suggested, at the top of the market for the amount predicted. For some reason he found that ironic. His previous experience of property sales had been of places he'd been living in; conveyancing fraught with anguish, buying and selling and sequential timing. Each time while the market was depressed. Not so the flat. His mother, with her usual foresight, had even managed to die at the right time.

After deducting sufficient to repay his mortgage, he had invested the remainder. He'd followed the advice of the same financial services group that his mother had used. There was no reason not to. They were well founded, they had his solicitor's endorsement, and it would have felt somehow disloyal to do otherwise.

Whatever the reasons, the results seemed satisfactory enough. With the investments carefully adjusted upwards to take account of inflation, the net yield, combined with the return from the rentals on the flats, had been greater than any of the predictions. His inheritance gave him a net income comfortably exceeding three times the average wage.

As the solicitor had remarked, it was not, perhaps, sufficient to leave the country for, but should he so choose, he would never need to earn a living again.

In the several years past, Simon's investments, beyond the Chiswick property, had coalesced. They were based on the widows and orphans principle; relatively low returns traded for complete security. For sentimental reasons he'd retained a large block of shares in his old company, accumulated over the years from various option schemes. And with it, the morning habit. Opening the newspaper at the business pages and checking the overnight share price, settling his mood for the day. Their performance had not betrayed his prediction. The price remained stubbornly depressed.

Whatever else, one thing seemed certain: his financial status was unlikely ever to be threatened. Once he'd removed the burden of debt incurred from a normal life, his affective wealth had increased at an almost indecent rate. In times of indolence, he almost regretted it.

four

Simon's house had a certain personality. He found it difficult to describe objectively, but he was certain it had moods. A brooding malevolence, mostly expressed benignly.

When he'd first seen it, it bore a passing resemblance to the sort of houses you drew as a kid in art class. Pitched roof, door in the middle, windows rising either side. Deceptive, for the doors were to the side and the windows varied in position but, like most children's art, the proportions were wrong.

It may have been called 'The Villa' but Victorian folly would have been a truer description. An example of mid nineteenth-century speculation, built in stone by a local builder eager to satisfy the supposed taste of a burgeoning middle class, it had remained empty for the first twenty years of its life. It had sulked thereafter. Its subsequent treatment had done little to lift its mood.

Eventually sold to another builder who added a floor by using the attic space then split it into semis, it was rented until after the Great War, then sold on as two. Fifty years of separation, various owners, varying degrees of sympathy, before being acquired by the previous owner before Simon. This unfortunate had taken on the task of reconversion into a single house. He'd failed, and the cost had been his marriage.

It had been on the market for a while before Simon had bought it at auction twenty years before; a lot of house for the money, though sad and incomplete. Slowly, an almost reluctant dignity had begun to re-emerge. It stood now, reunited with itself, structurally sound and functional throughout though with many rooms unfinished and, in part, unresolved. But resolute: stamped into the ground, unlovely but defiant.

And it had great panoramic views. It was what Simon had bought it for, and what at some future date, would sell it.

Typically for the period, it had been built for show, a demonstration, and the rooms reflected it. Those to the front were larger with higher ceilings, fourteen feet at ground level, whereas those at the back measured twelve. The pattern was repeated on the upper floors: twelve and ten to the front, ten and eight to the rear. Had the house continued upward with the same graduation, the floor levels would have begun to resemble a shelving unit.

For the first few weeks of his occupancy he had begun to convince himself that there was a resident poltergeist with flatulence. The heavy smell of gas would manifest in the corners of rooms and then dissipate. Weeks later he discovered that the old Edwardian gas lighting circuit, a myriad yardage of small-bore lead piping draped through voids in floors and within ceilings, was still live, and seeping.

That the house had never exploded or spontaneously combusted was surprising. At low points over the coming months, a fact regretted.

For the house had been buggered almost beyond redemption long before he'd ever owned it. A realisation slow to form and destined it seemed, judging by his more recent progress, to take many more years before it became an equitable conclusion.

Whereas all agreed that The Villa had been a bargain, the classic property investment, the work required to make it truly habitable had, naturally, been far greater than originally envisaged. Substantial hardly described it. Bought one November, his first winter had been grim. Simon had closed down most of the house and, when not abroad on work commitments, had camped out in three rooms until the following spring.

A two-week leave taken at Easter and an unhurried, sober, thoroughly unsentimental survey had led to a plan. The Plan. It ran to many pages, too many, and twenty years on was still uncompleted. It had also, as was the manner of these things, continued to grow. The roof, the foundations and the internal structure and services of the house were sound. The state of decoration of the individual rooms, however, varied.

There had been only the four main rooms on the ground floor, though two of these were combinations. The sitting room at the front had been knocked through either side of the central chimney breast and the wall separating the kitchen from the dining room on the east side of the house had also been removed. Around and loosely attached to the ground floor were variously decomposing extensions. To the east, a late nineteenth-century conservatory clinging precariously on. To the rear, the original kitchen sculleries, built on scrape foundations, were being squeezed between the house proper and the rising ground of the rear garden that their back walls were partially retaining. Their roofs sagged, the side walls bowed. A large wooden construction of uncertain use on the west side was fit only for burning, a fate it shared with the remains of an ugly garage which leaned on the forward boundary of the front garden.

The first floor had six rooms: two master bedrooms at the front, two other bedrooms and two bathrooms at the back. One, on the west, thirties grim; the other, sixties, functional in pink. The top floor had four further rooms, their ceilings sloping under the roof line, but light, with windows on two sides. Fourteen rooms in all plus the crumbling remains.

Simon had taken advice and instruction. A local builder, met at the auction, had taken him aside suggesting he might be of use. He was, as was his favoured plumber and electrician.

By the end of that first summer, the house was completely rewired and re-plumbed. A gas boiler of industrial proportions stood in one of the renamed crumbling utility rooms at the back from which issued around two thousand feet of pipework, the usual collection of water tanks and twenty-two radiators with ample capacity for more. Likewise the electrics. Four consumer units drove ring mains, power and lighting circuits to the furthest extremities of the house and beyond. Thousands of feet of wiring, power points galore. For the first time in its life the house was warm, nothing leaked and all the electrics worked.

Simon had increased his mortgage, had learnt plumbing from the plumber and household electrics from the electrician. The builder meantime had supplied him with trade accounts with all the local suppliers and had taught him the rudiments of building. He was competent in all but plastering.

That first year had set a pattern. His building season began at Easter and ended with GMT in the autumn. Winters meanwhile, dependant on funds and inclination, were devoted to the internals.

After demolishing everything around the house, Simon had spent his next few summers gradually rebuilding them. With his professional commitments increasing, it had taken him another eleven years. A side room with a shed behind it to replace the conservatory, moving the main entrance door to the front of the house. Two utility rooms, one wet the other dry, doubling the size of the original structures at the rear, and a large garage with workshop attached with a pitched roof, matching the new side room on the other side, to even up the house. In between, he'd replaced all the windows, built a small roof terrace over the void alongside the top room he used as an office and, with the surrounding constructions completed, he'd restored and extended the veranda to the front, recycling all the accumulated rubble and earth from the excavations.

The extent of the ground floor of The Villa had grown sixty percent. Maximising the count by including internals and externals, it now had ten rooms of varying proportion, giving the house twenty in total. Extending his lending in line with his salary had now tripled his mortgage.

It was, as Simon was only too aware, a ridiculous house for one. A folly perpetuated, justified as a retirement fund.

There was much about the house that Simon would have otherwise; trivial things mostly, bar one, fundamental and irreversible. It was, he'd decided, in the wrong place and the wrong way round. Houses, like cricket pitches, should be built north–south, with the south to the back. The Villa faced southeast. Likewise, placing it further back from the road, higher up the hill, might have been useful. After twenty years, it still tended to irk him.

With the mortgage paid off and notification received, a large plastic-covered package had arrived at his door some weeks later. It was ten inches thick and weighed over two kilos. The history of the house told through its various legal conveyances.

The documents themselves related 150 years of quality decline, from the double elephant-sized parchments of the original transactions, to the meanest sheet of A4 recording his own. It saddened his initial excitement. Somehow, he felt cheated.

Simon sat on the terrace at the back of the house, his hair wet and stiff from the afternoon's toil. A fresh pint of milk rested on the table before him, pipe and lighter to hand.

He stared at the wall of the terrace, recent dark verticals from the pick, considering each of the layers in turn. There were twelve strata so far, more than he'd expected in a depth of only eight feet. Clays of differing hues, a half-inch iron deposit and further down, soapstone with gaping voids seeded with layers of quartz. There were earthworms deep within the clay, curled and sleeping.

He looked along the terrace, gauging the dimensions of the remainder to be removed and comparing with his recent progress. Had he been in the mood to be depressed, the comparison would have dismayed him. He smiled; Sisyphus would have understood. He had before.

Somehow, there was an honesty in hard physical labour, however irrational. Or perhaps it was just stubborn stupidity, his rear garden excavations. Garden was a relative term, as were the excavations. All afternoon he had hacked through soapstone, the pink quartz bands squeezed between the levels. As the pick hit, something akin to shrapnel exploded around him. Four hours and less than half a ton shifted.

Later, he sat showered, aching, tired. An impact strike beneath his left eye showed a moderate bruise beneath a shallow cut.

Checking the television he saw the regional weather forecast for the following day. Dry, inclemently hot. Maybe another ton if he could get that large ridge shifted. He went back out to the terrace and listened to the evening birdsong tuning up around him. Some he could name, but most not. He didn't need to know the names to enjoy the performance.

The wind rose as the evening progressed. In the copse above him the undersides of broad leaves turned outwards, pale. Thin sheets of filmy cloud joined by scattered clumps began to glow. Swifts darted across the sky with their shrill conversation. There were groups of them, stacked at different altitudes. He counted one group and gave up at thirty.

A pair of buzzards circled above the trees, their wings hardly flexing, steering with their tail feathers. Then climbing, spirals, a hundred yards or so in diameter. And climbing still, until they disappeared from sight. Five minutes and gone; so ridiculously easy. Such apparent ease.

From the main road, some distance off, he heard the rapid, sequential gear changes of a high-powered motorcycle. They were expertly done. Simon knew that road and its moods, times of weather, seasons. He wished the rider well and wondered if he held a transplant card. At least an early, messy death might benefit someone.

He shifted his position, turning towards the house. The honey bees had returned to the eaves but the bumble bees were still working, seemingly random movements amongst the wild flowers. If he sat until dusk a pipistrelle bat would wind around the house in complete silence. Simon smiled.

It had been during the previous autumn. He'd spent an evening in his office at the top of the house. It had not been one of his better days. Giving up on the problem, he'd stretched out on the day bed that graced one wall. Unsurprisingly, he'd fallen asleep, the sound of a moth or butterfly somewhere distant for company.

Simon woke, vague, momentarily confused. Still half asleep, he'd headed down the stairs towards the bathroom. Something floated over his right shoulder, just visible at the edge of his vision, to disappear further down the stairs. He felt the hair on his neck rise: visions of every Hammer film ever seen recalled in vivid Technicolor. Boldly, he'd followed the spectre down.

He found it in the sitting room, hanging from the curtains: a small, exquisitely faced reddish-brown bat. Folded, it seemed very tiny. He opened a set of the French windows and, rather pathetically, waved his arms at it.

The bat ignored him to begin with, then started to fly, describing neat figures of eight around the central chimney breast. Simon, standing in the centre of one of the circles, turned each time it flew around him. He began to feel dizzy. It was not possible to know how the bat felt.

The display continued for some time. The bat circling, landing occasionally on the furniture and then continuing, Simon continuing to watch. It studiously ignored the open window however much he encouraged it. The silence was eerie, only the merest rustling accompanying its flight.

Suddenly, the bat changed direction, passed over his head and disappeared through the window. Simon, though relieved, had been almost sad to see it go.

five

It was getting worse. If asked to pick the one consistency throughout his life, Simon would have selected sleep. Irrespective of time, or place, or circumstance, he could always sleep, protractedly. He was renowned for it.

Countless days had been hastily rearranged as a consequence of his sleeping and, its complement, his inability to wake. If asked to list his leisure activities, sleep would take prime position. At least, it would have done.

Lately this, perhaps his greatest talent, had left him. Instead, he had developed an inability to sleep at a conventional time. Sleeping in daylight was easy; morning, afternoon, even early evening. But during the hours of darkness it eluded him. It was as if his sleep response had shifted five hours to the left; somehow his body was on US Eastern Central. ECT had replaced BST. For a variety of reasons, Simon was beginning to conclude that the life unstructured was the life impoverished.

He woke up, staring at the ceiling. Early light, strained by the curtains, cast gloomy shadows. He drifted for a while, returning to another troubled dream, talking to himself and choosing not to listen.

It seemed to be early for none of the shops were open. In some he could see lights coming on, in others he could even see people, but all the doors remained firmly closed.

Simon glanced at his watch, then looked at it more closely. Eight fifteen, it said. He was an hour ahead of himself – no wonder the car park had been so empty. He turned down a side street at random and began to walk in a wide circle to occupy the time.

With the threat of summer, the café had placed a few hopeful tables out on the pavement. He pulled a chair back from where it leant and sat down. The café's lights were on and he could see several people moving around inside. He pulled his jacket around him while he looked for a waiter. Giving that up, he lit his pipe instead. He'd passed the point of being pleased with himself for being out so early, now it was only the consequences that concerned him.

"You're our first customer," said the waitress, standing alongside him.

"So I see," he replied, and smiled. "I hope I won't be the last," he added, and ordered coffee. As the waitress left he looked up at the sky: the clouds had not lifted. Rain, he remembered, was forecast.

The coffee arrived. He'd ordered espresso and its bitterness stripped the skin from his tongue. He drained the cup and immediately ordered another. After the initial shock, the overall effect felt beneficial.

Simon enjoyed watching people, particularly when he didn't have to speak to them. The café was well sited, on a junction, at the bottom of a small hill in a pedestrian precinct. He watched the increasing tempo of the comings and goings between the streets. Some people looked consumed with their purpose. Others looked more vague, but all participated in some degree to what he saw about him. He was the only observer and his mind began to wander as he watched them.

People found their own way through, each to find their own excuse, a way to cope, suppress. Whatever it was that worked. It was called survival. No one could legislate for chaos. And civilisation was nothing more than a greater chaos within recognised boundaries. The art of government was specifying accepted and acceptable boundaries. Similarly: sanity was only socially acceptable madness.

The waitress passed, preparing tables, and after a brief thought Simon ordered another espresso. He continued to watch the people. He was just like them. Quite why he'd driven into the centre of town before eight in the morning thinking it was nine, not questioning the evidence before his eyes or listening to the radio, he was not entirely sure. Quite why he'd come into town in the first place wasn't obvious. Only that it had seemed like a good idea at the time.

Simon had decided that, by a small margin, the worst part of supermarket shopping was standing in the checkout queue, waiting to pay. Not that trundling around the aisles between the shelves, pushing a loaded trolley that had not enjoyed a service since manufacture and registered its displeasure by a determination to describe tight left-hand circles held much joy.

Simon stood in such a position now, and to pass the time was attempting to examine his fellow inmates. It wasn't proving to be entirely successful. People were too conscious of being on display; looking at customers was better done while purporting to stare at the contents of the shelves. But there were compensations: it was the perfect opportunity to examine at leisure the contents of trolleys other than his own. He'd never knowingly met anyone who ate Pot Noodles – now he thought he had. The afternoon was not entirely wasted.

Having gazed into several trolleys, he began to bore of it. Short of turning over the contents and interviewing the prospective owners on their choice, he felt he'd exhausted the immediate possibilities. He felt vaguely dissatisfied. The queue had not moved. He stared mournfully down at his own trolley, viewing the contents. One of the bottles of olive oil taunted him; it showed definite signs of leakage. Should he rush back and change it, always assuming he could remember where it came from, and possibly risk losing his place? Or should he hand it in to the checkout girl? He had two bottles after all. He decided to hand it in.

Extra virgin olive oil – daft name. Did it mean that not only had it never done it, but neither had it thought about it? It did look very green. He laughed. People stared at him. He stared back and tried to smile. They stared back and then, as if at a sudden signal, everyone went back to ignoring each other.

Looking in other people's supermarket trolleys wasn't half so interesting as looking in their refrigerators. That could be quite educational, if at times alarming. The oddest collection he'd ever come across was a single yoghurt, passion fruit, a selection of undistinguished tomatoes, slightly rotten, and shelves neatly stacked with photographic film. As he remembered, it had been an altogether odd evening. What people chose to keep in their refrigerators might form the basis of some rich pool of social research. He tended to keep potatoes in his which wasn't entirely normal.

At last the queue began to move. The queue moved again and his optimism of getting out sometime that day was renewed.

Simon stood at the checkout, leaning on his emptied trolley, waiting. He felt, and no doubt looked, rough. He'd not slept well and this additional delay was testing both his patience and his temper. Something ahead, a mumbled discussion over vouchers, had brought transactions to a halt.

A couple behind were giving him peculiar looks. Simon tried to ignore them. Suddenly the man spoke, triumphant.

"Didn't you used to be Dr Simon Kendal?"

Simon looked at him warily. "I still am. At least I was the last time I looked."

"I went to a lecture you gave. Very interesting. Very entertaining." The man turned to his wife, reminiscing.

Simon nodded and looked at the man more closely, but without result. He'd given a lot of lectures over the years, or rather the same lecture, occasionally updated. He still had the slides. An introduction to his subject, minimal, laced with considerable black humour. Legitimised death and destruction, always good for a few cheap laughs. Appalling otherwise. And he'd had some interesting videos. Unrelenting firings, unambiguous, horrifying, factual.

Simon apologised for not recognising him.

"It was a few years ago."

Simon nodded. "It would be."

"You were right then," the man continued, undeterred.

Simon smiled again, tolerantly. "I was? In what way?"

"You said the end would be unexpected, and surprisingly fast once it began. You expected to take early retirement."

Again, Simon nodded. He'd always said that. Though his reasons had little to do with the shifts in global politics. He thought he detected a note of pity and chose to ignore it.

"I did, eventually. I work from home now. Occasional consultancy."

"Must be hard that, after what you're used to. All the travel and that. Not getting out much."

Simon agreed, more to curtail the conversation than from any real conviction.

The impasse ahead of him suddenly dislodged and he moved to the other end of the checkout to pack his shopping.

"See you again," said the man as a farewell gesture.

Simon smiled. "Maybe."

Thoughtfully, he pushed the loaded trolley across the car park. He should have shaved.

Simon passed by on the other side of the road, quickening his pace. It disgusted him and his action disgusted him further. They shouted at him again and he stopped. They were four to his one; he counted them several times as he listened to the abuse. Simon reflected that he was neither Jewish nor homosexual. He didn't want to be, but as he stood there, part of him wished he was both.

He continued to listen as the largest of the four advanced towards him. The shaven head, the heavy boots, the tattoos, crude and inexpert – the whole effect was designed to intimidate and menace. He wasn't frightened, but he would admit to being scared. Simon adjusted his position slightly, feet spread apart, the left ahead of the right, ready to pivot. The law and authority would not help him if he chose to strike first, but common sense suggested he should. More common sense would have kept him from stopping in the first place.

He smiled, politely, and waited. He stared into a pair of eyes that shared none of his visions. Eye contact always challenged and his stubbornness denied him the luxury of looking away. Instead, he concentrated on keeping his smile, holding the eye contact, tensing his eyelids not to blink. A kick to the shin or a sharp straight-fingered blow to the solar plexus? He hung his left arm beside him, the right hung loose behind his back.

A car moved slowly down the street, followed by a large group of youths who came around the corner. From the side of his vision Simon noticed they were black. They shouted encouragement to him – at least, he took it to be that – and joined in. His protagonist, with a final insult, switched his attention and rejoined his own group. Not even they could call him black.

Simon was now marginalised, irrelevant. He lifted a hand to acknowledge his newfound allies, lingered a little, and then continued on his way. The situation had become a conflict that he wasn't part of. He no longer understood the rules, and worse, his skin colour would be an encumbrance.

There was a pub on the next corner and Simon made his way to it. It was crowded but the population seemed normal. He bought a pint of Guinness and stood near the door from where he could watch the street. It had emptied.

Simon put his glass on a shelf that ran around the wall and lit his pipe. He felt angry. Angry at the event, angry at his own reactions. An anger without an effective focus. He smoked his pipe and finished the Guinness. Leaving the pub, he walked on towards the car park. Faintly disappointed, he reached his car without further incident.

What he'd heard was like an old foul breath. A hag, resurrected, had crooked a finger.

Twenty years before he had been to Auschwitz. It had begun at the gate, the mocking iron legend, *Arbeit Macht Frei* – Work Makes You Free. The double barbed-wire surround with efficiently positioned watch towers. The buildings, full of careful preservations. Suitcases, clothing, neatly categorised into sex and type; the hair, the gold teeth. The Pope had returned to Poland only six weeks before. Auschwitz still bore witness. The grass had been cut short, the site was still tidy, kempt.

Simon had walked through the gas chambers, the masquerade

of showers, the ventilation shafts where the Zyklon B tablets were introduced, through the adjoining room that housed the ovens, cleaned and oiled, the doors swinging open at the lightest touch. The last remaining ashes, sunken, grey within. The overall effect had been one of homeliness, a casual domesticity belying bestial purpose.

There were few visitors, and most soon descended upon the Russian tourist shop housed profitably within the compound, offering for hard currency goods denied the Poles. A pilgrimage debased and sacrificed to shopping.

He had gone back into a gas chamber and stood in the dark and quietness. It was small, so small, the arched curving roof above his head. It was cool and peaceful. He had pressed his hands against the wall and reached up, running the tips of his fingers through the scratch marks, torn in terror into the concrete by dying hands. The fingernails scoring a last desperate witness.

The experience had not been cathartic, rather it had been a numbness that had taken time to comprehend. The twentieth century had been that time of solutions, of utopias promised. Utopias did not exist. Auschwitz of all, a final demonstration. And still, there had been others since.

It taught Simon never to trust, and it taught him other things. Simplistic solutions were always wrong. There were never simple, convenient causes. Simon remembered these things as he drove out of the car park. The symmetry, the quality of the buildings at Auschwitz compared to its more recent surroundings. Newspapers stuffed into holes in the pre-cast concrete apartment blocks that never dried due to the weakness of the mortar. Steel railings, fallen from their supports, hung drunkenly and rusting down endless dark stairwells where the lights had never worked.

He had no solutions, only some recognition of right and wrong. He felt somehow responsible. He always had. Six million had died because of ignorance, prejudice and bigotry, fuelled by tyranny. And still it was denied. He had never found the answer. It saddened him more that neither had anyone else. It was true: with continuous and repetitive memory the scar does the work of the wound.

He ran his fingers around the underside of the steering wheel, remembering the scratch marks.

Months before Simon had found it in the bottom of the supermarket trolley and without much thought had consigned it to the boot of the car with the rest of the shopping. It now sat on the dressing table in the bedroom, between the wardrobes, collecting dust: 'Next Customer Please'. It had been there so long he hardly noticed it.

He had read somewhere that Gandhi used to test his celibacy by sharing his bed with naked young women. Presuming that the women might have been willing, he admired his constraint. Simon smiled as he thought about it. Perhaps it hadn't been so much of a test, for he doubted if the women had been hooked in off the street, and Gandhi wasn't exactly unknown by his countrymen, or women. Neither, he suspected, were his idiosyncrasies. Their interests were better served by his compliance. No, he decided, it was unlikely to have been a real test – too public. Though for Gandhi, not a man without humour, his devilment, at least, must have been aroused.

Simon did not underestimate the ease of temptation. For himself, conveniently, he had always adopted the Saint Francis approach. 'Oh Lord, give me chastity – but not yet.' 'The easiest way to rid oneself of temptation is to give in.' And he had – that had always been part of the problem. A congenial evening spent with a woman had invariably, inevitably almost, led to a congenital conclusion.

Had he been a traditional moralist he might have described it as a short-term gain, but a sacrifice of the long-term good. The sins of the flesh, embraced, at the expense of the continual soul. Simon didn't know. Morality was a subject that confused him. Many things did, but morality was a class apart.

There were things that seemed Right and there were others easily described as Wrong. It was the ninety percent in-between, the infinite degrees of grey, that he could never decide upon.

He'd been of the generation that had questioned the strictures, the imposed rules of its elders, their taboos and double standards. The conveniently averted eye. Oral contraception, women in control for perhaps the first time in history, had made the freedoms far easier to express for both sexes. They had rejected all of the conventions in order to find their own. Except they hadn't, and fashions had changed. Simon wondered. Of all things, moral values seemed to be the lightest flotsam upon the tides. It was a paradox he didn't understand. He envied those with an understanding they could work to. He had only an insufficient appreciation.

His first tutor had accurately predicted it. He said it would be spoiling. Unfortunately, in common with several other of his predictions, he had been correct. In retrospect, it must have been easy to see. The first year at university, away from home, but close to what he knew. By the second year, a pattern well established and more repeated. Third year, culmination, confirmation of what had gone before. So easy it was, and easier it had become as the years continued.

Almost every woman he had ever known, he had slept with. Sometimes for comfort, sometimes for friendship, sometimes the opposite. And sometimes, even out of boredom. Rarely out of love. But, once the love had been tasted, the rest became as mutual masturbation. Eventually, without became even more meaningless than it had before.

It was a position that sensible women reached very quickly. Men, with sense, a little longer. That it had taken him the best part of thirty-five years saddened him. So did the years of consequences.

Perhaps it was simply because he didn't know any better.

That sex and reproduction were irrevocably decoupled from the mid 1960s onwards, and the resulting demands, or so it seemed at the time, of the active female population, had left Simon with an attitude to sex perhaps not found in other generations. An ease and a familiarity, and an expectation. The Martini attitude to sex – anytime, anyplace, anywhere. And for Simon, sex had indeed begun in 1963; midsummer, between Lady Chatterley and the Beatles' first LP.

When recalling something, Simon dated his life by the women

he had been with at the time. A life narrative punctuated by names and faces and failed relationships. Beginnings, ends, and a few precious middles.

Simon had a preference for thin women. Narrow and slender. The fashions for close-fitting clothing in the fifties formed his early adolescent eye. The sixties, reductions in every direction, confirmed it. Changing fashions, ageing and much experience since, had hardly dented his inclination. And while he understood the reasons, the rationalities did not overcome the prejudice. He did not excuse it, make any apology for it; it had become an almost hormonal response, a conditioned reflex. And he was thin himself, consistent of weight and size, irrespective of food or quantity. The final clincher.

That was the other part, the conceited part. As one aged, grew more comfortable with or used to the self, the more it seemed drawn towards the female similarity. What Simon wanted was the feminine equivalent of himself. It was not, perhaps, what he needed, but what he thought he wanted.

And he knew what he needed, wanted. It was a selfish definition. Someone who would help. To encourage, restrain, sympathise, to push and to pull unerringly; to recognise and realise the proportion of the potential. Potential, always as description: the hope, the threat.

In return he could give, would give, the whole of himself. He never had, and it was a measure of his failure.

Simon scrolled through the telephone's display until he found the number. Life would be so much easier, at least in some ways, if he'd had the ability to be a complete shit. Ethics and integrity had always intervened, the absolute need to tell the truth. An old friend, inviting herself for the weekend. Wine, food, maybe a little music, and leisurely, recreational sex. Except for her, Simon knew there was another agenda. Tears upon leaving, just like the last time, and the other times. Nothing had changed; it would be unfair not to remind her. He had promised to ring to confirm the arrangements. They would contain the unwanted reminder. And it would make no difference. She would never really believe him. So she would come, and then she would go.

Somehow, his generation, the sixties generation, the one that hoped to die before it got old, refused. Refused either to age and, increasingly, to die. Once they had driven the technological revolution, now they were leading the genetic one. They had stolen their children's clothes, their grandchildren's, and being for the most part slimmer and fitter, wore them with greater style. A complete inversion of their own experience. The sports jacket, cavalry twill trousers, pullover and always, whatever the circumstances, a tie. That parental ideal of the 1950s was long since dead.

It explained much. Whilst it was the duty of youth to revolt, now they were forced to be revolting. Inappropriate body piercing, tattoos, and truly boring, repetitive, alienating music. And again, perhaps it didn't. Nothing was so sure anymore. Another symptom.

He was of an age that had witnessed too many false dawns, so-called new orders, times of inappropriate hope both personal and otherwise, to be easily seduced by some new specious certainty. And as he was with ideas so he was with the manifestations of all-consuming fashion; from foods, through decor to lifestyle. And all between, and likely, beyond.

Like most, he supposed, occasionally his actions and behaviour appalled him. Savage, uncompromising, brutal. Words delivered with intent to harm, to wound. And target refinement with every added cut.

And like most, it was an almost illogical, emotional burst. Some form of cranial volcanic activity. Though triggered by some seeming inconsequence, to him it was based on considered, argued, coherent, articulate and rational thought.

The results could be devastating. And worse, when pushed, he didn't really care. Misanthropes of the world unite.

six

It was only eleven o'clock, but already the day was becoming oppressively hot. Simon sat on the terrace, under an umbrella, attempting to enjoy a late breakfast. The middle of May had suddenly become warm, surprisingly so.

Toast and honey, or rather toast, honey and flies, plus the odd wasp. Deciding the battle was lost, Simon abandoned the second slice to the insects and concentrated on the remains of the coffee and the orange juice. He turned his gaze to the garden: the spring surge had started. The teeming, uncultivated life continuing.

He watched two Red Admirals, then three, wafting around on a sprig of wild violets. Two of them together, the other looking on. He watched them fly; it was an erratic path, but accurate enough. Apart from the inevitable Cabbage Whites, they were the first butterflies he could remember seeing since the previous summer.

Later, much later, he furled the umbrella. There was little sunlight available at midnight. He sat at the table looking up at a clear sky, the remains of his evening meal scattered before him. The last of the second wine bottle was in the glass, a jug of coffee stood at his elbow. Tobacco smoke drifted quietly into the night air. He sat with headphones on, the lead trailing through the French windows. Occasionally his fingers picked out a percussion line, strumming noiselessly. He had always enjoyed eating in the open, within easy reach of the comforts of home.

Having noted the map in the bottom left-hand corner, he read the description of the wine from the label on the back of the bottle with care. The prose excelled itself. Not content to simply mention accompanying cheese and fish, soft white cheese and poached fish were specified. It did, however, answer the question as to what estate agents did on their days off. They wrote descriptions for wine labels.

He was faintly depressed. There had been a quiz in one of his less substantial Sunday papers that, it being the following Sunday, he had just finished reading. Someone, who no doubt would now make it their life's work, had interviewed a thousand successful entrepreneurs looking for common factors. On the basis that most social research sets out to prove a prejudice, unsurprisingly, common factors had emerged. From these the questionnaire had been formulated. He had scored zero. Not just low, but zero, and thus his worst suspicions had been confirmed. Never encouraging.

There was one Sunday task left to do. Simon checked that week's name and address in the *Radio Times* and wrote out a cheque for the usual amount. There were many thousands of registered charities in the UK, only a fraction featured on the radio, and he wondered, not for the first time, how they were selected. He sealed the envelope and put on a stamp. One of these Sundays he would get up early enough to hear the Week's Good Cause.

Feeling suddenly cold, he deserted the terrace and sought refuge in the house. It was very quiet. He sat at the far end of the kitchen, listening. He looked up at the clock on the cooker, the last number indexing as he watched: 02:17. The world was sleeping in preparation for its Monday morning. The refrigerator quietly humming, stopped, the compressor switching out with a final jerk. Now, the only sounds he heard were self-generated.

He reached for his pipe and watched the exhaled plume of smoke being drawn up into the light. It swirled, turning within itself, drawn up on quiet waves. He exhaled again, beneath the plume, and watched the perturbations. Nothing broke the silence. Gradually, the plumes dispersed to then reappear as gentle waves, the energy exhausted beneath the light. Somehow, it reminded him of death.

Monday mornings Simon thought of them. He had shared

an office with the same hardcore group of people over a period of years. Watching them change, watching them age, governed and conditioned by their occupations and ever increasing personal responsibilities. It saddened him, sometimes more than he could easily express. In ways he'd blundered into a type of luck. He hadn't been forced by circumstance to compromise. Now, if he chose, he didn't even have to adapt. He missed their company. He missed the polemics, the spontaneous good-natured but passionate arguments. It wasn't an atmosphere easily recaptured on the occasions he met them now, socially. Now, short of abusing strangers, he had to argue with himself. Simon smiled; the time to worry was when he started to lose those arguments.

There were other aspects of regular employment, previously taken for granted. Not only had the regular attendance shaped his weekdays, his time within the office had substituted for a social life. Having chosen to decline one, he had denied himself the other.

People went to work for a variety of reasons, that had always been clear. However, quite how necessary these reasons were, ignoring the monetary aspect, he now appreciated. The irony of so much time, but now, how little to do, did not escape him.

To make acquaintances was easy, an almost casual effort. Friends were much more difficult to attain, and he had not retained many for a variety of reasons. His friends now were few, widely scattered. And some, he remembered, had died for what seemed the most trivial of reasons. Walking far away on supposedly harmless mountains. It was a situation that, had he chosen to think about it further, would have considerably depressed him. It only proved that he should have planned his 'retirement' more carefully. That he now found himself in a situation somewhat different in detail than what he expected was not altogether surprising. Most of his life could be described like that.

There was an alternative: develop the consultancy, trail the expertise. A market unlikely to diminish within the foreseeable future. But thirty years dealing death and destruction seemed enough for one life. And, as he reminded himself, the constant refrain: *you don't need the money.* It would be retrograde, an admission of defeat. But again, he did need something to do. He watched another cloud of smoke.

Simon had finally given up smoking cigarettes at the millennium. The pipe had taken perseverance. And there was so much equipment, a lot of it. He'd found his ideal pipe – S-shaped, meerschaum, manufactured for some reason in the Isle of Man – and his preferred tobacco, but lighters had proved more problematical. A desk drawer of remnants bore witness. He was currently using a pair of poorly styled but reasonably well engineered Japanese examples. The search for the ideal continued.

His decision on cigarettes had not been prompted on either social or health grounds. His attitude was such that if he hadn't smoked already, he would have been inclined to take it up just to be irritating. Rather, finding that he was lighting many but actually smoking few indicated a change and, of late, he'd rather taken against the smell. A pipe seemed to suit him, and there was so much to play with. He spent longer lighting it than he ever did smoking it. After an evening witnessing these rituals, someone had recently described him as the heaviest non-smoker she had ever met. And maybe there was another reason. Somewhere he'd seen the suggestion that pipe smoking was indicative of a nipple complex. Perhaps it was, though Simon would prefer fascination to complication. The allure was simple.

There was another consequence from his adoption of a pipe. Hardly a shirt, sweatshirt or sweater remained without the signature burn hole.

Just within his field of vision, something moved. He timed the journey; a woodlouse transiting the floor diagonally, silent on the floorboards. Twenty-seven feet in two minutes. It had been a purposeful walk, not direct, perturbed by minute undulations, but constant. The house – the limestone walls, the ageing wood – was a haven for woodlice. Three million years of static evolution. Entirely benign. They'd fascinated his dog; she'd watched them walk by her nose, enthralled.

Simon watched them still. The night continued, his mind, unimpeded, drifted.

Something reminded him. Thirty years before, midsummer heat, morning. A miscalculation on travelling time from where he'd spent the night. An early arrival in the staff car park, the wide open empty space too tempting. A powered run and a 360° spin on the loose gravel. A long opposite lock slide into the end space. His fondly remembered Cooper S.

A man, vaguely familiar, old, leaning on a railing watching. An interception as he took a shortcut through the factory to his office.

"Dr Kendal!" Very formal.

He stopped, looked back, wished him a good morning, smiled.

"There are words for people like you."

"Sure, several."

"Cunt is one!"

Simon nodding, careful not to take offence. "Possibly." Indulgently, the look of innocent enquiry. "And what are the others?"

The old man, an odd expression, resigned. "To think I fought in the war for people like you."

"Thank you. I'm very grateful." He paused. "And what did you fight for?"

"Freedom."

"Quite. And I'm expressing it. Good morning."

True, and quick, and much too glib. The surety of youth. Few things done since excused that arrogance.

Some months before, and finding himself in that part of the country, Simon had looked up an old friend and taken him out to lunch. They had known each other for thirty years and had once shared an office, back in the days when one had jobs, not careers. Since then, their paths had much diverged and their conversation reflected the divide, settling into safe domestic territory by reviewing the progress of his friend's multiple children, the eldest of which, Simon learned, had just turned twenty-eight.

"How can he be nearly thirty?" his friend had said in mock confusion. "He was only born a couple of years ago!"

The perceptions of ageing compared to the appearance, more evident in his friend than himself. The generally accepted wisdom that children kept you young was, to Simon's observation, something invented by parents to make themselves feel better. The vast majority of the parents he knew seemed prematurely aged, to say nothing of the financial deprivations.

And there was another dimension. Accepting that nature cared nothing beyond reproduction – once the deed had been done, the life duty was performed. Biological destiny fulfilled. So, once the offspring were self-sufficient, the genes successfully perpetuated, there appeared to be no biological necessity to keep the donor alive. Indeed, taking account of resources, quite the opposite. Conversely, without issue, the life unfulfilled, the cycle incomplete, the span would be extended until the genetic destiny had been satisfied. Simon could live indefinitely.

It was a theory; somewhere, there would be figures to contradict it.

People became more tactile as one travelled south. Around the Mediterranean people touched each other. Simon had always been charmed by the French practice; the males shaking hands whenever they met, the women exchanging kisses. Fortunately, his exposure to continental male kissing had been limited, but he recognised his reticence as cultural.

In normal circumstances, the peoples of the northern latitudes never touched. There had been people he'd worked with for years that he had never touched; only to shake hands when he left. The northern latitudes kept pets, touched them instead.

Idly, he thought of the countries of Western Europe, the particular socio-economic similarities north to south. The heavy industries tended to be in the north, so was much of the real wealth. Those in the south, viewed by them with disdain, were seen as soft, benefiting unduly from the graft of the north and always faintly envied for their more benign climate.

And it was the climate that had determined attitudes, divided. He'd once read that the English reluctance and seeming inability for accurate medium-term planning stemmed from the changeability of the weather, and the inability to predict it.

If the climate was hot and the living easy, the spur to betterment had a blunted edge. Modern man may have emerged from Africa, but his technological advancement only really began after he'd experienced a few harsh winters.

He wondered if a similar trend, but inverted, existed in the southern hemisphere; industry to the south, the north leisured. He recalled what he could of Australia and New Zealand. Not sufficient. From what he remembered the industry of one was south, the other north. He thought of South America but his knowledge was even worse. Likewise Asia. He thought of natural resources, rivers as communication, colonisation, coastal ports, trade. Again, the lack of immediate knowledge precluded serious speculation.

His mind drifted back over its previous arguments, destroying each one in turn. Simon laughed at himself. Another specious theory.

There was such inevitability in this life. When he was younger, somehow the thoughts were different, new. But, as generations before had learned, reality settled; patterns ignored now dominated. All the brave new edges, blunt so soon, became the conventional middle. And the view changed. Sadly. Rail became discontent, discontent became begrudging acceptance. Those he remembered from his youth became old.

Simon had changed, but fundamentally very little. Old friends, when occasionally they met, commented. This meant either he was to be admired for his tenacity or he had learned very little. Neither consoled him.

Everyone was allowed to fuck up occasionally; that it had taken him to his mid fifties to do so indicated something. Late development probably. On good days he could view it dismissively, as a pause, a period of regrouping and reflection, consolidation before another advance. On bad days, he couldn't see beyond it. On other days, he oscillated between the two. And everybody failed eventually. But, by refusing to compromise at least you failed on your own terms. Or at least, so he thought. Now, just failure, with room to rationalise.

*

Simon's eyes had ceased to function as a pair and had chosen to work individually. He inclined his head and looked down to somewhere near his feet. One eye almost focused on the bedroom carpet, the other not. His brain fought to interpret the signals, and failed. Something beat monotonously deep within his skull.

Simon sat on the lavatory seat going through the contents of what used to be known as a sponge bag but now, with greater sophistication, had become a wash bag. It was large, black leather, two separate zipped compartments. About the only thing it didn't contain was a sponge. He turned over a bottle of salt tablets of indeterminate age. He delved again: a small blue jar he didn't recognise. Vicks VapoRub, long past its smear-by date. And then the paracetamol. It was a while since he'd had a real hangover. He had forgotten the awfulness of it.

He awoke suddenly, his mind confused by its own reality. The news summary played in his ear, its content immediate and familiar. Several more seconds and he recognised where he was. Since the alarm had gone off an hour before, every item on the Today programme had enmeshed itself in his dreams. It had been a busy hour. He sat on the side of the bed, exhausted.

It was a Thursday, he could tell, for a discussion had begun. Fundamental particle physics: difficult, uncompromising. He turned down the volume with faint guilt. He could listen later and, failing that, the programme was repeated in the evening. In another twelve hours there was the possibility, even the probability, that he would be more receptive, his mind engaged.

He opened the bedroom curtains and stared out at the day. Peonies may be the national flower of China, but Simon had always found his small clump something of a disappointment. They bloomed every year around the date of his conception in early May, bursting forth in vivid crimson, and just as he was beginning to doubt his reservations, the petals promptly fell off.

Scattered by the wind they lay sprinkled forlornly across the drive, fading. If there was a parallel, he chose to ignore it.

*

There was one universal insult, applicable to both sexes, though with a more certain effectiveness when applied to women.

Turning a corner, he glanced down the street before crossing over. A woman, an old acquaintance, not seen for some time through choice, was crossing in the opposite direction. They met in the middle of the road. He accepted her excited greeting with grace and allowed himself to be propelled back across the road.

He waited patiently for the gushing to cease, giving cursory responses to too many questions. They reached a pause.

"So, how's the diet going?" he enquired.

"I'm not on a diet!"

He paused. "Ah," he said, with heavy emphasis.

She was proving difficult to shift and Simon, conscious that he was already late, had exhausted his supply of platitudes.

"Look. I'd love to stop and chat, but I really can't. I'm late. Sorry."

He raised a hand, and turning, rapidly walked away. The expression he left behind showed hurt and disappointment. He felt mean, but it was preferable to how he might have felt, and what he would have said, had he stayed longer.

"Have you been ill? You don't look very well to me."

Dressing for spring weather always presented Simon with problems. He listened to the forecasts, studied the sky, and then invariably spent part of the day carrying a coat or wishing he had one. The day had proved typical for the season. Hit by a sudden hailstorm he had taken refuge through the first available doorway.

He stood in the entrance hall, shedding hailstones from his jacket onto the floor, and looked about him. Judging from the literature on the racks lining the walls, he appeared to be in a museum. The city had sprouted a lot lately. Someday, no doubt, the whole town would be incorporated into some kind of giant theme park. He glanced back through the glass doors. The hail had turned to rain, heavy. He put his jacket back on, paid the entrance fee, and began to tour the exhibits.

It was an industrial museum, or rather a collection specialising in the history of small manufactured goods. He walked down the lines of cookers, irons, vacuum cleaners, washing machines, from the earliest manufactured to the present day. The displays drew no conclusions, the accompanying text restricting itself to a brief description and the manufacture date of each exhibit. But there was a common theme, so obvious he was surprised never to have noticed it before. Each class of object showed smoother and cleaner lines as the years progressed, much less of the workings showing. It wasn't just a question of technology level, or fashion, or economics. And it held for the smallest domestic appliance, he realised, to aeroplanes and ships. The function remained for the most part unaltered, but the design style became less and less cluttered.

He turned a corner and was greeted by a display of sewing machines. The observation held. Simon felt quite pleased with himself and completed his tour with renewed vigour.

He stood in the little souvenir shop, placed predictably at the exit, looking for a book on industrial design. There wasn't one. He tried to remember where the main library was, and what street he was in.

Simon loved thunderstorms with an almost primeval fascination. So much celebratory power, an energy impossible to either harness or predict. He watched the lightning sheet and fork, and reacted to the thunder. A streak shot between two clouds, rising upward. The ground was lit as if by instantaneous daylight, brilliant enough to read by.

The rain lashed at his face as the wind rose behind it. He closed the window reluctantly but continued to watch, rapt enjoyment at the majesty of the display.

Imperceptibly the moon rose, lambent. It was full, the darker patterns on three quarters of its surface etched sharp and clear. It shone. Simon stood in wonderment, as might an earlier man. How big it seemed, that seemingly perfect circle, traversing his sky.

Thirty years before, men had walked upon its surface; small steps, not yet transformed to leaps. Another promise of his youth that time had not fulfilled. Though those pictures of the Earth, such unexpected beauty, isolated against the blackness, had spawned the ecology movement.

Humanity, for its survival, needed giant undertakings, enterprises that shared three characteristics. Political unpopularity and seeming pointlessness, huge expense and technical innovation. There were few now he could think of. Clouds covered the moon as the rain continued. There was nothing left to see.

after

seven

Simon felt stale. He stared at the floor between his feet and wondered idly as to the last time he'd cleaned the floor. He couldn't remember. He felt guilty at the thought, but not sufficiently chastened or encouraged to do anything about it.

Simon stood up to make more coffee and, as he waited for the kettle to boil, his eyes came to rest on the pile of paperwork on the kitchen table. The files for the various jobs in hand and a few newspaper cuttings. One limp sheet stuck out from the rest and he pulled it clear to tidy the stack. It was a review from an exhibition. He checked the dates: it was still on.

He read the review again and debated with himself whether to go. He had no excuse not to, and the alternative of several hours' housework was a dismal thought. He headed for the bathroom, coffee in hand, for a shave and a shower, to emerge from the house, freshly laundered, half an hour later as the heavens opened.

'It was a dark and stormy night' might be the archetypal beginning but, as a shaft of lightning disintegrated a tree in the middle distance, it threatened to become a premature ending. He drove on, the windscreen wipers struggling to redirect the deluge. Also, as he reminded himself in the gloom, it was only early afternoon.

Negotiating the steaming remains of the tree spread over part of the road, the verge and part of the field beyond, he turned another bend and reached the junction with the main road. Water cascaded across the tarmac towards him and he climbed the final rise like some amphibious animal. Unsurprisingly, there was no other traffic.

The rain continued. He had to park several hundred yards from the gallery and he arrived thoroughly wet. His mood was not improved. Rather, the feeling of some impending doom that had clung to him since waking was further confirmed. He entered the doors, already defeated, doubting the expedition.

Once inside the entrance he was greeted by a swarm of schoolgirls, vying with each other to buy postcards. With difficulty, he picked his way through them and headed for the nearest available open space.

It was a very large painting, dominating the room. Somewhere, he'd read that a painting should automatically position the viewer into the most appropriate spot. He tracked sideways, then backwards, seeking it. It was learning how to look. Any fool could see. Looking was harder, and looking told. Seeing merely hinted.

Concentrating, he had not heard her enter the room behind him. The shock of their collision unbalanced him. His shoes, still wet from the rain, gave little purchase. He fell sideways, his outstretched arm collecting her handbag on the way down. As he hit the floor he watched as the contents scattered before him, his eye settling on a small marble egg, highly polished, that spun and then slowly rolled across the floor.

She stood over him, looking faintly perplexed.

"Are you all right?" she asked, her voice a mixture of concern and irritation.

Simon stared at the toe of a black high-heeled suede boot and nodded, getting his breath back. He rose to a crouch and, still on his knees, retrieved the egg. She bent down and scooped the remaining contents back into her handbag.

He rocked back on his heels and looked at her. She was one of those types of women that were invariably found to be with somebody else. He looked around for the male companion, but failed to see one.

She continued to look down on him with a neutral expression.

"Can you see better from down there?"

Simon smiled and stood up. She was taller than he was.

"Only if I open my eyes." He handed her back the egg. "I don't think it's damaged," he said. "Though I fear it may never hatch."

She turned it over in her hand. He watched her expression, but it betrayed nothing. Simon hadn't stood so close to such a beautiful woman for some time. He was surprised to find it made him feel nervous.

Apparently satisfied, she put the egg back in her bag and smiled at him.

"Are you sure you're all right? It looked like a heavy fall."

"More style than content," he said, and smiled back. He paused, summoning boldness.

"Tell me," he said, slowly, "what would you say to a pot of coffee?"

She glanced at the picture, and then back at him, pausing long enough to make him blush. Her smile changed to one of amusement.

"That was a careful choice of words." She looked back at the picture. "I'd say yes."

They walked from the room, following the signs to the coffee shop on the first floor.

"I think you'll find that they only sell it by the cup," she said.

Reaching the café, they divided the responsibilities. He veered left towards the service counters while she walked out towards the covered terrace to secure a table. He stood in the queue and watched her walk. She walked well, the head steady, the stride proud without being overstated. He would have no difficulty finding her. The hat would help.

The coffee, as predicted, came in cups. He put them on a tray with a selection of sugar and creamers, and skirted around the room to join her. He sat down as she emptied the tray. She tasted the coffee, wrinkled her nose slightly, and added a little sugar. They sat in silence for a while, Simon watching, his boldness persisting. It had stopped raining.

"So, why did you come here?" he asked, after a pause that felt too long.

The hat was black, with a broad rim. She took it off, laying it on the seat beside her. Stretching a hand back, she lifted her hair, held in a snood at the neck, and let it drop.

"You're very inquisitive," she said finally.

Simon shrugged. "Possibly." The gesture was not entirely convincing.

She opened her bag and took out a packet of cigarettes, following with a lighter. Selecting a cigarette, she lit it. The moves were deliberate, unhurried.

"Why did you?"

"It seemed like a good idea."

"And was it?"

He smiled. "I haven't yet decided."

She wore a fitted black jacket over a white T-shirt; with the jeans and the boots, and the hat, it made an arresting image. He looked at her hair, pulled tight back upon the head, held in the light net at the neck. Examining the roots, he decided it was probably natural. It was the kind of blonde that chemistry hadn't managed to emulate.

She sat sideways, across from him, looking out towards the old docks redevelopment. Turning back, she reached across the table for the ashtray, her eyes continuing to slowly scan behind him. He began to feel nervous again.

"You didn't answer my question," he said lightly.

She turned to face him.

"I came for a little peace."

Simon immediately felt contrition.

"I'm sorry," he said. "I've disturbed you."

She gave a small shrug. "It doesn't matter. I needed a cigarette anyway."

Her tone was quiet, polite without being particularly interested.

This was not, he thought, going quite the way he might have intended. The light breezy conversation, an afternoon's enjoyment leading to an evening's consequence. He was at once disappointed and relieved. She was, he noticed, left-handed.

He reached into a pocket and found his pipe.

"Why do you carry the egg?" he asked.

She looked at him, a very direct look. Clear blue eyes, almost defiant.

"It's my comforter." She paused and gave a self-deprecating smile. "I prefer to have it with me." The smile faded. "I'm told it's very childish."

He drank some of his coffee and resting the cup on the table, reached into one of his jacket pockets. Separating it from a paper clip and an elastic band, he took out a dilapidated piece of soft plastic.

"No. It's not."

He turned the piece of plastic over in his hand, remembering. Once it had been a squeaky toy, a yellow and purple locomotive with a face on the front. On the piece he held, only an impression of the face and half of one wheel remained. The edges were serrated with a multitude of teeth marks. She watched him as he held it.

"It belonged to my dog," he said. "The house is still full of them even though she died years ago. Every jacket I wear has one of these somewhere in the pockets."

He smiled, more for himself, and put the piece of plastic back in his pocket. He glanced up at her, feeling slightly embarrassed.

She was leaning forwards, the cup of coffee cradled between her hands. Great globs of tears streamed down her cheeks, dropping into the coffee.

"I'm sorry," he said. "I didn't mean to upset you."

"You haven't," she said, after a pause.

She drank some of the coffee and took a tissue from her bag. Simon felt distanced, estranged by some private pain that had been exposed. Resisting the impulse to take her hand, he turned away slightly as she blew her nose.

The composure re-established, she sounded brisk as she finished the coffee.

"I should be going," she said.

Simon turned back to her.

"Why?" he asked, softer than he'd intended.

"Because I think I ought to."

He paused. "May I see you again?"

She gave a small, suspicious smile, and looked at him. That same direct look.

"Why?"

"All the usual reasons." He smiled. "And a few others."

They stared at each other for a few seconds. To Simon, it felt like a long time. She reached into her bag and taking out a small black business card, placed it face down on the table between them.

"Should you wish to, you can reach me on that number." She gave him a farewell smile. "Thank you for the coffee. Mind how you walk." As she stood up she glanced down at him, critically. "Your hair needs cutting!"

Simon watched her go until she disappeared around a corner and then reached forward for the card. It was stiff, and he had to use both hands to prise it from the table. The lettering was small, in silver. 'The Gallery' it read, with an address and telephone number. He did not recognise the street name, but the postal district was familiar. There was no name on the card.

He put the card carefully inside his diary, and then finished his coffee. It was, he'd noticed, the sixth of June. The anniversary of D-Day.

eight

Again Simon wondered, it was Thursday. It had been over a week – long enough to not appear overly keen, but not long enough to have forgotten. He picked up the card for the second time that afternoon, and dialled the number.

The day had started poorly and had not improved. Belinda was drafting a sign. It would be A3 and prominent. She scanned what she had written.

should you wish to
eat, drink, smoke, copulate
or use a mobile phone
you are requested to do so elsewhere

She crossed out copulate, thought again, and wrote it back in. The telephone beside her rang.

A female voice answered; it did not sound familiar.

"Good afternoon. It's Simon Kendal – we met at the exhibition the other afternoon."

There was a pause. "Not me. I expect you mean Belinda. Hold on and I'll see if she's available."

Simon held on, trying to listen to a muffled conversation in the background. There was a click as a receiver was picked up.

"Belinda Barnfather. Good afternoon."

"Hello, it's Simon Kendal – we met at the exhibition last week."

"So we did, last Wednesday." He heard her lighting a cigarette. "What can I do for you?"

Simon felt his nervousness returning. "I wondered if we might meet."

There was a pause. "Did you. When?"

"I hadn't got that far." He paused. "Saturday?"

Another pause. He heard a page being turned. "No, I can't make Saturday."

"Tuesday then," he said, pulling another day out of the air.

"Tuesday's fine, convenient even. I suspect I'll be needing somewhere to go that evening."

Simon didn't understand the comment, but let it pass.

"Good," he said, trying not to sound too relieved.

"Where? Or haven't you got that far either?"

"A restaurant," he paused, becoming efficient. "I'll book a table somewhere and let you know."

"You did mean Tuesday evening?"

"I did," he replied, realising his mistake.

"That's fine."

"Oh yes. And I've had my hair cut."

"Not before time."

Simon waited for her to say something else, but she didn't.

"Fine," he said finally. "I'll ring before Tuesday."

They said goodbye, and rang off.

Simon put the telephone back in its cradle and stood up. Well, she hadn't said no, but equally, she hadn't exactly sounded enthused. He began to think about restaurants.

It was a long time until Tuesday.

nine

They were to meet at the restaurant. With effort, Simon had managed to contain his excitement and remain relaxed. So successful had this been that he'd fallen asleep in the afternoon, not waking until the early evening. He arrived in haste, his hair still damp from the shower, a few minutes early. The restaurant was beginning to fill up, but she had not yet arrived.

Relieved, he confirmed the booking and reserved a corner table, smoking, on the opposite side to the kitchen. That done, he positioned himself at the far end of the bar from where he could watch the door, and ordered a weak Pernod. He sat, sipping it occasionally while he waited, and lit his pipe.

It was a small family restaurant, the older members having come from Naples. Simon had grown fond of the place and used it often. That it was only a short drive from his house was an added benefit. He sat at the bar and watched the easy charm that greeted each of the customers as they arrived. Had it not been for his concern at her lateness, it might have been a pleasant enough way to wile away an evening. He compared the time on the wall to that on his wrist. The readings coincided. He concentrated on the surface of the Pernod, trying to determine a description of the colour.

"Hello," she said. "I'm sorry I'm so late."

Simon slid off the stool and stood beside her. He smiled. "No matter, I wasn't worried."

Belinda looked at his sleeve, still pulled up to expose the watch.

"Really," she said, and smiled back.

"What would you like?" he asked, indicating the bar.

"Thank you. Anything but sherry. I've had enough sherry and warm white wine this afternoon to last me months." She noticed his glass on the bar. "Pernod would be fine. Just a little water, no ice," she said to the barman who had appeared in front of them. She watched the drink being poured. "That reminds me, where do I find the facilities?"

Simon gave her an enquiring look.

"The lavatory?" she suggested helpfully.

The barman answered and they thanked him.

Simon watched her legs disappear up a flight of steps to the side of the bar. She was wearing a close-fitting black suit with a pencil skirt, a black hat with a medium brim, and court shoes. Apart from the small jet earrings, mounted in silver, she wore no jewellery. He wondered where she'd been. Her Pernod appeared beside him, the glass gleaming. He felt a little underdressed by comparison in his habitual jeans and suede jacket. At least the jeans were clean.

He heard her footsteps coming back down the stairs. She was carrying the hat and her hair hung loose over her shoulders.

"So, where was all the sherry and warm wine?" he asked as she rejoined him.

She groaned. "I went to a viewing this afternoon. It turned out to be rather tedious."

"Did you buy anything?"

"Lord no. I didn't go to buy, just to look, and to see several people I knew would be there. Keeping contacts warm." She examined her glass. "It's important to know what's being shown – it sets fashions, and fashion is what sells." She smiled at him. "I like to know what it is I'm ignoring!"

"You must explain your business to me," said Simon.

She looked around as a waiter greeted them, and they followed as he led the way to their table. It was the younger son, and Simon watched as he flicked his eyes over Belinda in true Italian fashion while he made just a little too much of seating her. Simon received an approving nod as he sat down himself, unaided. The waiter departed, promising to return directly. Simon opened the menu.

Belinda seemed amused. "Did he approve?"

Simon laughed, and ignored the question.

She really was alarmingly attractive. Beautiful. Everything about her – her hair, the shape of her face, the clear skin and the large blue eyes – came as a new and delicious shock.

Simon knew the menu almost by heart and pausing only to confirm the listings, turned his attention to the wine list. He pondered the Barolo – too heavy – settling on the Montepulciano, and plenty of water. Belinda arranged her hat and bag on the seat beside her and ran a hand through her hair. Simon suggested his choice of wine and received approval.

"You've been here before I think," she said.

"Many times. I come here about once a month, sometimes more, it depends. I'm quite fond of it."

"Your local?"

Simon confirmed it was one of them, amused at having been so easily found out.

The waiter reappeared and took their order: onion soup and tagliatelle for Belinda, whitebait and lasagne for him. The wine was opened and, after a precautionary sniff of the cork by Simon, poured immediately.

He raised his glass. "Your health," he said.

"*Salute!*" Belinda responded.

Simon smiled. "*Prost!*" he said, by way of reply.

She looked surprised. "Do you speak German?"

He chuckled. "About ten words on a good day, and that includes *scheisse*! And comic-book German of course."

She frowned. "What do you call comic-book German?"

"Oh, you know. *Achtung Spitfire! Gott in Himmel!*"

Belinda laughed. "You must have some bizarre conversations."

"The phrases do have a limited usage I grant you."

The soup arrived, rapidly followed by the fish.

"You do?"

"Speak German? Yes. I deal a lot with Germany."

"Is that why you learnt?"

"No, but it's how I keep in practice. Conversations and reading their trade mags, and the odd book." She reached for the bread. "I lived there as a child."

"Is Barnfather a German name? It doesn't sound like it."

"No, I don't think so. My father was in the RAF and served there. It's where I was born."

"Whereabouts?"

"Gütersloh, but I spent most of my childhood near Frankfurt. I didn't really live in England until I was eleven."

"Coming back to school?"

"Yes, boarding school. There wasn't any family left here by then." She gave a rueful smile. "And sending the child back to England allowed my father to take up a Hong Kong posting. He and my mother had a wonderful time."

Simon thought he detected a slight change of mood; a cloud seemed to have appeared. Perhaps he'd been asking too many questions.

"I've worked with Germans on occasion, spent a lot of time there," he said, after a while. "In fact I had a friend there who lived just north of Frankfurt. Most of them are nice people."

"Most people are."

"I suppose there's not really an awful lot of difference between any nationality. The same preoccupations, worries."

Her soup finished, she moved the bowl away from her. Simon had abandoned his fish some minutes before, succumbing to the reproachful stare of their eyes. Besides, he was enjoying looking at Belinda. So too, he noted, were the waiters.

"Femme," he said as she looked up.

"What is?"

"Your perfume. I just recognised it."

She smiled and nodded. "I put on a top-up while I was in the loo."

"Thank you," said Simon.

"You're welcome," she replied without rancour, and gave him

a quiet smile. She glanced at the depleted whitebait. "If you're done with those do you mind if I finish them?"

"Not at all." Simon lifted the plate across and watched them disappear. She was obviously hungry.

The plate empty, she thanked him and smiled. "May I smoke?"

Simon smiled back. "Of course, as long as you have no objection to my pipe."

"Not at all. Though you may object to mine."

She opened her bag and took out a slim packet of cheroots. Leaning forward, she lit one from the candle on the table, exhaled, and removed a loose piece of tobacco from her lip.

"You smoke cigars as well?" asked Simon, surprised.

"Very occasionally, though more so lately." She smiled. "I blame my father. When he discovered I'd started to smoke he insisted thereafter that I join him for a cigar after dinner."

Declining to join her, Simon stuck with his pipe and refilled her glass.

"When do I see you again?" he asked casually.

Belinda frowned slightly. "This is an odd time to ask."

Simon felt himself blush. "Well, I could wait until the end of the evening – it is traditional. But, by then, I might be nervous about your answer." He paused and smiled. "More nervous." He smiled again. "Equally, you might be on edge in case I didn't ask you."

"No. I wouldn't get nervous. Should I have wondered, I would have asked you."

"Thank you. Pretend you're nervous."

She looked at him for what felt like a long time.

"You also presume that I would want to." She smiled quickly. "I'm busy for most of next week, and this weekend I'll be away. How about the following Sunday?"

Sunday week was further away than he'd wished, but her explanation had not sounded evasive.

"Sunday week then."

Nervous or not, Simon thought he detected a slight relaxation. Or was it just himself?

They smiled at each other.

"You seem much more cheerful than you did the other day."

"Do I?" She smiled again. "Can't be anything to do with the company. Hormones probably."

Simon picked up a piece of bread. "So, The Gallery?" he said, with a hint of enquiry.

She gave him a tired look. "My shop."

"What do you sell?"

"Pictures."

"What sort?"

"All sorts."

He paused. "I see."

She took a roll from the basket, noting the ironic tone. She broke off a piece and reached for the butter and the oil.

"I'm sorry, I'm not being very forthcoming."

Simon nodded.

She broke off another piece of bread. "I sell pictures, all sorts of pictures, from nineteenth-century landscapes to twenty-first abstracts. And I do it well." She gave a self-deprecating smile. "Well enough to cover my overheads and make a reasonable living for the last twenty years. And I enjoy it. Well mostly."

She chewed for a while. "Sometimes though, it gets tiresome. Like today." She sighed, the fresh memories swirling wearily.

Simon took another roll and broke it open.

"May I ask why?" He paused. "You don't have to answer."

Belinda chewed for a little longer. It was not a subject she particularly wished to discuss, but she now owed him at least a brief explanation. She recalled something written to introduce her last showing earlier in the year.

"In essence, the contemporary art market." She smiled briefly at him, not wishing to patronise. "In your terms, modern art is riven with fashion. The factionalism is appalling. Normally, I try to keep well clear. But I've just spent the best part of the last two days being pitched at and I'm sick of it. At least for tonight." She had a sudden, horrible thought. "You don't paint do you?"

"No."

"Thank God for that."

He smiled, relieved. "Now I understand what you meant when I rang you."

She frowned. "Which was?"

"You said you needed somewhere to go this evening."

"Sounds awful." She laughed as she remembered, embarrassed. She laughed again, but this time her tone had a hint of challenge. "Perhaps I meant I needed something to look forward to."

Somehow, Simon did not feel reassured. "I'd like to see your gallery sometime," he said.

His tone questioned and she noticed it. She reached for the water beside her. "Sure, we always welcome new customers. I'll give you a tour and you can judge what I sell for yourself."

Simon laughed. "I don't know that I'll be able to judge."

"Maybe not, but you'll have an opinion. Everybody does."

Their second course arrived.

"Tell me about your German friend," she suggested as they began eating.

"Oh, Peter." Simon sighed. "He died a couple of years ago. Heart attack, massive and complete." He shook his head. "Sadly, we chose different directions, different reasons. I still haven't forgiven him for dying. Silly bugger." He smiled. "Though we did laugh together, a shared disrespect for attitudes."

Simon laughed, remembering. "We were at a dinner, in the States. One of those sort of evenings you get after a couple of days of business meetings. You know the kind of thing – someone puts 'Social Evening' on the agenda to soak up the blood.

"It was hosted by the Americans, one of whom was female, and it was her birthday. So, predictably, towards the end of the evening they brought out a cake to the table. I say cake, a piece of limp sponge, typical American, with this damn great candle stuck in it, but thin. It looked like a very long pencil with a flame on the top. So, after a rousing chorus of 'Happy Birthday', she blew the candle out. It was all very sweet really. She cried. So did Peter and I.

"After this exhibition one of the hosts suggests that we sing all our national anthems – there were Italians and Spanish there as well. You know how Americans love to make a noise, especially after a few drinks. I was sitting next to Peter and we exchanged a look."

Simon laughed again. "'No!' says I. 'We could sing yours, we could sing ours – they have, after all, the same tune. We could even sing the Spanish and Italian. But then we'd have to sing the German. And that means we'd have to stand up and put our right arms out, and I refuse to do that.'"

Simon realised that he was half standing, acting out the scene. "Sorry," he said. "It's a bit graphic, this story."

He continued standing. "At this point, Peter stands up alongside me and pulls down my arm. 'No, no, Simon. I've told you before – we don't do that anymore. What we do is this.'" Simon put out his hand with the palm downwards. "'This is how high the snow was last year.'" He raised his hand. "'Oh, hello there!'"

Simon sat down, conscious that apart from their laughter, the restaurant had gone very quiet. He indicated the room and grinned at Belinda.

"As you can imagine, the effect was much the same as this."

Belinda smiled back. "It sounds like you had a lot of fun together."

Simon nodded. "Yes, we did. We'd asked all those questions of each other that only a German and an Englishman of our generation could ever ask. Our friendship was based on a mutual trust."

Belinda picked up her glass. "What is it that you do?"

Simon gave what passed for a dismissive shrug. "It's more what I did. I've sort of retired at the moment, with pension. I'll tell you about it another time."

She smiled, and Simon realised that he'd only repeated her own deflection to a similar question.

He sketched a rough outline. "It's a complicated story," he added, by way of an explanation.

"Lives usually are."

They talked generally throughout the remainder of the meal and when Simon thought back over it the following day, he remembered the conversation more as a mutual exploration. Subjects introduced, dimensions assessed, and then seemingly stored away. Little said, but a lot of ground covered.

Unusually, she was widowed.

"Oh, I'm sorry."

She shrugged. "Thank you, but there's no need to be. It was a long time ago, a very long time." She thought for a second. "1980, June. We'd been separated for a while and I'd not seen him for months. The divorce was going through." She gave an approximation of a smile. "One set of legal fees replaced by another. James, his name was. It was not what one would describe as a long and happy marriage."

Simon tried to read her expression, but failed. "How did he die?"

"Bizarrely." She laughed. "Typical somehow."

Simon didn't reply, but let the question hang. It was several minutes before she spoke again.

"He fell off the Albert Bridge," she said at last.

"Careless," said Simon, almost without thinking.

"Wasn't it! We'd lived near there, he'd stayed. James had always wanted to cross it by walking over the suspension cables. One night, a little pissed or high, he tried it. He fell off near the second tower, hit the balustrade and then the Thames. The river police found his body the next morning. I'd moved out of London by then, so it was several days before I heard. His parents were very upset. Well, so was I. Stupid way to die.

"Death by misadventure seemed a fair verdict. He was a painter, a good one. Perhaps even better had he lived." She laughed, though without much humour. "His work fetches a good price these days. Rarity value. I sold one of his larger canvases last year."

"Did you keep any, afterwards I mean?"

"Just the one. A portrait of me, a present for my birthday."

"I'm sorry," Simon said again, unable to think of anything more appropriate.

"It's a long time ago. He never was very stable. He drank and he was violent. There was never any future in it."

Their coffee was finished, and the restaurant had taken on a deserted, abandoned look. They were the last to leave. They stood in the street outside as the doors were locked behind them. Simon looked up and down the street.

"How did you get here?"

"By taxi."

"I drove," he said.

"I had the impression you did. I noticed you drank very little."

He smiled. "In some things I'm almost sensible."

Simon looked back along the street, relieved not to see any taxis. He turned to face her.

"May I offer you a lift?"

"Thank you, that would be kind."

"Which way?" he asked, once they were seated in the car and the engine started.

She indicated straight on. "Just follow the road."

"I warn you, I have a rotten sense of direction," he said after a while. "I will need constant instruction."

She didn't reply, and Simon realised it may not only have been his navigation he'd been referring to. He braked to avoid a suicidal cat.

"And when in doubt, I always turn left," he added.

"Why left?"

"It's easier than turning right."

Belinda laughed.

He followed her directions and pulled up a few yards beyond what he saw was The Gallery. There was a small entrance door between it and what looked like a florist next door.

"As you can see," she said, "I live above the shop."

They climbed out of the car and he walked with her to the door. He had been careful to remember not to lock the car. She opened her door, and then turned around to face him.

"Thank you for a lovely evening. I really have enjoyed it." She smiled. "I've not laughed so much for a long time."

Simon smiled back. "I'll ring you next week about Sunday."

"Yes, do."

He paused. "If you'd care to lean forward, I can kiss you goodnight."

She smiled again, and leant forward.

Simon kissed her gently on the lips, and was more than pleased to feel an equally gentle response.

"Goodnight."

He walked the few steps across the pavement to his car, and heard the front door close behind him. He listened to the ticking sounds of the engine cooling, and glanced back at Belinda's door.

He could taste her lipstick.

Simon drove down the street, trying to work out in which direction he should be heading. He stopped at a junction and leant across the passenger seat to read a sign. No help. Belinda's perfume lingered. As he straightened up he caught his reflection in the rear-view mirror, and smiled. It was somehow reassuring. So many years of this made absolutely no difference.

ten

Belinda had rung him during the morning cancelling their lunch, but suggesting a drink somewhere later in the afternoon.

Simon picked her up from The Gallery around four and drove out of the city, intending to find a country pub still open on a Sunday afternoon.

Belinda looked tired. It was not the woman he had spent the evening with at the restaurant, rather the vulnerable girl he had met at the exhibition. It was unexpected and Simon wondered why. He did a quick calculation in his head. It seemed unlikely to be hormones. She was dressed entirely in black. Black suede jacket, T-shirt and jeans, topped and tailed with a beret and boots. She reminded him of somebody, or something, but he couldn't remember what.

There was an enforced cheerfulness as they drove south of the city that Simon soon grew tired of.

"You don't seem very happy," he said, after a while.

Belinda paused before she answered. "I'm sorry," she said. "I'm feeling rather tired."

He drove on. The traffic was light and soon they were clear of the edge of the town. The grey of their surroundings turned to shades of green as open fields replaced buildings, but she did not seem to cheer; if anything, rather the opposite.

"What happened to lunch?" he asked, his tone conversational.

"I'm sorry. I was delayed this morning."

Simon didn't ask why, and the reason wasn't volunteered. He glanced at her through the driving mirror. She was staring straight ahead, though not looking at the road. She sat stilted, and while she did look tired, some greater strain seemed evident. He thought of probing, deliberating between the tactful concerned diplomatic, or the direct approach. In the end, he chose silence.

"I didn't sleep very well last night," she said finally. "I've not slept well for some time. Maybe it's starting to catch up with me." Her voice tailed off. "I fear that I may not be very good company today."

Simon waited a while before he answered. "It's a difficult time," he said.

They began to pass through a village and Simon scanned for a pub that looked open. He pulled into a car park that still had a few occupants.

"I think we may be here," he said.

They walked across the gravel and Simon pushed open the entrance for her. A choice of doors faced them to the left and the right. Hearing noises from the left, he led her through the right-hand door. It was a small, old-fashioned saloon bar, very brown and warm, unoccupied apart from a large dog that lay asleep in front of the empty fireplace. A long sofa, deeply upholstered, lay to the right of the bar and Simon walked over to it, putting his pipe and lighter on the accompanying table. Belinda sat down and put her shoulder bag on the floor beside her. She stretched back into the sofa and crossed her legs, a hand resting either side of her knees.

She sighed. "This is comfortable."

"Good," he said, and smiled at her. "What will you have?"

He walked the few steps back to the bar and, reading the instructions, rang the bell and woke the dog. After a while, the landlord appeared.

"I'm sorry," he said. "I thought I'd locked the door." He saw Simon's expression and grinned. "It's all right, we're still open."

Relieved, Simon ordered red wine for Belinda and a half of Guinness for himself. He carried the red wine to the table, and then returned with the Guinness. As he sat down beside her the dog got up, walked slowly across the floor, and flopped down beside him.

"You've found a friend," she said, as Simon reached down to stroke the dog's head.

The dog had been patted by many strangers and did not respond. Simon gave its head a final rub and picked up his glass.

"Cheers," he said.

He lit his pipe. They sat in silence for a while until Simon tired of his own reticence.

"So, what's wrong?" he asked.

Belinda did not respond immediately, instead reaching into her handbag for a cigarette.

"It's boring," she said finally.

Simon analysed her tone and decided it did not match her words.

"Sunday afternoon is not the time for major excitements."

He turned slightly on the seat and looked into her face. He smiled. "I'll try not to be too bored."

She smiled back, but it was not a smile of amusement, more of resignation.

"Come on, tell me." It was encouragement, bordering on instruction, but he said it softly.

She leant forward on the sofa and picked up her wine glass in her left hand. The cigarette burned in her right and she rested it over her left, the whole balanced on her knee. Simon thought it a curious, almost confessional posture. She seemed to sigh.

"You've been married, haven't you." It was not a question.

Simon was surprised. "Yes," he said. "Though not currently. Not for a while now." He smiled. "Several times. I'm not very good at it," he added as an afterthought.

"I thought I was," she said. "I did try. I did this time too. And I have."

He looked quickly at her left hand. There was no wedding ring, or any evidence of one.

"It never struck me that you might be married."

Simon had a rule about married women, or those in similarly described circumstances. The rule was no.

His concern must have shown in his voice.

"I'm not married," said Belinda. "At least, not in the way you mean."

Simon didn't reply immediately.

"I'm getting confused," he said.

"Don't be." She smiled. "There's a simple explanation. Perhaps I'll tell you in a while."

"I look forward to it."

Belinda ignored his comment and asked a question instead.

"Did you try in your marriages? How many times? Several means more than two."

He smiled at her pedantry. "Twice," he said. "Seven months and seven years. No children." He lifted his glass. "As to did I try… At the time I thought I did, but reviewing them later, as you do, I concluded that I hadn't tried hard enough. That was the problem. The second time certainly. You compare yourself to others, get complacent, take it all for granted. And then, one day, you find it's gone."

He paused and watched the dog who, now bored, wandered back to its rug in front of the fireplace. Simon watched it lie down, stretch its back legs and adjust its head. He envied the dog its comfort.

"To find it suddenly gone is a dreadful shock," he said. "I've not forgotten it. Never take anything, or anyone, for granted."

Belinda nodded.

"Even oneself," she said, quietly.

Simon looked at her.

"It must be so much harder if you've made the conscious effort to try, and then it fails. Perhaps women always try harder."

There was another pause. Simon heard the landlord behind him and took the opportunity to get them both another drink. He carried the glasses back to the table. The dog looked up, disturbed by the activity but, seeing there was nothing on offer, resumed a somnolent position.

Simon sat down and crossed his legs, reaching for his pipe. It needed a refill and he began emptying it.

"Does anyone get it right?" she asked, after a while.

"I'm not sure, it's not something you can ever know. Some people certainly think they do, and others think they have. But you can never be sure. There's not an absolute right, there never is, about anything. The 'happily married' are simply together. For most, I suspect, it's an acceptance. With some others, a conscious measure between the known and the unknown. A sort of happiness, set against a frightening, perhaps terrifying risk. Constant compromise. There's no formula, no magic state of grace. People just stumble along as best they can, just like they always have. And, I suppose, just like they always will.

"Sometimes they fall over and can't get up. Society and the law intervene. They call that separation and divorce."

His pipe refilled, he drained the remains of one glass and picked up the next. Belinda, he noticed, was well ahead of him.

"If one has children," he continued, "the complications are so much greater. Fortunately, I've never had to find out. But the fundamentals don't change. My parents stayed together because of me, but only succeeded in crucifying each other."

He took a large mouthful from the glass and put it back on the table. He laughed, but there was no humour in his voice. "Everyone fucks up. It only seems a question of how, and when."

He lit his pipe and watched as the smoke curled away from them.

"I seem to have talked rather a lot," he said after a while.

Belinda gave a small smile, and nodded. Simon smiled back, a little ruefully.

"My intention was, as I remember, that you should."

"I know," she said.

She emptied her glass and Simon recognised his cue.

He stood at the bar and rang the bell. As he waited, the dog came over to join him. He reached down and rubbed its head, receiving a lick of the fingers in return. It was a while since a dog had licked his hand; he had forgotten how it felt and a raft of memories surfaced. The landlord had to speak to him twice before he could reply.

Simon ordered another red wine for Belinda and a mineral water for himself.

"Oh, and a packet of crisps for the dog – if that's all right?"

The landlord thanked him and smiled. "She's not that fond of crisps. She likes peanuts though, and pork scratchings."

They settled on peanuts and the now excited dog followed Simon back to the table.

"You've bribed him!" said Belinda reproachfully.

"Her," corrected Simon.

"I do beg her pardon. Peanuts?"

He laughed, beginning to feed the dog a nut at a time. "I took advice."

The dog's patience matched his own as he fed her. Gently, she took each one, chewed and then swallowed quickly, before immediately presenting her mouth for another. She did not bore of the repetition. Again, he remembered.

"You loved your dog, didn't you?" Belinda's voice was soft, concerned.

"Yes, I did. Still do," he replied. "She never let me down. Dogs don't, not mongrels anyway. I've no experience of pedigrees, but I guess they're the same."

He continued feeding until the nuts were gone. He split the wrapper open and put it on the floor in front of her. She pushed it around with her nose, and then lay down several feet from the table, watchful, her eyes open. He took some tissues from his pocket and cleaned his hands.

"So," said Simon, turning towards Belinda. "You were going to tell me."

"So I was." She picked up her glass and held it. "Are you sure you want to hear? It's not a particularly savoury story."

He smiled encouragement. "I'll tell you afterwards."

She gave him a small smile in return. "I'm not sure where to start."

She took a cigarette from the packet on the table and appeared to examine it, turning it around in her fingers.

"I first met Richard a couple of years ago. He was a customer. He came in a few times, bought a couple of small prints, and then he asked me out to dinner. Initially, I refused. It's best not to socialise with clients for obvious reasons, at least, not in that way. Anyway, on a weak day, I agreed. One meal was followed by another and for the next couple of months we established a sort of pattern. Initially Thursday, then Friday evenings. I'd not long finished a relationship and it was a comfort to have a new friend."

She shook her head slightly. "I was vulnerable, and so was he. He'd recently separated from his wife and children, and was living by himself in a flat in the centre. It's strange the things that bring people together. I suppose we each fulfilled a mutual need. The Friday evenings went on for a while, and then we started spending the occasional weekend together."

She smiled again – at least Simon would have described it as a smile, but he noticed that while her mouth smiled, the eyes did not. She picked up her glass, drank a little, and then lit the cigarette from Simon's lighter.

"Our weekends always ended just after lunchtime on Sunday when he would leave to see his kids. I didn't mind of course, quite the opposite. I encouraged it. They were his kids, he loved them, and I'm not too fond of people who don't accept their responsibilities. After the afternoon with the kids, the four of them, Richard and Hillary plus children, would have supper together and then he'd put them to bed."

She looked at Simon and shrugged. "I know all the details, he used to tell me."

She rolled the ash from the end of the cigarette. "Richard wanted to buy a cottage in the country and we went looking together. We found one and he bought it while I furnished it. After that, we settled into a routine. It was an easy relationship, understanding. I suppose he was keener than I was to begin with, and then we levelled off."

She stopped speaking and picked up her glass again.

"So what went wrong?" Simon asked, after a suitable pause.

She put down her glass. "It was last Christmas. My parents were going to Germany, and we were flying out to join them for the New Year. They'd never met Richard and it seemed like a good opportunity. Well, it didn't happen. He spent Christmas with

Hillary and the children, and I spent it at the cottage, alone." She shuddered slightly. "I've never liked Christmas much, and last year seemed to confirm it."

She smiled. "How did you spend the last festive season?"

Simon remembered and laughed without humour. "The festive season. Endured rather than enjoyed. I slept as much as possible."

She laughed. "So did I."

"What happened after Christmas?"

"There was one hell of a row. And, after a couple of weeks, Richard announced that our relationship was over and he was returning to his wife and family."

"And did he?"

"Oh yes." Belinda was looking beyond the table, down towards the fireplace. "I've not spoken to him for months."

Simon stared in the same general direction.

"How do you feel about it now?"

"Resigned. Occasionally a bit numb. If you're no longer wanted, it doesn't matter what your feelings are." She paused, returning her gaze to the table. "Superfluous."

She paused again, and then she smiled, though more to herself.

"It's ceased to be the first thing I think of in the morning when I wake up, if that's what you mean. Getting over it. Most of the time," she added.

"Where do you spend your weekends now?"

She laughed. "It hasn't changed. I stay in the shop until late on Saturday, then I go to the cottage. It's where I was this morning when I rang you." She laughed again. "Not particularly sensible, but I suppose there's a certain reassurance in old habits."

She drained her glass and put it back on the table.

"So there you are. I did warn you. It's not a very edifying tale."

"Have you decided anything? I mean about what you're going to do?" Simon's voice was concerned but neutral.

"Not really. The relationship is over and I wouldn't want to go back to it. I have the use of the cottage for as long as I want. When I no longer do, I'll leave. Till then...who knows?"

She lapsed into silence.

Simon waited a while before he spoke, unsure of what to say. In the end, practicality prevailed.

"More wine," he said firmly, standing as he spoke.

Belinda shook her head, but then changed her mind.

"Why not? I don't open tomorrow. Monday's my day for catching up on the paperwork. Yes please."

The dog had retreated to the fireplace while Belinda had been speaking. It raised its head as Simon crossed to the bar, but chose not to move otherwise.

Simon returned with more wine and mineral water, sparkling this time. Belinda picked up her glass and stared into it.

"Have you ever studied red wine in the light? There are so many colours in there."

She tilted the glass as Simon watched, then drank a little.

"Damaged goods," she said. "Boring."

"It wasn't boring," said Simon. "Just sad."

Belinda nodded and looked away from him and, although he could not hear her, he sensed her crying.

It was very still around them. A clock, previously unnoticed, ticked quietly polite in the far corner. Simon listened until it became oppressive. Belinda's right hand lay in her lap, the fingers clenched.

He reached for her hand and held it. He gently lifted her fingertips and removed the soggy tissues. She was quiet now and he stroked the now empty hand with his thumb.

She took a sip from the wine glass, and then another, then reached for a cigarette. Simon lit it for her. They continued to hold hands while she stared through the smoke towards the window.

He passed a finger gently over the back of her hand, following the path of a vein, a blue trace under the light tan. He coughed slightly and took a deep breath, thinking before he spoke.

"There comes a time, with sharing, when you are left with only the one who gives, and the one who takes. What was once the addition of two people becomes the subtraction of one from another."

He wrapped his fingers around her hand and lifted it.

"There comes a time when you have to abdicate responsibility, and then walk away from the wreckage."

Belinda continued to stare out of the window.

"From what you've told me, I think you've reached that point."

He paused for a moment.

"You must leave that cottage. There is no reason left to stay."

They sat for a while in silence, though Simon felt it to be a more positive silence than the one before. He looked at his glass and decided that he was heartily sick of mineral water, sparkling or otherwise.

He stood up, and leaning over Belinda, kissed the still inclined forehead.

"Don't worry."

He went to the bar, returning with two further glasses of red wine. He put one within easy reach of Belinda and added a fresh pack of cigarettes to the table.

"I'm going to feel dreadful in the morning," she said.

She drained her previous glass and replaced it with the new one, moving the empty to the collection they had assembled at the end of the table. She took hold of the stem, turning it between her fingers. Simon held onto her right hand, their arms resting between them.

"You're right, of course," she said at last. "I know it. The logical part of my brain screams it. But, it's so very easy just to say it."

"I know."

She sighed, a heavy lifting of the shoulders.

"Perhaps I'll spend a few weekends at the flat, alternate, visit my parents. Catch up with friends." She smiled. "Go for long walks in the dark, avoiding large stretches of water and high places. I don't know."

Simon took another deep breath.

"You could always spend the odd weekend with me," he said, slowly.

Belinda did not reply, but reached for another cigarette. When it was alight she turned to face him. Simon felt the blue of her eyes examining his face. It was that very direct look and it made him feel uncomfortable. He felt himself begin to blush.

"I'm making this up as I go along," he said, managing a smile. "No suggestions or implications."

She seemed to smile and turned back to face the table.

"I get my own room, do I?"

"Of course," he replied, sounding shocked, but rather too hurried. "A choice if you wish. I have several spare bedrooms – more than two. Though some are a bit rough, like no bed."

She picked up her glass and appeared to be studying it.

"It's an open offer," he said, softly. "No demands, though I might develop natural preferences," he added, a little laughter in his voice.

She smiled. "Would there be a lock on the door?"

Simon thought for a moment. "It would depend upon which room you chose. I could easily fit them to the others."

He smiled at her mischievously. "Alternatively, I could put a bolt on my door, just in case you weaken!"

She looked at him. "How very thoughtful."

Simon caught the chill of her expression and regretted his levity.

She continued to examine her glass. He picked up his own and emulated her position, rocking the wine slowly backwards and forwards, watching the reflections.

"It's two years of my life," she said. "Wasted."

"I know," he said. "But for some, it's the rest of their lives."

She turned lengthways on the sofa and put her feet against the armrest at the far end. She pressed slowly down on her feet, her back pressing into him.

"Hold me," she said.

Simon went to place his arms around her shoulders, but as he moved she raised her arms, and so his arms wrapped almost naturally around her chest, a breast cupped within each hand. She covered his hands with hers, and he felt her nipples rise and press against his touch.

They sat like that for some time, her head leant back against the side of his face. He felt very close and protective towards her.

Eventually, she peeled his hands away and turned within his

arms. He kissed her softly and she gently responded.

"I have to go to the lavatory," she said.

Simon laughed in surprise. "That's a pity. I was getting used to that."

"So was I."

Simon stood up and moved the table back to allow her to pass, watching as she walked away. After five glasses of wine she seemed surprisingly steady.

She returned five minutes later, her hair brushed, fresh lipstick. She sat down, eyeing the empty glasses on the table.

"And I wondered why I felt the worse for wear. Shall we go?"

Simon nodded, smiling as he stood up.

"First though, I think I'd better follow your example."

He returned and gathered his clutter from the table, their debris to the bar. Belinda stood up and together they made their way to the door. As they left, the landlord reappeared and Simon shook his head. He glanced over at the dog, watching them from the fireplace.

"What's her name?"

The landlord smiled. "Shirley."

Simon smiled and said goodbye to each of them.

The outside air was fresh and the sun had come out. Simon opened the passenger door, turning to find Belinda standing behind him, a hand resting on the car roof for support. For some reason her pose reminded him.

"Juliette Gréco!" he said, a note of triumph in his voice.

Belinda raised an enquiring eyebrow and looked at him.

"Edith Piaf? I'm sorry, but I seem to have missed something of this conversation."

"No. I've been trying to think of who you reminded me of when I collected you. Dark-haired French singer, early sixties." He laughed. "A formative image of my adolescence."

"Thanks," she said, climbing into the car. "I've always wanted to be somebody's fantasy figure."

"That's not what I meant. Besides, your hair is the wrong colour. No, it's the black clothes and the beret."

He closed the door before she could reply and walked around to the other side.

She smiled to herself at his observation. It was not, she remembered, original. She'd started to wear black at college when the fashion was for bright colours. It had become her signature.

Simon turned out of the car park and gave thought to their destination. The clock in the dashboard registered around six thirty – too early to start looking for a restaurant. The Villa was a lot closer than The Gallery.

"I thought we might go back to the house?" he suggested, just a little too casually.

"Fine. I like looking around other people's houses."

Simon thought he detected a slight mocking in her tone, but did not respond. He consulted a signpost at a junction and turned sharply right.

Belinda groaned. "I don't want to be tiresome, but do you think you could slow down a bit. My eyes are having trouble keeping up with the corners."

Simon slowed down, and drove the rest of the way at an unhurried pace.

He turned off the main road and drove the half-mile until he reached the tree that marked the beginning of his own road. He turned into the narrow lane that led to the house. Lane had become something of a misnomer; with the recent surge of growth, it more resembled a wide footpath.

Belinda looked around her in what Simon took to be mock alarm.

"Oh God…you live in a trailer park!"

Sensing genuine concern, Simon snorted. The lane widened into something more of a road. They passed the occasional respectable dwelling.

Belinda continued to look around. "How do people ever find you?"

"Sometimes, they never do."

"I'm not surprised."

He pulled into the driveway and parked under the cherry tree.

Belinda was staring at the garden as he let her out.

"It's looking somewhat forlorn," he commented, casting a critical eye over the growth.

She nodded agreement. "I've had periods when I've really enjoyed gardening."

"Help yourself, anytime."

She looked up at the house as he led her up the steps.

"High, isn't it."

He opened the front door and let her through, then unlocked the inner door and led the way through to the kitchen. He sat her down on the larger of the two sofas at the far end, and turned on the kettle.

"Coffee?"

She nodded and looked around her. She stood up and crossing to the window, looked up towards the trees at the far end of the garden.

"The back garden matches the front," he said, slightly apologetically.

"It's consistent."

Simon carried the cafetière and two cups across to the table in front of the sofa and she followed him. She took off her jacket and dropped it over the back of a kitchen chair. Simon waited for her to sit down.

He pushed the handle down, compressing the grounds.

"Black, as I remember."

Simon sat beside her and poured the coffee.

Belinda took off her beret and raked a hand through her hair. The hair lifted from her shoulders, fell back, and resumed its previous position. She reached for the nearest cup and sipped at the coffee.

Simon watched her, faintly amused to find himself nervous.

"I thought we might go out to eat later on?" he suggested.

She leant back into the sofa, nestling the coffee cup, and took another sip.

"That would be nice," she said. "I'd like that."

Simon picked up his own cup and leant back alongside her. He laughed slightly and she asked him why.

"I think I'm feeling nervous."

She smiled at him. It was a very open, wide-eyed smile.

"I can't imagine why."

"I can," he said.

Belinda continued to smile, but did not reply.

Her coffee cup empty, she put it back in the saucer and watched as Simon refilled it from the pot.

"Bathroom?"

"There's a choice of two. The best is upstairs, first door on the left."

He listened to her climbing the stairs, thought briefly about following her, rejected the idea and drank his coffee instead. He glanced out of the window and watched as two blackbirds chased each other through the trees.

Belinda reappeared and stood alongside the table.

"Why don't you show me the house? I really do like looking around houses."

"Really?"

"Seriously."

He took her over the ground floor first then the top floor, sketching out the history.

"In 1919 the rental for this side of the house was £26.10s." He laughed. "The other side is three feet wider, downhill, holding this side up. £28 a year." He laughed again. "A year," he repeated wistfully.

They retraced their steps to the middle floor and he showed her the larger of the spare bedrooms. She looked at the inside of the door and smiled at him.

"This is the one with the lock on the door?"

Simon nodded and laughed.

Belinda looked out of yet another window. "You really must do something about your gardens, it's such a waste."

"I know," he said. "They're on my list."

She followed him out of the room.

"So," he said. "The best bathroom is there, as you've seen, and this is the main bedroom."

It was a large bed and she remarked on it.

"I had a waterbed for years but it burst last autumn." He glanced at the floor. "That accounts for the interesting patterns on the carpet and the stains on the sitting room ceiling."

She climbed onto the bed and rolled across it.

Simon watched, his mind pretending not to consider alternatives. He carried on talking by way of diversion.

"I siphoned off over a ton of water, two hundred gallons, out of the window."

"That's a lot of water."

"It was a big bed."

She leant up on an elbow and looked at Simon who was still standing at the doorway. She looked at him quite hard before turning her head away, appearing to look out of the window.

"I have no unfortunate diseases," she said quietly. "I give blood regularly."

Simon tried to smile, registering both the words and the meaning.

"Likewise," he replied, his voice a little harsh, his throat suddenly dry.

Belinda turned to face him.

"Well? Are you going to join me – or do I have to tell myself a story?"

Simon climbed onto the bed and lay sideways alongside her, resting on an elbow. He leant over and kissed her.

"Hello," he said.

They had laughed a lot in the restaurant, at one point sharing an attack of the giggles. All the earlier tensions of the afternoon were long since past.

At Belinda's request, Simon had driven her back to The Gallery.

"Thank you for a lovely day," she said, as she walked to her door.

"I'll ring you during the afternoon."

"Fine. About three."

She opened the door and turned to face him.

"It's been a big day," he said.

She smiled. "I hope so."

She kissed him.

"Sleep well."

Simon drove home slowly. He could still smell Belinda's perfume in the car, and it was only with the knowledge that the perfume was repeated within the house and in his bed that enticed him out of the car.

He walked into the kitchen and found her beret lying on the floor under the table by the sofa. Simon made coffee and sat at the kitchen table drinking it. It had been an important day.

He sat, occasionally stroking the beret lying on the table in front of him.

eleven

It was an odd reaction, considering: euphoria postponed.

Simon opened the back door and walked around the overgrowth described as lawn to give himself a change of scenery. It was dusk. A blackbird passed low overhead, startling him with its alarm call. The trees above sank broodingly into the sky. He completed two circuits, a path trodden behind him, and carrying the by now empty glass, re-entered the house. It felt enclosed, oppressive.

Simon sat on the wall, midway down the garden, leaning on a pillar for support. An opened bottle and a fresh glass rested beside him. He poured a little of the wine and looked beyond the house over the valley to the far horizon, and the sky. Clouds to the southeast, the reflected light from the setting sun. First a gentle gold, rapidly deepening to apricot, and then the final palette of pinks to red before the grey crept over. It was as if the sky had bled to death.

He now recognised his feelings. It had been a gradual realisation; feelings that he had not allowed himself for a long time, almost forgotten. He had ceased to be alone; now, he was lonely. There was a world of difference.

The approaches were opposite. Women tended to commit beforehand, the act in confirmation. With men, the exploration, the conquest featured first. Recognition and commitment sometime afterwards.

The night air began to chill.

*

Simon repositioned himself around the bed several times. He tried each side and various diagonals without success. Tiring of it, he gathered the pillows into a heap behind him and, sitting up, switched on the light. He looked at the clocks either side of him. By mutual agreement they read 03:32.

There was half a cup of cold coffee left. He drank some and then lit his pipe. His body was tired but the mind, active, refused to let him sleep. Simon sat, his head facing the mirror above the dressing table, unseeing, his eyes unfocused. He thought about Belinda, and he thought about Belinda and himself.

He thought critically, adopting the position of the detached, uninvolved observer. It was difficult and he failed at it. There was a slope, coincident with inclination. He could feel the frictionless, inexorable slide, the delight and terror of every movement.

He smoked and drank the remains of the coffee. His thoughts did not come to any conclusion.

He turned off the light and settled back into the bed, pulling the duvet around him. Worrying was neither helpful nor constructive. Simon rolled over, forcing his mind to drift. It had registered its concern. His body and his mind consulted and, after a brief while, concurred. He slept.

What the heart declares, eventually the head accommodates. And, intellectually, what the head does recognise, the heart eventually accepts. And then, perhaps, agrees with.

twelve

Their telephone conversation had been brief. Simon had made a suggestion and Belinda had agreed. As he put the phone down it felt more that he'd arranged a business meeting than a social encounter.

Planning ahead, he booked the theatre seats, a table at a restaurant to follow, and a taxi to collect them from The Gallery, timed for ten minutes after his agreed time of arrival. It lacked spontaneity, but at least it was efficient. It suited the tone of their conversation.

Late Friday afternoon found him wondering what to wear and, more particularly, what to take with him. A change of clothes for the morning? A toothbrush? Turning up clutching an overnight bag was, perhaps, a little too presumptive. Equally, going completely unprepared indicated something else. After some thought he settled on a T-shirt, black suede jacket with black jeans and a bag, suitably prepared, to be left in the boot of the car.

Misjudging the traffic he arrived early, parked outside The Gallery, and pressed the button on the video entryphone. Belinda's face appeared on the screen.

"You're early," she said, smiling as she opened the door.

She stood aside for him to enter, and closed the door. Simon waited for her in the hallway. She joined him, pausing as she came alongside. As she looked at him Simon smiled and kissed her. It was a light kiss, on the lips, a kiss of greeting. Simon noticed he wasn't wearing any lipstick.

Belinda gave him a faintly conspiratorial look and led the way down the hallway to the stairs.

"You're early," she said again over her shoulder.

"Overeager I expect," he replied. "And I didn't get as lost as I expected. I didn't want to be late," he added.

"Very commendable."

There were a lot of stairs and Simon talked as he climbed.

"I've arranged for the taxi to pick us up at seven forty. In about twenty minutes."

He reached the top of the third flight and followed Belinda into a large sitting room. There were French windows on either side of the far wall leading out to a balcony. Both sets of windows were open.

Belinda turned to face him.

"Twenty minutes you say?"

Simon nodded.

"In that case, I'd better finish getting dressed." She plucked at the oversized T-shirt she was wearing. "Let me get you a drink in the meantime. White wine?"

Simon thanked her.

"Do sit down," she said, disappearing out of the door.

There were several armchairs, and a sofa, to the right of the room. Simon selected the sofa.

Belinda reappeared and handed him the wine. The glass was very cold.

"I won't be long."

She paused at the doorway and glanced back at him.

"I'll be upstairs. Wander around if you want to."

Simon sipped at the wine and put the glass down on the coffee table in front of him. Her final look had puzzled him. It was almost as if she was checking on what he was wearing. He glanced down. His shoes matched, so did his socks. Perhaps he should have worn a tie? Surely not.

He stood up and walked around the room. It was a large room, almost thirty feet long by about fifteen wide. He guessed it extended the whole width of the building. Against the wall, between the French windows, was a dining table with four chairs, black with leather seats, matching the sofa and armchairs. On the far wall was a long open unit running the width of the room, also in black. Books, a stereo unit, and a small television rested within it. There were a lot of books. He resisted the obvious and chose not to inspect the titles on the spines. A large plant sat plump on the edge of the unit, facing the window.

He turned back to face the centre of the room. The walls were a pale grey. The carpet, like the curtains, a soft pink. There were five pictures on the walls, none of which he recognised. Closer inspection showed them all to be originals. Then, of course, they would be.

Simon smiled to himself and collecting his wine, walked out onto the balcony. There were matching rectangular plant troughs at each end, crammed with flowers that trailed over the railings. A garden table in wrought iron to match the railings and two chairs stood in the centre. Simon leaned carefully over the railings and looked around.

He was on the opposite side of the building to The Gallery entrance. A service road ran beneath him, each building having a reasonably sized yard at the rear. The buildings opposite him were similarly served. He looked down into Belinda's yard. There was a lean-to up against a side wall and beside it, parked well back, an old Golf GTI. There seemed to be a small dent towards the back of the roof, dead centre, just behind the glass of the sun roof.

He looked up and down the service road, and across to the buildings opposite. There were balconies on each side, all to the same pattern, each decorated differently. Not entirely to his surprise, hanging washing did not feature on any of them. This was a tumble-dried neighbourhood. Starlings were beginning to roost on a roof a few buildings away. He was watching them as Belinda joined him.

"Don't jump," she said lightly.

Simon glanced down: the drop was forty feet. He turned and smiled at her.

"I'll wait and see how the evening progresses."

"Suit yourself. But try not to land on my car." She smiled at him. "I dropped a wine glass on him the other week and he still hasn't forgiven me. I'd hate to upset him further."

Simon gave an expression of concern. "I'll try and remember to miss."

He followed her into the sitting room and took the opportunity to look at her full length. She was wearing a simple dress, a deep ivory, sleeveless with a high neck. She wore no jewellery apart from a pair of long drop earrings. Her hair was brushed over to one side of her head, falling back over the shoulder. Simon caught the scent of her perfume, but did not recognise it.

"You look lovely," he said simply.

She smiled at him; it was an open look. "Thank you," she said. She continued to look at him and Simon, feeling himself starting to blush, turned away.

He was about to ask something about the pictures when the entryphone rang. He looked at his watch.

"Taxi," he said. "Time to go."

Belinda picked up an evening bag from the table and gathering up a beaded shawl from the back of a chair, led the way down the stairs.

Simon found the play more adequate than inspiring. Enjoyable without being memorable is how Belinda later described it. More entertaining had been the interval; the scrum at the bar for the pre-ordered drinks and the rapid consumption of tepid gin and tonic, the flat beers. A seemingly intrinsic part of the theatrical experience.

"How often do you go?" she asked, as they walked to the restaurant.

Simon thought for a moment before he replied, "It's very variable." He smiled. "Sometimes it depends on whom I'm with."

Realising he may have given the wrong impression he added, "It's been a while."

That didn't sound right either.

Simon had an ambivalent attitude to theatre, occasional attendance. Perhaps he was just too aware of the mechanics of it, but he had been rarely touched by a play. Unlike film. He could lose himself in a film, either cinema or television. Theatre, more difficult. The theatre was about illusion, but too often it had been disillusion. And it was a disproportionate amount for three hours in an uncomfortable seat without adequate legroom.

He explained as much to Belinda as they walked. He laughed after the comment on the seats. "It's like flying budget short-haul, without the journey."

She didn't respond immediately and he wondered if he'd sounded pompous. He apologised, but it was how he felt.

"How about you?" he ended lamely.

"It rather depends what's on." She paused, conscious of her pragmatism. "Though I understand what you mean." She paused again as she mounted a kerb. "There's more to it though. The surroundings. The theatre is more of an occasion than the cinema – there's more tension with a live performance, more risk. Not just a technological demonstration." She laughed. "Now who's sounding pompous."

Belinda laughed again, her tone becoming ironic. "And, of course, in common with most little girls, I had my ballerina phase, so I suppose it's not so much the theatre, more the stage."

They reached the restaurant. It was an interesting menu, both in content and in wording for there were a variety of languages. Simon found the English peculiar and Belinda confirmed so was the German. There was even some Russian.

Simon decided on goat's cheese and vine leaves followed by something that seemed to involve four types of fish. There was no smoking.

He looked across the table at Belinda.

"What have you decided?" she asked, noticing his attention.

Simon told her.

She listened, smiled slightly and closed the menu. "I'll have the same." She turned to the wine list. "White?"

The intrigue of the menu was sustained by the food. The fish came with a variety of sauces, none of which Simon could readily identify. Belinda, to his relief, seemed to enjoy his choice.

They talked throughout the meal, mostly exchanging stories

and remembered anecdotes, the conversation unhurried, flowing easily. Colours and perspectives being shaded in, explorations continuing.

With the wine glasses empty and the coffee exhausted, Simon followed her suggestion by paying the bill and ordering a taxi.

Once back at The Gallery he followed her up the stairs and towards the sitting room. A picture stood at the top of the next flight, hung high to the ceiling. It was a full-length life-sized portrait of Belinda, naked. She stood side on, looking down at the viewer over her left shoulder. The viewpoint was close to the floor. Simon paused and looked at it.

He was unqualified to judge it as a painting, only for likeness. The pose was striking and Belinda's body shape appeared entirely familiar. Her expression, however, was not. A cold, harsh stare, showing absolute contempt. It challenged the viewer to look, and then dismissed the interest.

Simon continued to look at the painting until he heard increased sound from the kitchen. He entered the sitting room as directed.

"Coffee, wine, or would you like something else?"

He could feel her looking at him. Perhaps it was his imagination, but there was something in her tone that suggested something other than beverages.

Simon sat on the sofa, hesitating.

"Perhaps a little of both," he answered, conscious of sounding calm.

"Fine. I think we finished the last bottle, so you open the wine while I see to the coffee."

Simon stood up and followed her out to the kitchen adjacent to the sitting room. It was large and brightly lit.

Belinda put a screwpull on the kitchen table and took two long-stemmed glasses from a cupboard. She opened the refrigerator door and handed him a bottle of German Riesling.

She smiled at him. "If I change colours, I get a headache."

He smiled back. "Please don't. I'm getting used to you as you are. I'll get confused otherwise."

It was a weak joke and he was gratified to hear her laugh.

She loaded the coffee maker, switched on the kettle, and turned to face him.

"Could you keep an eye on things, I want to go and change."

He watched her go, disappearing up the final flight of stairs. He then watched the kettle, adding water to the coffee at the appropriate time.

She reappeared wearing a black wraparound silk dressing gown that ended at the knee. Red toenails showed on bare feet beneath.

He offered her a glass of the wine, opened and poured in her absence.

She thanked him. "Please go and sit down, I'll bring the coffee through in a moment."

Simon picked up the glasses and returned to the sitting room. He put hers on the coffee table and stood in front of one of the pictures, looking at it.

"It's part of my stock," she said from behind him. "I tend to rotate them through."

He nodded. "I did wonder." He turned to face her, putting his glass down. "Bathroom?"

"Up the stairs, on the left. Above the kitchen."

Simon mounted the stairs, and turned left. The bathroom was the same size as the kitchen, the ceiling sloping down towards the end. There was a large skylight, covered by a blind, let into the ceiling.

As he came out of the bathroom, he met Belinda emerging from the doorway opposite.

"Hello," he said. "I remember you from downstairs."

She ignored the comment.

"I've brought the coffee up, I was just going down for the wine." She didn't wait for him to reply, but disappeared back down the stairs.

Simon walked into the room she had just left and found the coffee on a tray, standing on a table just inside the door. He sat on the one available chair and contemplated the large bed, slotted under the eaves against the far wall. A full-length wardrobe dominated the other wall, a small dressing table built into the side of it. There was a floor-length mirror mounted on the wall opposite him, and Simon shifted his position slightly to avoid looking at his own reflection.

Belinda reappeared with the wine and put his glass within reach on the dressing table. She opened a drawer of a bedside cabinet, took out a pack of cheroots and, borrowing his lighter, lit one. Then, with her wine glass in the other hand, she sat down on the bed, opposite his chair.

Simon lit his pipe. She gave him a small smile, crossed her legs and raised an eyebrow.

After a silence that seemed almost indecently long, Simon started to laugh.

"This is going to sound ridiculously coy," he said. "But I'm not really used to this."

Belinda gave him a disbelieving expression.

"I meant the approach," he added lamely.

Belinda shrugged slightly. "You seduced me the last time as I remember."

"I'd not forgotten."

"That's reassuring," she said.

Simon picked up his glass and drank a little. Then he put his pipe in an available ashtray. He drank a little more of the wine, conscious of exhausting the immediate range of diversionary activities.

Belinda continued to smile at him indulgently.

"I was rather expecting you to bring a bag," she said.

"It's in the boot of the car." He smiled, embarrassed. "I didn't wish to appear presumptive."

She smiled back at him. It was an enigmatic smile Simon thought, all things considered.

"Perhaps I ought to go and get it?"

"Perhaps you should."

The stairs, he noticed, were getting shorter with each ascent. Wonderful thing, hormones.

Belinda was propped up in bed when he returned. The coffee, and the remains of the wine, were on top of the bedside cabinet. Her dressing gown lay draped over the chair.

He put his bag near the door and, as casually as he could manage, rapidly added his clothes to the dressing gown. He slid into the bed alongside her.

Simon smelt toothpaste, and realised that Belinda had cleaned her teeth in his absence.

"It's raining," he said.

"It was forecast. Thunderstorms. I like thunderstorms."

thirteen

Simon awoke feeling warm and comfortable, not needing to remember where he was. Belinda had got up, but her warmth lingered in the bed. He rolled over and closed his eyes, pulling the duvet around him, enveloped in the smell of her body. It was a private, personal fragrance. It was, he remembered, a Saturday.

He re-awoke to find her leaning over him. Her hair was damp and he could smell the conditioner. She had just kissed the top of his head.

"Good morning. Did you sleep well?" she asked, an amused expression on her face.

Simon peered at her, one eye above the duvet. "I don't remember, so I must have done." He leant up, exposing the rest of his face, and smiled at her. "Good morning, are you coming back to bed?"

It was a question more in hope than expectation.

Belinda frowned. "No. And you're not going back to sleep."

She turned, and picking up his bag, dropped it on the bed onto his feet.

"Breakfast, ten minutes, downstairs."

Simon watched her depart, the long towelling bathrobe sweeping across the carpet. It must be something they taught in the English public school system, he thought. They were always so hearty in the mornings.

He could smell baking as he descended the stairs. Following his nose, he joined her in the kitchen.

Simon did as he was bid and sat down. Orange juice and a large pot of coffee were on the kitchen table. These were joined by a pile of croissants, fresh from the oven. Butter and jam were beside him. Belinda sat down opposite him and began to pour the coffee, while Simon sat enjoying the ambience.

"You provide a very good service," he commented. "I may consider staying here again."

Belinda gave him a rather neutral look.

"If I'm invited," he added.

He took a croissant and broke off a piece, adding a little butter. He could hear a radio playing from the sitting room, but the voices were indistinct. He had the rest of the day for the news. He looked across at Belinda instead.

She drank her coffee hot, and he watched while she poured herself another cup.

"I know this may seem like an odd question," she said, putting down the coffee pot, "but how did you find the bed?"

Simon was immediately reminded of the questionnaires found in hotel rooms that he never bothered to fill in. He said so.

"It's new," she said, explaining. "I've only had it a few weeks."

She paused and looked at him over the remains of her orange juice.

"You're the first person to use it, other than me."

Simon listened to her tone, but detected nothing. He thought about his answer.

"Firm, but pliant," he said at last, attempting to restrict himself to the subject of the bed, and failing.

Belinda blushed slightly and Simon returned his attention to the table.

"Personal things, beds," he said eventually, raising his head.

Belinda caught his expression and laughed.

"Quite."

Simon reached for the coffee. "You're spending this weekend with your parents?" he asked, confirming something she had said the night before.

She nodded. "Until Monday."

"When shall I see you?"

Belinda smiled at him. "When would you like to?"

"When you get back?" His tone was light, but there was a seriousness in the question.

She glanced at him. "Lunch, sometime next week?"

They settled on Wednesday.

Simon examined his coffee cup.

"Next weekend." He hesitated, watching her expression. "Next weekend," he repeated.

"What about it."

"I wondered if you'd like to spend it with me?"

Belinda smiled at him again. It was a positive smile, he decided, though she could have made it easier.

"Planning ahead are we?" she asked, teasingly.

"Moderately." He smiled, refusing to be put off. "Knowing what one is doing saves worrying about it." He continued to watch her expression. "Me worrying about it."

"When next weekend?"

"Saturday evening, Sunday?" He laughed. "As usual, I hadn't got that far."

She relieved him of his, by now, empty coffee cup.

"Fine. We can discuss the details on Wednesday."

She closed the front of the dishwasher and turned the machine on.

"Its nine thirty," she said. "I open at ten, and I have to put a face on and dress."

"Time for me to leave."

"If you wouldn't mind." Her tone was apologetic, but firm. "I'm sorry, but I've some clients coming in at eleven, and I need to do a couple of things before they arrive."

Simon found his bag at the foot of the bed, his remaining clothes from the night before neatly folded and packed.

Belinda was sitting at the dressing table and he leant down to kiss her neck, a hand resting lightly on each shoulder. She swivelled round and kissed him.

They stared at each other for a few seconds and then Simon straightened up.

"I'll ring you Monday evening about lunch."

"Do."

"I'll see myself out."

"Please," she said, and smiled. "You know the way now."

"Just keep walking downhill until I run out of steps."

Simon removed *The Guardian* from the letter box, resisted the impulse to complete its delivery, and left it at the foot of the stairs.

He felt cheerful: it was only four days to go until Wednesday. Even the parking ticket, flapping hello from the windscreen, failed to sour his mood.

fourteen

Simon laughed as he read the sign on the car in front.

HIRE A TEENAGER – WHILE THEY STILL KNOW EVERYTHING.

As he drove he listened to the radio. Another survey, another sad conclusion. Half the population was illiterate, the other half enumerate, and neither half cared.

It was a warm, fuggy day. More thunderstorms were forecast.

He was half an hour early. Simon sat by a window overlooking the street and watched the display. It was going to be a long lunch. A waitress hovered, ominously.

He gave up trying to ignore her and ordered a beer, accompanying the request with his most winning smile.

"Did you book, sir?" she asked, returning with the beer. It was not a question, more an accusation.

"For one o'clock."

She glanced up at the clock above the bar.

"It's twelve thirty."

"You know, I noticed that. Is it slow?"

The waitress ignored the question.

"Sir is early."

Simon agreed. Satisfied at having won, the waitress departed.

He returned his attention to the street and then glanced up at the sky. Statistically it rained only seven per cent of the time in Western Europe. There was hardly a real cloud in sight, but the English, pessimistic as ever, had gone out prepared. If not carrying an umbrella, then a coat instead. Some were even wearing them, hot, flustered. As he watched he did a quick survey. Of ten coats being carried, eight were folded inside out. As a child he'd been taught to do the same thing. Why? The coats were not wet, it hadn't rained.

Surely it was more sensible to carry the coat the same way as it was worn, outer outwards. Or perhaps it was just typically English; inside out to keep it nice, dear. Keep it nicer still: leave it in the wardrobe, in the wrapping. No matter that your indoor clothes were filthy, the visible coat remained unsullied. The pristine outer garment, over the soiled suit, over the ragged underwear.

For some reason he remembered Double TWO shirts. Weren't they sold with two collars? No, a collar you could cut off and stitch back on the other way round. But that was a long time ago. Things were different then. People repaired things. They could sew.

She was only a moving blur but he recognised her immediately. He would now, within any crowd. And, of course, the hair: white blonde, heavy, rain straight. She joined him in the café, draped her jacket and hat on the chair, kissed him on the top of the head and disappeared to the lavatory. Simon watched her go, those limbs with body attached.

While he waited he looked again down the street. They were lucky with their constant size and shape, the recognisably thin in a society of the increasingly overlarge. Fifty percent of women were now size 16 and above. With men, the beer belly was being replaced by the solid doughnut, thick at the centre, flabbing over the lowering belt line. They looked awful enough dressed, let alone naked.

Obesity was nature's contraceptive. Alas, it had far to go to become entirely effective.

"You're late," he said hopefully, as she rejoined him.

"Nonsense," she replied, and sat down. "You're early, again."

"That's the second time I've lost that argument today."

Simon was absorbed – it was a fascinating sight; Belinda meanwhile, had chosen to ignore it. The normal method of feeding was taking food by mouth, but this individual appeared to be supplementing it by some form of osmosis through the facial skin.

Eating spaghetti could be a messy business, and the area around the mouth and chin displayed ample evidence of carelessness. But, to get sauce thickly smeared across the forehead indicated, at the very least, poor co-ordination.

"Did you know," he asked.

Belinda glanced up at him. "Probably not."

"I heard something appalling as I drove over."

"Radio Four?"

Simon nodded, and remembering her definition, smiled. Radio 4, defined as the lazy way of reading and for years, his entertainment and his education.

"The three most widely recognised images of the twentieth century were the Coke bottle, the Swastika and Mickey Mouse – in that order. The imagery of icons. It says something about the relative power of advertising, political creeds and popular entertainment."

"But no sex." Belinda laughed. "That says even more."

fifteen

There was an expectancy, an imminence which he found difficult to describe. Suddenly, short of time, he bustled around making preparations.

Magazines and newspapers tidied into reasonable piles, a squashed cushion beaten back into shape, piles of books rearranged into more decorous order. He changed the bedclothes, in reasonable expectation without automatic presumption. This attitude was a departure from the normal and he pondered it without reaching a conclusion.

His tidying was partial; the majority of the house remained unaffected. Over years, objects had migrated. With no shortage of space, rooms had taken on individual, peculiar usages. One was full of electrical items: reels of wire and wound lengths, various ratings and types. Sockets, connectors and junctions; fittings, pieces of kit yet to use and those of the all-encompassing description – all might prove useful. Another room, plumbing. A building room, although without the materials, or the mixer. Yet another, wood and woodwork; sheets of ply of varying thicknesses and size, softwood and hardwood lengths, useful and otherwise. Boxes of offcuts. A fifth room housed everything mechanical, as well as jars and boxes of screws and nails, nuts and bolts, metal fittings various, and anything that didn't fall naturally into one of the other four. It was the larger of the unused rooms. The workshop still housed the majority of his tools, but these too were prone to movement.

House as shed becoming shed as house.

Simon finished his preparations just as the appointed time

approached. He need not have hurried: Belinda was late.

Finding himself hovering by the window, he sat down to wait. He looked around the sitting room with a critical eye and then rearranged a few more books. His eyes rested on the floor. A sweep would not have come amiss, but it was too late now.

He thought of the rest of the main house, particularly the bathroom. Unable to be sure, he began to run up the stairs. He'd just begun pouring bleach into the lavatory as the door bell rang.

He arrived breathless, the smell of bleach on his hands. As Belinda stepped over the threshold he kissed her, arms outstretched. She gave him an inquisitive look.

"Lavatory," he said.

She gave him a faintly amused smile. "No thank you. I went before I left." She smelt the bleach and raised an eyebrow.

"Putting out the guest roll," he said.

"Instead of the torn-up newspapers you mean."

"Cut," Simon replied indignantly. "One does have standards."

He led her into the sitting room.

"What can I get you?" he asked as she sat down. His hands were still suspended outwards and he began to feel like a second-rate vaudeville singer.

Belinda looked at him and smiled. "Whatever you're having."

Simon retreated to the kitchen to wash his hands and put on the kettle. He returned to the sitting room to find Belinda standing by a window, looking out over the valley to the wooded slope beyond.

"It really is a lovely view," she said, turning to face him as he joined her.

Simon looked at the trees, noticing how dirty the windows were.

"It's one of the reasons I bought the house."

He heard the kettle switch itself off, excused himself, and returned to the kitchen to make the coffee.

Belinda sat at the other end of the sofa, to the left of him, her right foot tucked under her left thigh. She was wearing jeans and a white T-shirt, both of which fitted tightly. Simon found himself staring at the crotch of her jeans and returned his attention to his coffee.

"What would you like to do this evening?" he asked.

Belinda looked up and smiled at him.

"After a Saturday in the shop, nothing too strenuous." She paused and looked at him again; it was that wide-eyed innocent expression he was beginning to recognise. "At least, not to begin with. You choose."

Simon returned his mind to its original subject. "I thought I might cook," he said.

His suggestion surprised her. "Do I get to help?"

"No."

"Do I get to watch?"

"Certainly. But only if you applaud."

"I'm a woman. Anything I don't have to cook gets applaudeed – well almost."

"Thank you for that vote of confidence."

She smiled. "Watching someone cook is always interesting. No one does it quite the same."

Simon laughed. "A bit like sex."

"Possibly. More recipes though."

Belinda was making him nervous. "How soon would you like to eat?"

"That depends on what you propose to cook."

"And that depends on how soon you want to eat," retorted Simon. "In ten minutes, you could have a salad, with dressing. In two hours I can cook the leg of lamb I'd intended. And a salad. In between, something else, with salad. And we can eat outside, if you wish."

She smiled at him; it was a warm smile. "Let's eat late, outside."

Simon glazed the lamb with honey and fresh orange juice, carefully laying strips of bacon across the skin before placing it in the oven. He noted the time it went in on a sheet of paper and added the time of its removal. He prepared new potatoes and baby parsnips and put them together into a saucepan, sprigs of mint in the water. A variety of beans and sugar snaps, topped and tailed, were packed methodically in the steamer. Finally, he prepared the runner beans, passing them through the cutter and laying them on top of the other vegetables in the tray. The steamer took its place on the hob with the saucepan, and he added the time to switch them on to his list.

Belinda sat on a spare working surface, a glass of red wine to hand, watching him. The ease and casual thoroughness of his method impressed her.

"Do you always wash up as you go along?" she asked. "It's very efficient."

"Usually." Simon checked his notes and poured himself a glass of wine. "It's probably a throwback to the time spent in labs. Always keep the equipment clean and ready for use." He opened a cupboard and put away the honey. "Also, living alone, there's no one else to do the clearing up."

Belinda slid off the working surface and amused herself by inspecting the contents of his cupboards. There were many of them and all were full. She commented on it.

Simon laughed. "It's the rationing mentality. I inherited it from my mother. When she died she had twenty kilos of sugar in stock, and she never took sugar. It was enough to keep her in jam-making for years."

During the time while they waited for the lamb, Belinda collected her bag from the car and emptied its contents into the empty wardrobe in the bedroom. Simon meanwhile had carried everything they might need onto the terrace. He was sitting there when she rejoined him. She exchanged her T-shirt for a silver sweatshirt, her hair newly brushed, and he could smell a fresh application of perfume.

"We eat in half an hour," he said.

"Good," she replied, sitting down and taking a freshly filled wine glass. "I'm beginning to feel quite peckish. It's very black out there in your road – the street lights seem to be out."

"There aren't any, it's an unadopted road."

She looked at him quizzically. "I assume that doesn't mean that the road is condemned to spend the rest of its life in a children's home." She looked at him and laughed. "Though, I don't know."

Simon ignored the comment. "Unadopted by the council – the access is too narrow."

"But you get all the normal services, rubbish collection and so on."

"Mostly, except they don't sweep it. It's the same as a private road in that we all own a piece of it. Bureaucratic nightmare to get anything done – you've seen the state of the surface. A graveyard for exhaust systems."

They ate unhurriedly, their conversation blending into the dusk becoming night around them, the remains of the wine before them.

Belinda looked up at the sky. The air was clear, the stars bright.

"It's going to be a hot day tomorrow."

"Agreed." Simon followed her gaze upward. "How can you tell?"

She laughed. "I heard the forecast!"

"That's cheating." He smiled and picked up his pipe. "Assuming it is, is there anything that you would like to do tomorrow?"

Belinda picked up her glass. "No. Get up late, listen to the radio, read the papers. Why, do you have anything in mind?"

Simon emptied the remains of the bottle into their glasses. "No, I tend not to do anything particular on a Sunday." He gave a small laugh. "Much the same as most of my days."

Belinda noticed the change of tone.

"I've been meaning to ask you about that. You still haven't told me what it is you do."

He smiled at her; it was an apologetic smile. "I think I'm deciding that I've retired," he said. "I'll tell you about it tomorrow." He gave another self-deprecating laugh. "I get depressed if I think about it without daylight!"

She gave him another enquiring look, but let the comment pass.

Condensation was beginning to form on her glass and she ran a finger around it before draining the contents. Simon followed her example and put his empty glass on the table next to hers.

Their eyes met and Simon smiled at her.

"Time for bed said Zebedee."

Belinda grinned.

"Boing," she said. "As I remember."

*

Simon woke. He could feel her along the length of his back, their contours moulded, set. He stretched his legs back; thighs, calves, heels touching. He leant his head and her head moved into his neck. They touched from head to foot, skin on skin, warmth on warmth. Touch on touch. The smell of her hair, drifting.

There was something excitingly different about a woman's body. Compared to his own, reaching up there were additions; reaching down, an inverse replacement. And while the surprise had long ago disappeared, the excitement of the differences, and the delight of the exploration, had never ceased.

And, as it was with faces, so it was with bodies; each unique, never the same. The subtlety of contour and shape, the individuality of skin texture. The touch of a female human being.

The whole experience transcended simple sexuality. He found it almost magical, and revelled in its mystery.

He lay on his side, his arms around Belinda's shoulders, a hand lightly stroking her head. Her breathing was deep and regular, and he thought her sleeping. She moved slightly and lifted a hand to reposition his left arm under her neck. Simon thought he could feel her smiling.

It was a significant act, sleeping with someone the first times. A significance that went beyond the obvious, for it either marked another beginning, or the beginning of the end. With the hormones and the pride satisfied, the feelings could be honestly examined, and the knowledge of the person compared to the hope.

Simon had never entirely understood it, but the recognition had always been immediate. He only regretted so many mornings of inward remorse. In the dark, boldly through the front door. Back door exit with the coming of the light.

He lay and listened to Belinda's breathing. A regular, even pace. Simon gently stroked her head, half hoping that she might wake. He curled himself along the length of her body and closed his eyes. For almost as long as he could remember, he had not awaited the coming of a morning with so much anticipation. Looking forward to the day.

His mind continued drifting. Does one make love to the body, or to the mind within, or a mixture of the two? It was a stupid question.

One made love with, and to, the whole. And first times were complicated times. The definition depending upon the innermost feelings.

Simon did not know. And while he knew the action, after several days beyond, he could not decide upon description. With thought, intervened to complicate, he could reject but not select. Effect had begun to dominate cause.

Peril and delight.

sixteen

Boiled eggs and soldiers, orange juice and two varieties of coffee contributed to a restful Sunday morning. Simon was amused that Belinda had thought to bring her own, a box of filters, a brand unknown.

"I prefer these in the morning," she'd explained. "I'll leave them here. You can try them for yourself," she added lightly.

They exchanged expressions. "Next time, perhaps," he said.

Simon stowed the box in the appropriate cupboard. Carrying coffee was something he'd done himself.

Later, they walked down towards the river, stopping at the pub guarding the lock. They didn't stay, choosing instead to continue the walk. Belinda led the way, climbing over the stile towards the bank of the river.

The water level was low, the flow slow, reluctant. The banks arched out above the surface, reflected. It was very quiet; the heat lulled everything into a somnolent quintessence.

"It's daylight," she said, when they had absorbed the mood. "Tell me about your retirement."

After a token protest, Simon told her. She listened with little interruption.

"Have you decided what to do?"

Her voice was quiet, reflecting his own, the tone concerned. Had he had a family, it was how they would have spoken. Simon registered the care and was grateful for it.

"So far, I've only rejected things." He told her some of the discarded ideas, and the reasons. "I seem to be burdened by choice more than anything." He laughed. "A unique experience."

They walked on until they reached a bridge. Crossing it, they walked back on the opposite bank.

"I'm not in any hurry to choose," said Simon, finally.

They came across a small clearing with a low construction, impressively fenced, in the middle of it. An electricity substation. Prominent yellow signs were secured to the fencing. They contained a warning triangle with a lightning flash skewering a fallen human. Beneath, the words: DANGER OF DEATH. KEEP OUT.

They walked on, Simon frowning.

"I think that sign is ungrammatical. Death is the result, not the action. Danger of dying would be more correct."

Belinda looked at him, smiling. "It's a warning sign."

"Yes."

"It got your attention."

seventeen

There was a natural rhythm to things, an organic scale, an easy pace that if ignored, at best distorted, at worst destroyed.

Simon had driven to a country pub for lunch and, encouraged by the weather, had taken himself for a walk before driving back to work off the alcohol. As he walked, the fresher air and the time eroded the effect. He traversed one field and, crossing another, climbed onto a stile to be greeted by an undisturbed field of what he took to be barley. A slight breeze was blowing and he watched the effect on the standing grass. He made himself comfortable and lit his pipe. Again he thought about Belinda. It had become his preoccupation.

Too fast a pace would lead to a rapid termination, too slow would lose purpose and direction. It was a nice divide, a fine ridge flanked by canyons either side. He smiled to himself as he wondered just how much was led by conscious thought.

There was another truth and he knew he should confront it. Too often before it had been ignored, and too often before it had conspired to defeat. Ever too eager, impatient, he would rush onwards towards an obvious conclusion. Except that this time, no obvious destination suggested, or even hinted.

And there were other predilections to be aware of. Investing others with virtues they may not have. A transference of hope rather than the recognition of reality.

Everyone had preferences, things they would like to change, but this was dangerous when applied to people. People didn't change, they gradually evolved. And if one had vested them with untrue attributes, made that step from preference to belief, the truth had gone. For lovers, that most important truth. With a basis of fallacy, failure was the eventual consequence. The rejection of one by the other, the other thought betrayed.

He sat on the stile and looked over the field. It was a large field, sloping from right to left. Simon stared over it but did not see it; his eyes were looking out, but his mind was looking in.

The analysis had started; comparisons, calibrations, a tactile chill. Love the mind, hate the attitude. It was a response littered with failures, and he remembered them. Names and circumstance, so easily recalled. His mind moved on, rejecting recollection, while his eyes scanned for relief. There was something about Belinda that didn't fit the pattern. Something that while he suspected, recognised, he could not as yet describe.

Perhaps it was that she didn't take him seriously, the acerbic thrusts didn't cut. Perhaps it was simply that she chose not to react, ignored the invitation to rise. Whatever it was, so far it seemed to work.

So far he had been encouraged, reassured when needed, and then in turn, restrained, without reacting with resentment. He was, he recognised with irony, being managed rather well. Better than he could himself. Another unique experience.

Simon shifted his weight, his eyes still staring at the field. Whatever was growing was still relatively short and green, even within the furrows, climbing towards the light. He thought about Belinda, and he thought about himself and Belinda, Belinda and himself. It wasn't perfect, but it was better than what he'd known, or cared to remember. No feelings of compromise embittered his taste.

Simon focused his eyes and watched the lighted specks breaking on the breeze. Time would tell – it always did. Sometimes it would shout, sometimes it would scream. And, at other times, it merely whispered. For once, he chose to listen.

Sliding off the stile to the ground he took a last look at the field of barley. It continued to wave at him. It was not drowning.

He would be guided by events, not impose a direction. Relationships had to keep moving forward. It was like riding a bicycle: you had to keep moving, however slowly, otherwise you fell off.

eighteen

Apart from a couple of midweek lunches, events had conspired to prevent them spending an evening or a night together for two weeks. Belinda had been busy, and even Simon had been less indolent than usual, having taken up several long-standing invitations to visit old friends.

The London supernova of the late seventies, friends scattered to unlikely places around the country and abroad. Just like himself. It was months since he'd seen most of them; some, years. It was a hectic couple of weeks and his motives were mixed, not least to have something new to report when he saw Belinda again.

She had spent the previous weekend with her parents and he had been lonely without her. Listening to *The Archers* had not been the same.

Simon was more organised for her second weekend; he'd even managed to clean the floors. With most of the afternoon to spare, he stretched out on the sofa with the magazines from the morning papers.

The sound of the door bell woke him.

"Hello," he said, after he had kissed her.

Belinda examined his face as he bent to pick up her bag.

"You were asleep."

Simon laughed. "How can you tell?"

"You have that same vacant look you have in the mornings."

"Thanks."

She chortled at his tone and immediately vanished up the stairs into the bathroom.

Simon followed and dropped her bag on the bed, sitting down beside it. She glanced at him as she came into the bedroom and raised an eyebrow. Simon responded with what he supposed to be a suggestive expression.

Belinda laughed and gently reminded him of their last experience just after he had woken up. Simon had not forgotten.

"I've earthed myself this time. Besides, I have no reason to suspect the condition was anything other than temporary."

Belinda started emptying her bag. "Terrible thing, suspicion." There was laughter in her voice. "What are we doing this evening?" she asked over her shoulder, lifting a dress and hanging it up.

"I've booked a table for nine." Simon read the time from beside the bed. "We have over two hours."

Belinda put her bag in the wardrobe and closed the door. Turning around to face him she grinned and climbed onto the bed.

"Two hours?"

Simon nodded and read the time again.

"Two hours and seventeen minutes."

"Well," she said, slowly. "If you'd care to fetch me a glass of wine, I might just be persuaded to investigate the state of your affliction!"

Simon awoke. Belinda was breathing quickly, harsh gasps, short and panting. He pressed himself along the length of her back and matched his breath with hers. Slowly, he reduced the rate, and she followed.

He kept their breath in unison until both were deep and slow. When he was satisfied, he nuzzled into her neck and fell asleep.

Belinda woke with a start, eyes open, struggling to focus in the partial light. The ceiling glowed, unnaturally, sharp shadows from the window frames. She slid from the bed, crossed the floor, and stood at the bedroom window looking out.

The external lights had triggered, the front garden bathed in light. An insouciant fox loped up the drive, paused and then moved to the side of the house. Intrigued, she changed rooms to follow the progress.

As she moved, the back of the house and the garden beyond lit up. She watched as the fox made a brief inspection of the excavations and then leisurely climbed the steps. Unhurriedly, it continued strolling, pausing occasionally, until it disappeared into the trees. The lights went out. Momentarily blinded, Belinda continued to watch, but there was nothing more to see. She heard an owl, distant, calling.

She returned to the bedroom window: again, nothing to see. The night had returned.

Simon slept on, oblivious. Belinda turned, leant an arm on the sill, and looked at him. He lay on his side, his shape still moulded along the contour of where her back had been. She glanced at one of the clocks, the figures a luminescent red: a while after four.

She was fully awake now, the air by the window cool on her back. She pondered; a brief, quick decision. Moving quietly, she retrieved her handbag, felt around the bathroom door for a robe, and descended to the kitchen, the sensored lighting at floor level casting ethereal un-day-like shadows.

The sky was lightening rapidly. She made tea and, finding something for her feet, followed the trail of the fox onto the terrace. The day began around her. That curiously seductive arrival of a summer dawn, inexorable, the seeming rapid bursts of acceleration. A hedgehog, suddenly startled, scurried across the ground above her. A blackbird swooped low, its alarm call shattering the active silence. Soon, the features of the trees, their individual leaves, became discernible. The birds began to call, and then to sing.

She made more tea, the strengthening light more noticeable as she carried the pot back to the garden. She leant back in the chair, cradling the cup in her lap, another chair for her feet. The air was warm; she could feel the residue of the previous day's heat rising from the ground. An old resolution to rise earlier, enjoy the summer dawns from the sensible side, was remembered. She felt relaxed; apart from her own flat, she felt as comfortable here as she did in her parents' house. More so, possibly. It was a significant realisation, and she recognised it. This was not as she had planned her summer, not at all. It was, she realised, another beginning. All the hopes, all the fears. And all the demands and compromise to come.

She finished the second pot of tea and stood up, stretching her legs. She walked slowly up the garden and climbed through the copse and continued climbing to the top of the bank where Simon tipped the spoil from his terrace dig. A sudden lifeless smear of pallid brown against the green, stretching to the boundary wall. The field beyond, ploughed and drilled, green shoots spiking through the even rows.

In need of a pee, she undid the bathrobe and leant back. The range surprised her. She did the action, not done since a competition at school. And not something ever contemplated in her parents' garden. She chuckled, amused and appalled in equal measure.

nineteen

With a mischievous expression, Belinda gradually pulled back the duvet. Simon did not move, his face remaining buried in the pillow. She leant over and kissed the tip of his penis. Still no reaction. She stood back and looked at him. Were it not for the body hair, he would have looked like any other little boy of nine.

She took his penis in her hand and slowly began to pull. She felt the beginnings of an erection and continued to pull. Simon woke up, feeling himself sliding down the bed. Then he realised why.

"Time to rise," she said.

He glanced down in confirmation.

"I am," he said.

"Most impressive."

Belinda flicked a finger hard at the underside of his penis, near the base. Simon gasped as it fell back, limply, onto his thigh.

"That was cruel – I might never get another one."

Belinda laughed at his expression. "Never mind, you'll always have your memories."

She looked at him, still laughing lightly. "You know, the male body, naked, is really very untidy."

"Thank you." He looked at himself, disinterested. "Real insult to real injury."

"Come on, up," she said sternly. "We have things to do today. It's ten thirty, you're missing *The Archers*."

He watched her exit from the bedroom and fell back on the bed.

"Bugger *The Archers*."

Concentrating on the night before, he smiled contentedly at the memory. He heard the lavatory flush as Belinda reappeared at the doorway. Her expression was malevolent. Simon nonchalantly climbed off the bed and wandered across the carpet.

Eventually, reaching the living room, he sat on the larger of the two sofas and looked around in vain for the Sunday papers. He failed to find them. Belinda put a large cup of espresso on the table in front of him.

"We leave in ten minutes."

Simon stared at her, uncomprehending. "We do?" he asked, without conviction. The haste seemed indecent, inappropriate to either day or hour.

There was a large backpack on the floor, near to the refrigerator. Simon had noticed it as he came in. He continued to ignore it. He drank his coffee and enquired as to the whereabouts of the papers. Belinda seemed not to hear him, choosing that moment to leave the room instead.

He rose quickly and crossed to the backpack, bending to pick it up. At his second attempt, he succeeded. It was surprisingly heavy.

"Caught you," she said, re-entering the room behind him.

"I gave up camping in my twenties," he said, dismayed at being discovered.

"Who said anything about camping?"

Simon feigned disappointment. "It's never my turn to wear the make-up and the lipstick!"

Belinda ignored him and walked out up to the terrace. She returned immediately with the sun umbrella, furled like a lance, and placed it on Simon's shoulder. He reached up and caught it as she let it go.

"It's more traditional to use a sword. Shouldn't I be on one knee or something?"

"You'll be on both knees if you don't get a move on."

As she locked the back doors, Simon reached for his shoes. They were leaving. He picked up the backpack as instructed.

"What have you got in here, concrete blocks?"

"Ice."

He followed her to her car, the engine still warm. As he swung the pack into the boot he took the opportunity for another feel: inconclusive. He loaded the umbrella, a further smaller bag, and took his allocated position in the passenger seat.

"Picnic," he said, in a moment of inspiration.

"Correct." She smiled at him. "By that lake we saw on our first Sunday."

Simon smiled back; already they had anniversaries. His smile faded as he realised it was at least a twenty-mile drive.

"How nice," he said.

Ignoring his tone, Belinda started the engine, drove down the drive and onto the lane.

"You'll love it when we get there."

Having negotiated a suicidal ball, dog, small child of indeterminate sex and a terrified parent in quick succession, she turned onto the main road and began to accelerate. Simon felt uncomfortable and lit his pipe, trying not to look at the speedometer. It was always faster from the passenger seat, no matter how good a driver she was. He made a conscious effort to relax and enjoy the scenery.

A ten-minute walk found them at the side of the lake in the place that Belinda had selected. Glad of the rest, Simon knelt down and began to unload the backpack.

He peeled the rugs and Sunday papers off the top and then a red gingham tablecloth. Belinda knelt beside him, taking each of the items in turn. Bread and fruit followed, then plates, cutlery and glasses. There were two cold boxes at the bottom. Removing a strong cardboard box that, he was informed, contained a blackcurrant cheesecake, he lifted out the larger of the two. Within was a selection of cold meats, paté, a bag of mixed salad, cheese, coleslaw and potato salad with chives and spring onions. Pots of butter completed the picture. He looked in vain for the chicken drumsticks wrapped in foil. Perhaps they were in the other box. They were not. The other box contained wine, water and ice.

He looked at her appreciatively. "You've been busy. How many days are we planning to stay here?"

She returned his expression tolerantly. "I like a selection. We don't have to eat it all at once."

Few things were more alluring than the sound of a descending zip. Buttons were tiresome and Velcro did not excite in quite the same way, the initial reaction being alarm, the tearing of fabric. Nothing compared to the illicit zip.

Simon looked out of the window and watched as two jackdaws dive-bombed a buzzard, harrying until it changed direction. Further towards the horizon, a loose straggling vic of seagulls headed west. A distant sound of running water reached him from above.

Women bathed for psychological reasons; men, physical. Men mostly showered, women mostly soaked in the bath. A woman bathed every day, sometimes twice. For men, traditionally, it depended on their level of filth. Belinda, oddly, both showered and bathed.

She lay in the bath, the water lapping at her shoulders. She was watching Simon who, balanced on one leg, was going round in small circles. He seemed to be doing some form of complicated toe step. She tilted her head to the side to get a better view. He succeeded in getting a foot on the opposite hem of his jeans and pulled his leg clear.

She leant back into the water. "Why don't you use your hands?"

"Too easy," he replied. He glanced over to her. "You look comfortable in there. May I join you?"

"Foolish person," she replied, laughing. She shifted sideways, allowing him a little more room. The bath water threatened to spill over the side.

"You might at least have done the gentlemanly thing and taken the tap end."

"The bath's the wrong shape. It's more interesting this end." He kissed her shoulder and gently moved a hand. "You feel nice underwater."

She thanked him. "Don't get too excited, I'm getting out in a minute."

Simon reached out a foot and hooked the plastic duck, sitting by the edge of the bath, into the water. Plastic bottles toppled and fell in. He splashed his foot about, making waves to drive the duck towards them. Belinda countered, making waves with her hand. The duck bobbed up and down, confused as to its direction, out of reach. He moved his arm further around her.

"It's getting crowded in here."

Water began to lap over the bath and onto the carpet. She moved an arm.

"This is not entirely comfortable," she added, and rolled around to face him. "If you wanted to indulge in these practices, you should have fitted a bigger bath."

"Had I known you then, I would have done."

Belinda leaned over him and, with difficulty, climbed from the bath. She rescued the shampoo and conditioner bottles and giving him an enquiring glance, stepped into the shower. She was not surprised when he joined her.

She would go home in the morning.

Belinda levered herself up on an elbow and watched as he sorted through a drawer.

"I shall need to borrow some clothes."

"Certainly," replied Simon, pulling on a pair of knickers and straightening up. "What would you like?"

"Apart from those, jeans and a shirt?"

"That I can do." He opened a wardrobe. "Jeans above, shirts below. Twenty-eight, thirty-two and fourteen and a half. Please help yourself."

She joined him in the kitchen, barefooted.

"I borrowed a belt too."

Simon looked up. Blue denim shirt, sleeves rolled up, and jeans, equally faded, the belt taking up the slack at the waist. The jeans were noticeably short.

Belinda glanced down, lifting a leg. "Yes," she said, and grinned. "Thirty-two. My inside leg is closer to thirty-six."

Simon thought for a moment. "Perhaps you should keep some clothes here." It was casually said.

"Yes, perhaps I should," she replied, aware of Simon's meaning. She laughed. "Actually, I already am. There's a bra and a pair of knickers in your laundry basket."

Simon, his mind elsewhere, wandered into the bathroom. There were changes. They were tiny, insignificant in themselves, but to him, almost shocking. It came from living alone, the knowledge of knowing automatically where everything was without looking. Belinda, left-handed, left the soap on the opposite side of the wash basin. Both racks of the towel rail were now occupied; the waste bin had moved. He could almost track her path across the room.

He closed the bathroom door and descended to the kitchen, thoughtful now of a departure. The journey was beginning.

twenty

Simon was tired. He lay in bed, vacantly staring at the ceiling, trying to remember what day it was. Either a Tuesday or a Wednesday. He leant up and looked around. The radio alarms told him the time, nine thirty or nine thirty-one, but not the day. The dressing table now sported a newly arrived, radio-controlled weather station, courtesy of Belinda; why, he couldn't for the moment remember. It displayed the day, but he couldn't read it from that distance.

He fell back on the bed and again considered the ceiling, the patterns made by the sunlight through the window frames. Start with the easy ones, he decided. He remembered his name without difficulty. It wasn't much, but it was a start.

It was a conundrum this, or perhaps an irony, or simply just the nature of it; this, the most serious of relationships. The sheer strain of it. Initially, physically tiring; then emotionally exhausting. The formative period, so many escalations to contend with: excitements and worries, delights and fears. The last few days had worn him out. Belinda also.

Worse still was this constant feeling of warmth. It unsettled him. A state, unwanted but familiar, supplanted by another. Something akin to happiness. Much more alarming.

With the morning papers read, three cups of coffee (varying degrees of tepidness) consumed, he consulted his diary for the schedule of the day. Wednesday, nothing critical. The sky from the window confirmed the overnight weather forecast. The cloud layer had thinned, but not sufficient to allow any sun. A heap of magazines from the weekend papers, close to a pile from previous weeks, failed to tempt.

He made more coffee, took some bread from the freezer, and thought what to eat in the evening. Fish. The clouds continued to lift. It might be an afternoon for a walk.

Someone had once complained to him that his small talk lacked trivia. At the time he'd protested, his position being that her statement was a contradiction. In retrospect, he could see why he'd lost the argument.

He sat in the pub and listened to the conversation at the next table. He'd been tuning in for the last twenty minutes. He found it both interminable and fascinating. Boring because it lacked any substance, compelling because of it. To be able to idly chatter was, he decided, another talent he lacked. He could talk, but only about something. When he was younger he had talked to think; now, he talked as he preferred to think. Something with meaning, beyond mere noise. It was a practice cursed and blessed in equal measure.

He thought of his previous failures. The series of relationships over the years. The marriages. Self-evidently, none had fulfilled their early promise. His last wife had told him he was exhausting to live with. He'd reminded her of it recently and asked her to elaborate. Intensity seemed to be her answer.

Marriages depended on a lot of things, and many lubricants. Small talk was an example. Relationships didn't need, couldn't use, a continuous diet of meaningful. What they needed most of the time were insubstantial sharing noises, allowing each to slide across the other with minimum abrasion. Living with another, he remembered, required a constant effort. Marriage, however defined, more so.

He ordered another drink and returned to his table. The couple, and their conversation, had left in his absence.

Simon wondered if Belinda might move in. The thought delighted and appalled him. He thought of the irony. It was what he most desired, and what history had shown him he was least capable of.

He thought of the conversation he'd overheard. There was something comforting in simple, uncluttered views, unhindered by layers. He had the habit of complicating the simple.

As he walked back through the village, Simon noticed that people were looking at him in a slightly different way. That indulgent look that only middle-aged women can give. Perhaps it was because he smiled more, some new expression of well-being. Or the stoop he felt he should be developing. Whatever it was, there was a shift, subtle but discernible.

There was, he recognised, a difference between being lost and not knowing where you were. It was similar to not knowing the way forward until you knew which direction you were facing. It was easy to navigate backwards; confirmation by recognition. Exploration was altogether more difficult.

He had loved several times before, or thought he had, which amounted to much the same thing. He remembered the joy of it, and he remembered the pain.

twenty-one

Belinda carefully rolled the ash from the end of her cheroot into the ashtray. She pulled the cardigan, borrowed from Simon, further around her. The evening air was beginning to chill, and she could feel the dampness of the dew. It had been a warm day and they had chosen to eat on the terrace, watching the sun disappear behind the trees. The remains of their meal were still on the table. Belinda absently picked at a piece of bread and refilled her glass. She rested the side of her head on a hand and looked across the table at Simon. He seemed to be studying the trees that leant protectively around them. He had a quiet, reflective expression.

She stubbed out the cheroot and, after a moment's thought, lit another. It was, she noticed, the last one in the packet. A breeze stirred and a leaf blew down and landed in her lap. She picked it up and put it on the table in front of her. It was whole, symmetrical, each side of the stem perfectly reproduced on the other. She looked up again to find Simon watching at her.

"It's getting colder," he said. "Perhaps we should go in?"

"Not just yet," she said.

Simon lit his pipe and picked up his wine glass. Belinda had a distant, preoccupied expression.

"This is the third weekend I've spent here," she said, after a while.

Simon thought for a moment, and then nodded. "Several weeks ago, last weekend, and now this. Are you counting?"

She smiled. "No. Are you?"

He smiled back at her. "Only retrospectively."

She picked up the leaf from the table and turning it in her fingers, felt the underside. There had been a time, long ago, when she had drawn leaves. Fine delicate pencil studies, the veins of filigree setting off the texture. She been proud of those drawings, if a little too figurative. She wondered what happened to them. Lost, with the rest of her portfolio, when she'd left the Slade.

She looked at Simon.

"I'm moving out of the cottage."

"Good," he replied. "It's about time. Do you have much to move?"

She shrugged. "Clothes, bits and pieces. A few items of furniture."

"Will it all fit in the flat?"

"I was wondering if I might bring some of it here?"

"Why not. There's plenty of room."

"Physical accommodation was not my concern," she said, irritated by his practicality.

"I did realise that," he said, kindly.

Simon's spirits soared and he made a valiant effort to contain them.

"I'd be very pleased, delighted," he added.

He emptied the remains of the wine bottle, sharing the contents between their glasses.

"Would you like any help with the move?"

"No, I don't think so. It's something I'd prefer to do by myself."

She looked down at the leaf, still in her hands. It had begun to wither.

"It's getting cold out here," she said.

twenty-two

The weather had held and they continued to take advantage of it. A rough fire burnt in the corner of the terrace, giving a background glow to the guttering candles. A second bottle of wine grew empty as Simon refilled their glasses.

Belinda thanked him, picked up the glass and then turned her head at the sound of something moving in the trees above them. Another rustle, then silence.

It had been a very pleasant Sunday, restful. They had read the papers over a protracted lunch and then walked in the late afternoon sun. In the evening Simon had cooked a duck, heavy with garlic. They had talked, amused each other, and said very little.

Somehow, the day seemed to anticipate a conclusion. Neither had approached it, not wishing to spoil the mood, opportunities carefully circumvented.

The fire crackled and sent up a small shower of sparks, extinguishing as they blew towards the trees. She caught Simon's eye and smiled.

"Do you mind if I ask you a slightly indelicate question?"

Simon gave a half-laugh, wondering. "No, of course not."

"Does garlic make you fart? It does me."

Simon, momentarily taken aback, laughed louder. "All the time."

"Oh good, I can blame you then."

Squatting down, Simon added wood to the fire and then gave it a couple of prods. Another shower of sparks drifted away as Belinda watched. He continued to squat, poking at the fire.

He turned and saw her looking at him, that same deep look.

"Are you having second thoughts?"

Simon straightened up and sat opposite her. "No, not second thoughts. Just thoughts."

He kicked at a stone somewhere near his feet and gave her an apologetic expression. "I suppose…" He looked at her, watching for a reaction, choosing his words. "With your things coming here, it's much the same as if you were moving in. Not that I don't want you to," he added quickly, unable to read her expression. "If you'd like to, of course."

Belinda continued to look at him. It was, perhaps, a little quick, but it had a kind of logic.

"Are you asking me to live with you?"

"Yes, I think I am."

They looked at each other. Belinda seemed to smile, but it was Simon who broke the silence.

"But, I'm just wondering if we shouldn't give it some kind of trial, give it the best chance – a better chance. I've been here before. Perhaps more often than you. Big leaps, little thought. And it's not a bridge you land on, it's a raft. Floats well, but no direction, prone to hazards. Easily destroyed. Another pile of debris clattering off down the river, wreckage clinging." He laughed at himself, breaking his line of thought.

She looked at him. "Very graphical. Thank you for the encouragement." She laughed at his presumption. "And I haven't said I will yet."

"I know." He shrugged. It was, in its way, a positive gesture. "I didn't mean to dissuade you. I'd be thrilled, of course, but…" he hesitated, "I don't want to…" He hesitated again, searched for another phrase and failed. "Just fuck up again."

He gave a short, reluctant smile. "It matters. You matter. If you didn't, I wouldn't worry. You'd just be one of a number. Repercussions. And I'm getting tired, too tired of all the repercussions."

Simon was staring into the fire, the reflection in the half-light softening his features. He looked, she thought, sad.

There was a long pause.

"I'd not thought of myself as one of a sequence," she said eventually.

It was an unaddressed statement. There was another pause, longer.

Simon reached for her hand. "I'd love it if you moved in. I really would. And you're not just one of a sequence – please don't think that. It's just," he looked back at the fire, "I seem to have spent half my life having relationships, and the other half recovering from them. It's not indefinite. There is a limit. Sometime, there is a last time." He gave a rueful smile. "Like first times, last time every time."

She gave him a mixed expression. "You do know how to make a girl feel wanted."

He went to interrupt, but she raised a hand.

"But I do know what you mean. And don't think I haven't had the same sort of thoughts. There is a lot of debris behind us." She paused. "Or should that be beneath us? You've got me at it now. Whatever. Neither of us are very good at this. And just like you, I don't relish another failure."

She paused, attempting to find the words to say exactly what she felt, meant.

"I'm not sure, but we won't know unless we try. And now, unless we do, we'll be going backwards." She gave him a challenging expression. "It's either forwards or backwards, no in-betweens."

Simon nodded. "I know."

"This trial," she skipped the imagery. "Trial period. How long?"

"I don't know. I haven't thought."

"Well, it doesn't need a fixed time. I guess we'll know soon enough."

Simon, alarmed, began placating. "We don't want to give up at the first problem."

She smiled at him indulgently. "I wasn't suggesting we do."

The relief on his face, even in the half-light, was palpable.

"Tomorrow then," she said. "I'll start moving things in."

twenty-three

He trooped up the stairs for the umpteenth time, and drooped another armful on the bed. Feigning exhaustion, he slumped beside them and watched her unpack.

Belinda had chosen to transport most of her clothes in the large flat cardboard boxes she used to ship pictures. He was only grateful she was not using the wooden ones. Flattened boxes crept around the walls as his wardrobes and drawers filled. Hanging space in the other bedrooms was already exhausted.

"You have a lot of clothes," he said, as she decided on an appropriate depository for woollens.

"I do seem to. I suppose it comes from keeping two separate wardrobes. I'll be taking some of this to the flat. And there are some things there that should really be here." She looked thoughtful. "And a lot to the charity shop."

With the boxes emptied, she turned to the suitcases. There were three of them. One seemed to be entirely composed of more shoes, another of boots. The last was full of underwear.

"This is a transvestite's dream," he said.

She turned to him, an eyebrow raised. "Is this something I should know about?"

"No."

"That's a relief."

Simon laughed as he remembered. "When I was an adolescent, we used to worry about changing sex."

"Why?"

"I don't rightly know. Perhaps it was just coming into fashion."

For the want of anything better to do he went downstairs to make coffee. He returned with two mugs and put one on the window sill, next to a teddy bear that had taken up residence in his absence. It looked well used, the look of an old and trusted friend.

"Who's that?" he asked, sitting on the one remaining space left on the bed. "The bear."

Belinda crossed to the window and thanked him for the coffee. She patted the bear on its head and straightened its bow.

"He's called Him." She smiled. "He has a twin called Her, but they don't get on. She lives at the flat. I've had them since I was two."

Simon nodded and, after a little thought, picked his way across the floor and into the bathroom. He returned minutes later, carrying a rather scruffy and dirty little bear. He beat off the dust and sat it next to Him.

"Who is that?" she asked, looking amused.

"That is Quark," he said. "I don't think it has a gender. It was a special offer with Boutique tissue in the seventies," he added, remembering. "I think it was ten bob with box tops."

"Quark, from Lewis Carroll?"

"Almost. It was used to name a particle in atomic physics. It seemed appropriate. Teddy bears are a sort of fundamental particle."

Belinda appeared unimpressed with the explanation. "It seems an awful name for such a little person."

She picked it up, adjusted the bow, and rearranged its seating, further away from Him. She looked at them together.

"I hope they get on."

"I expect they will, if we do," he said, with more seriousness than he had intended.

She continued sorting her underwear for several minutes and then returned to her coffee by the window. She rearranged the bears again, their backs to the light.

"That, Simon, I suspect, rather depends on you."

*

Another hour and another load, books this time and yet more clothes.

"Oh. There's a few things in the car. I got them in, but I'll need your help to get them out."

There were four boxes. One occupying the whole of the back seat and very heavy, the others in the boot. Carrying them in and building the stand was the hard part. Once plugged in the equipment was self-setting.

Remembering the adage *If all else fails, read the instructions*, Simon read the booklets first: many pages, most comprehensive, some almost comprehensible. Simon stood back, impressed. Sony's finest, in full working order, VCR and DVD to match. The size of the widescreen TV dwarfed his old set. It looked and was, he knew, very expensive.

"You haven't just bought this?"

"Lord no. It was a Christmas present from Richard. It's been in the storeroom at the shop ever since. Seems a shame now not to use it."

He looked around, and thought.

"Not that I'm worried, but is there much more to come?" His tone betrayed concern.

"Some, if you want me to do this properly."

Getting no reply, Simon mounted the stairs in search of her. The sight that greeted him in the bedroom was, at the very least, curious.

Belinda was kneeling on the bed, her upper torso and head buried deep within the duvet cover. Her naked bottom meanwhile was stuck high in the air, the archetypal ostrich position. It reminded of a particularly rude joke, several. The contents of her handbag were strewn across the floor.

Wisely, although tempted, he had the sense not to touch. Instead, he located her head inside the cover and spoke to it.

"I know this is a silly question, but what are you doing?"

"Sewing."

"There's no need to be shy about it!"

There was a grunt accompanied by movement as she slid out to emerge with her hair full of feathers. She was clutching a sewing kit, reading glasses perched on the end of her nose.

Simon laughed and enquired again.

"I shook out the duvet and got covered in feathers. I've found the hole and stitched it up." She looked at him accusingly. "I found patches of gaffer tape in there."

Simon nodded. "Burn holes." He paused. "If you're interested, I've have a couple of buttons that—"

"Don't even think about it," she interrupted.

Simon no longer did.

Belinda stepped from the shower, her body dried, and walked to the far end of the bathroom, and the airing cupboard, for a fresh towel for her hair. The airing cupboard was of an impressive size; she'd had bathrooms not much larger. So was Simon's collection of towels, mainly off white, all sizes catered for. Most bore a woven 'S' in the centre. She suspected but hadn't asked.

Clad in T-shirt and knickers, a towel swathed around her head, she found him sitting on the veranda immersed in a newspaper. He poured coffee as she joined him.

She released the towel, gave her hair a vigorous rub and then combed it straight to dry in the morning sunlight. She shook out the towel and hung it over the back of a vacant chair.

Simon followed her gaze as she indicated the letter.

He smiled. "S for stolen. Or, more precisely, Sheraton. It was the company's hotel of choice in the States – I stayed in a lot of them. Some used to present me with a parcel of them when I left. There's a selection from around Europe as well."

She looked at him, pityingly. "Like the ashtrays."

Simon nodded, unabashed. "And the cutlery."

Come the evening, and lacking the inclination to cook, Simon suggested they eat at one of the pubs by the river. There was a choice of three within walking distance.

Belinda remembered an earlier comment. "And I'll pay," she said. "Just don't get too pissed and fall in."

As they walked she talked about her parents, filling in a little background.

"And you still call them Mummy and Daddy?"

She laughed. "Yes, still. I'm not sure why. I always have I suppose, it's how I think of them. Feels natural. We have pet names too, like any family."

"Oh yes?"

She smiled, more to herself. "They depend on the circumstances."

Simon was intrigued. "What are yours? I promise never to use them," he added.

She laughed, gently mocking. "Oh yes. Very likely." She thought of one of the more unusual. "Daddy calls me Sticky sometimes."

"Why Sticky?"

"Old story. They used to entertain – a lot. You did then, stationed in Germany in the fifties. Lots of Americans. They all called me honey. Hence Sticky." She thought for a moment. "At least, I think that's where it comes from."

Simon thought back. "I don't know that I've ever had a pet name." He laughed. "Apart from 'Come here, you little sod.'"

"Why, do you want one?"

"Not especially. Why, do you have anything in mind?"

"I'm sure I could think of something. With you it would have to be an opposite." She laughed. "Simple. That goes with Simon."

"Too easy."

"I don't agree. It works both ways."

Simon was not convinced. "Then I'd have to call you Ugly."

"I quite like that."

"You would."

Simon steered the conversation back.

"I should like to meet your parents sometime."

"Oh, you will." She paused, roughly calculating how long they had known each other. "The summons for an audience should come any day now."

twenty-four

After a lifetime of forever late, Simon was becoming early. He parked in the yard behind The Gallery and walked around to the front entrance. He glanced into her neighbouring shops as he passed, thinking of their late-night shopping expedition to come. Bed linen and towels, the life domestic.

Belinda was busy with a customer, a well-dressed woman in her late thirties. A rather serious little boy, presumably her son, was sitting in one of the chairs by the reception desk. Simon joined him. The boy acknowledged him as he sat down but didn't speak. Simon guessed his age at around eight.

They sat for a few minutes, Simon watching the transaction, the little boy staring at some distant point towards the street. Simon spoke to him, as much to reassure himself as the boy. He was useless with children, never knowing what to say.

"I'm sure your mummy won't be very much longer."

The little boy nodded, a curious, almost forlorn gesture. He seemed troubled somehow and Simon asked if there was anything wrong.

The little boy looked at him for the first time, that same serious expression.

"May I ask you a question?"

Surprised, Simon replied, "Yes, of course you can."

"Do you know what death is?"

"Yes, I do."

"Could you tell me please."

"I can try." Simon, shocked, thought quickly. "Just give me a moment to compose my answer."

Simon believed in the soul, although he couldn't entirely describe to anyone else the full implications of the belief. Likewise, an afterlife. Death, in itself, was not the end. There were too many indications otherwise. The understanding he lived with involved quantum physics and parallel reality, superposition theory, the Schrödinger principle. Simultaneous states, many worlds, continuous. And while he could live with his certainty of something beyond death, his muddled explanation would hardly be appropriate for a troubled eight-year-old. Religion might struggle to convince, and so might any description of heaven.

Simon drew breath.

"Death is an end, but it is also a beginning," he said, slowly. "We can see the end, but we cannot see the beginning. And we are not supposed to. But I'm sure there is one." He paused, trying to judge the reaction. "Does that help?"

The little boy didn't react immediately and Simon wondered what else he might say.

Then the boy nodded. "I think so."

Simon looked up to see Belinda and the woman standing close by, listening. He stood up and the little boy followed, wished him goodbye, and joined his mother. The woman gave Simon a kind, almost grateful smile, before Belinda showed them out.

Simon was leaning on the counter when she returned, looking vaguely at one of her pictures. Belinda took his hands in hers and kissed him.

"His uncle died this week. It's his first experience of death."

"It won't get any easier," said Simon, bitterly.

As they set off, Belinda noticed his expression and laughed. "You look worried."

"I've just thought. This is our first shopping expedition together."

She laughed again. "You make it sound like some grand Victorian exploration. It's only a shopping trip."

Simon was not convinced. "Buying or shopping? As activities, as I remember, they're not to be confused."

"I'm shopping to buy, if that's what you mean. If I just wanted to shop, I wouldn't ask you. No fun at all."

They reached the mall, agreed on where to park and walked through the chosen entrance. Simon's mood was mixed. He was unsure as to how social he was feeling and these places required a degree of fortitude. Not inaccurately, they had been described as the new cathedrals. The nation's retail activity in a single day was equivalent to that of a whole year fifty years ago. He took a deep breath as they plunged into the delights of John Lewis.

In the event, it was relatively painless. Some discussion, little disagreement, though more extensive than he'd supposed. With the towels and bedding secured, Belinda suggested a break for coffee. While she ordered, Simon took the bags to the car. Walking back into the café, he followed a waitress to their table.

It was sad. So often the difference between plainness and attractiveness was separated by a few millimetres. True ugliness, like true beauty, is rare. Simon gave an involuntary grimace as the waitress left.

Belinda commented on it.

"A two-bag woman," said Simon, without malice.

"Two-bag?" Belinda smiled. "I've heard of brown paper bag jobs, but not that."

"Similar, but much worse," explained Simon. "A two-bag woman is one bag for her, and another bag for you in case her bag comes off!"

As they began round two, Simon, seduced by the sight of a bookshop, veered off. Belinda, not to be distracted, pointed to a shop further down. Later, Waterstones bag in hand, Simon went in search of her.

It was one of those dress shops whose supposed exclusivity was advertised by an external button, pressed to gain entry. The interior was a surprise to Simon, dark, his reaction oscillating between intrigued and appalled. Clothes shop metamorphosed into art gallery. Each garment displayed in isolation, an added mystique with, no doubt, a price to match. There were chairs, deep, somnolent. Simon sat.

An assistant slid to his side. "Good evening, sir, how may I help you?"

Simon peered into the gloom, but to no avail. He smiled at the assistant instead.

"Yes, I think you can. I'm looking for a wife!"

Her face became an interesting mixture of contrasts, but remained calm. He admired her for it – perhaps she was used to strange customers. The assistant decided on the impassive approach and carefully framed her reply.

"Did sir have anything particular in mind?"

"Tall, I thought." He indicated with his hands. "About so high."

The assistant's expression didn't change and he began to enjoy himself.

"But small," he brought his hands together. "About a size eight, or ten, depending on the height. And blonde, definitely blonde, long hair. Maybe foreign-looking, but nothing too obscure."

As he spoke, his eyes continued to roam around the shop, adjusting to the light. In time, he might even be able to see. As it was, he heard her before he saw her.

"Ah," he said to the assistant, who was beginning to show the first signs of irritation. "I think I see something over there." He set off purposefully in the direction of the sound.

He found her standing at the cash desk, and sidled up.

"Excuse me, but would you like to come home with me?"

Belinda's expression was one of aghast tolerance.

She turned and looked at him for several moments, taking in the worried expression of the assistant who had caught up. She glanced at her watch, paused and then swept her bags from the floor.

"All right, but for no more than an hour," she answered briskly. "I have another appointment later."

Simon thanked the assistant and followed her out.

"Very amusing. I may never be able to go back there again after that." Simon thought she didn't sound particularly put out. He took hold of the bags. "I just hope I still like this dress when we get it home."

"Never mind. Should you need to change it, I'll come with you and apologise. They'll find it awfully romantic."

Belinda snorted. "Anyway. What did you say to that poor girl? She looked terrified."

Simon told her.

"I'll go back by myself if I have to." She paused. "And who ever said I would marry you?"

"I've been waiting for you to ask me."

"Don't hold your breath!"

He continued to enjoy himself. Sometime, a former life perhaps, Simon wondered if he had been a woman. It would be an explanation. His appreciation of all things feminine had not been developed merely as an aid to seduction. He really did derive genuine enjoyment. He was reminded of the truism that a woman can never have enough tops.

Another two hours, a dozen shops behind them, and four carrier bags containing her purchases swinging from his hand, Simon suggested a quick scour of Marks before they closed.

With a confidence that he now knew want she wanted, he took responsibility for tops while Belinda looked further afield. He sorted through a few rails, rejecting each in turn, mostly on style of sleeve, a particular concern.

An example displayed on a mannequin caught his eye. Black, small cap sleeves, a sparkly star motif. He took one from the rack, carried it to Belinda for inspection and approval, and returned to look for one in the appropriate size. There were no size eights and particularly no tens.

Irritated, he glanced again at the model, standing on a step, mounted on a plinth, its arms demurely placed behind her. He climbed the step, reached over a shoulder and checked the size tag at the neck. Size ten, and no visible dust. He climbed down and searched for an assistant, spotting two gathered at a till some way off.

"Could you remove a garment from a mannequin for me please."

Simon's tone did not imply a question.

"Possibly. The display staff have already left. What is it?"

"A T-shirt."

Simon didn't wait for a reply but led them across the store. They paused for a few seconds before Simon climbed up. He rotated the body on its plinth. It was surprisingly heavy.

"OK. How does this thing come apart? Presumably the arms rotate."

"They slot in."

Simon grasped the right arm and immediately the hand fell off. He caught it and passed it down.

"Could you hold my hand."

Easing the arm upward he felt a click as it cleared its slot and lifted it off. He repeated the process with the other arm and it came away, this time with the hand attached.

A customer passed, looking on with amusement.

"Are you interfering with that woman?"

"I am," replied Simon, laughing.

A weary-looking supervisor appeared just as he succeeded in removing the T-shirt. He was intrigued to notice that the exposed breasts showed just the hint of a nipple at rest. Simon cupped a hand over each.

"Poor girl, and we haven't even been introduced."

The supervisor eyed him with a commendable lack of suspicion. "Should you be holding her like that? Don't worry, we'll redress her." She glanced at her staff, the older of the two looking sour, the younger amused if a little embarrassed, each of them festooned with an arm. "Leave those for the display staff in the morning."

Simon climbed down, clutching his prize.

Belinda was standing a few yards away, a couple of items draped over an arm. She had watched the performance, unsurprised, but had wisely thought better than to interfere. He grinned at her and she grinned back.

"Changing room?" he asked.

The outer door was unlocked for them to leave and they stepped out together, a fifth bag now swinging from Simon's hand. Belinda took his free hand in hers and gave it a gentle squeeze while they discussed the possibility of a drink before returning home.

"You enjoyed that, didn't you," she said, laughing.

"Hugely. When can we do it again?"

twenty-five

Belinda was installed. More clothes, a microwave, cooking utensils and the odd item of furniture had arrived at spasmodic intervals during the week. Their bedroom, and the bathroom, had undergone a distinct change of character, not least because of towels and bedding: the smells had changed. And fresh cut flowers for the sitting and living rooms. So far, Simon had enjoyed the transformations. As Belinda had remarked, it was just as well, for there was more to come.

With the first few days successfully negotiated, they had begun a moderate exploration of future plans. Belinda had suggested an early visit to introduce him to her parents. Simon was at once flattered and alarmed. It was a long time since he'd been introduced to 'the parents' and he said so.

Belinda laughed. "I'm not seeking their approval. It's more to satisfy their curiosity."

Simon understood the point. "You're very close to your parents aren't you?" he said.

She smiled. "Very. I've known them a long time."

Belinda spoke without any sense of irony, and Simon smiled in turn.

"I'm envious of you – I didn't have that with mine."

Simon paused and looked out of the window. It was fully dark now; the threatened rain earlier had not materialised.

"Boys are favoured, developed by their mothers. Girls, by their fathers," he said.

Belinda glanced at him, troubled by something in his tone. "You speak of your mother often. I almost think I know her." She paused, framing her thought. "It's an odd emotion this, but I feel deprived, cheated almost that I never had the opportunity to meet her."

"She was a formidable woman. Every nightmare, every joy." He smiled. "There are similarities. Your birthdays are close and you are both left-handed. You would have got on. Eventually."

"I would have hoped so."

She stopped what she was doing and looked at him. There was an omission. She wondered how to broach it, but there was no subtle way.

"You never mention your father."

"No, I suppose I don't."

Belinda's expression conveyed the question.

"He's been dead a long time. Longer still to me."

Something in his expression worried her, and she said so.

"It's nothing to worry about – at least, not now."

He lit his pipe and continued to stare from the window. He didn't speak for a while and Belinda chose not to interrupt his silence.

"We didn't like each other. I loathed him, and he hated me. And we didn't know each other. We never did. By the time we could have done, he'd died."

Simon's pipe had gone out and he turned to relight it.

"My mother was preparing to leave my father when she found she was pregnant. So, she decided she would wait until I was five, then seven, then eleven, then thirteen, sixteen, eighteen. And then I went off to college. And so, by twenty-five when I left college, she thought she could. And when I was twenty-seven, they finally divorced.

"My grandfather, mother's father, had made a lot of money during the war. He was a greengrocer. Had this amazing talent to make money. No ability to keep it, mind you, but a prodigious talent for making it. At the end of the war he set up all his kids in houses. So my father never had to buy a house, pay a mortgage, do all the things that people struggled to do in that class they considered themselves to be in, in the fifties. My mother had the whip hand

– the house was in her name. To stop her leaving, my grandfather always said, and it worked. Meanwhile, my father bought new cars every year, to the obvious envy of the neighbours.

"Their problems together got transposed onto me, into me. And then, I suppose, I became the primary cause. I don't know. It's difficult. I never really asked my mother about the early years. By the time I could have done, she was old and we'd forged ourselves into the mother and adult son relationship. I didn't want to risk it. It had taken a long time coming."

Simon took a drink from his wine glass and relit his pipe.

"So I remember my father for all the wrong reasons. I remember those silences, never understanding the snide comments, the sarcasm, the mockery he gave me to the questions I would ask. I mean, you're a little boy, you're seven years old and you ask a question, and you get an answer. And you can't comprehend the answer, the spite and the irony. It's lost. And he's using you to get back at your mother. And your mother's using you. But at least Mother was open about it.

"Christmas. One in particular. I must have been about twelve or thirteen. We used to have the dinner at one o'clock, and it was silent until two thirty – that's when he went out. That's when Christmas Day started.

"My father was a wonderful parent from the outside, and a non-existent father on the inside. So nobody knew. I didn't say anything. You don't. You don't want to appear different from anybody else. My mother didn't say anything, because she didn't want to admit anything to her brothers. God knows what my father said.

"He was perfect, he would be everybody's friend. You had a problem, he'd be there. Sympathetic, understanding, helpful. Yet for my mother and me, he was non-existent. So it was, if you like, everything you needed on the surface was there. So you had a father, he lived at home. It was a mother, father, son household. Everybody accepted it, he saw to that. But once that front door had closed, it ended. The pretence stopped."

Simon picked up his glass and drained it. He refilled Belinda's and then his own. He lit his pipe, the movements swift and hurried.

"I've never told anyone about this before." He smiled, a brief apologetic smile. "I don't want to bore you."

"You're not boring me."

She resisted the impulse to reach for his hand, and Simon resisted the impulse to take it. He drained the wine glass again, and then refilled it. He felt thirsty.

"I had a bicycle when I was seven. A curved frame with these strange things in the middle, which I subsequently worked out were hinges, because it was a BSA commando bike that had been welded up. And I had a train set, bloody good one, an early Hornby electric, pre-war. Be worth a lot of money now. And then there was the Meccano. Did you know that you can correlate the decline in people reading for mechanical engineering degrees in the eighties with the decline in sales of Meccano sets ten years earlier?

"I had an amazing Meccano set, I even had pre-war bits. The colours were a sort of washed-out brown and green, post-war was red. It was my father's big treat to build me something enormous and elaborate and present it to me on Christmas Day. This must have been up to about seven or eight. And I would delight, so my mother told me, in taking it to pieces, after he'd spent all those weeks building it. The little bent wire screwdriver and the double-ended cranked spanner. And I would get it to its component parts by Boxing Day.

"I didn't do it spitefully, but he had built this, and I wanted that, and I wanted to build it myself. So I would take his to pieces. Just as my mother had done with his life. Or rather, the life that he'd wanted, which didn't include me. I lost track of the stories of the things that she had been forced to take to try and get rid of me. Even down to the bottle of gin and the hot bath. God, the ignorance was pathetic.

"Anyway, that Christmas. I got all the usual things from my mother. The caring things. The stocking at the foot of the bed, filled with the new coins, the golden money, the chocolate coins in gilded paper. The Mars bar and the chocolate. The orange. It was a tradition she kept up until she died. Once, one year, when we weren't speaking, she sent it by Datapost." He paused. "I miss those Christmas stockings."

Simon picked up his glass and stared down at the table.

"You asked me how I spent last Christmas and I said I slept most of the time. That's why. Stupid things, silly things, break your heart."

Tears were running down Simon's face and he put his hands over his eyes and brushed back the tears with his palms. He paused, lit his pipe, and emptied the wine glass. He stared out of the window.

"This is a long way back. I never talk about this. I don't even talk about it to myself."

While he continued to stare, Belinda took another bottle from the refrigerator, opened it and refilled their glasses. Simon thanked her. After a while, he continued.

"So, this particular Christmas I'd emptied the stocking from my mother, knowing that, at the end, there would be some personal present, something she had decided on months before and saved up for even longer. And there were the expensive, daft things from my uncles, still to open. The surrogate fathers. The things that soon break, but give enormous pleasure in the meantime. And my father gave me an envelope. It was a thick brown envelope. And inside, there were three other, small envelopes. It was exciting – I'd never had a present that was envelopes before.

"So, I tore them open. I picked the thickest one first, and that had three pound notes in it. The second had a postal order for five shillings, and the third, another postal order for twelve and six. He'd sold my bicycle for three pounds, my Meccano for five shillings, and my train set for twelve and six. Three pounds, seventeen shillings and sixpence. There was a lot you could do with three pounds, seventeen and six. When I was twelve, in 1958.

"I never forgave him for that. It was so mean, mean in deed and mean in spirit. But, the decline had started long before that, when I was about seven. I remember when it began. We had a running race, on a beach in Wales, and I won. He had asthma. He couldn't run more than forty yards. We ran perhaps a hundred, so I won.

I could throw much better than him too. It was a bad week. After that he saw me as a rival.

"So, from recollection, and this is difficult because of my mother, so how much is truth and how much just received I don't know. But, I think my father ceased to be a father to me that week, when I was seven. He didn't speak to me much after that. Apart from one incident I do remember. It was grotesque."

Simon paused and shook his head.

"It was at school. Everybody's getting to seventeen, rushing off to get their provisional driving licences. I talk about it to my mother, she speaks to my father, and reports back to me. And, eventually, he will teach me to drive. I was really pleased – I mean, this was an adult thing. Perhaps we could be son and father again. It wouldn't be son and father like everyone else, but it might be the beginnings. I'd tried before. I knew our situation was wrong, how we were, but I didn't know why. I just wanted it kind of normal. You do when you're that sort of age, you're very idealistic. It should be like this, so why isn't it. And please explain to me why it isn't. And they can't. So you don't accept it.

"So, off I go, late January, and get my provisional licence. And there are guys by then who've already passed their tests. Here you are, you can't drive, you're not part of the group any longer. Peer pressure's important at that age. It's important at any age when you're a child, but at that age especially – boy, verging on what you think is a man." Simon laughed. "I've yet to meet a man under the age of twenty-five," he said. "Women, perhaps, would say older."

Belinda interjected. "Forty, if ever."

"It depends on how you define man. I wouldn't disagree with fifty. I trot back, fresh from the licensing office in Ealing, clutching my brand new provisional licence. The little blue linen cover. And, over dinner, I present it to him proudly. I'd spent my ten shillings. My entry fee into manhood.

"'What's that?' he says. 'It's my provisional licence,' I say. 'I've never taken a test,' he says. 'You have to now,' I say. 'Oh,' he says. 'Who ever told you I was going to teach you to drive?'

"To me, that ended it. The promise and then the final rejection. The intended cruelty. That was the end of it. I picked sides, and I chose my mother's. And between us, we crucified my father. Until the day he left, his life was dreadful. And I worked on it.

"You pick your side, whatever the reason, whatever the truth. And then, you live with the consequences. Just like life.

"I began to leave home that year. According to my mother I left home some while later. But, to me, I left home then. Nights out, and then many nights out. The times I was there, perhaps just to overcome her hostility to whatever she thought I was doing, we united against my father.

"And, in retrospect, it's just sad. There's more to life with parents than taking sides. But you don't know much when you're young. You just react according to how you're treated. You don't compensate, you don't empathise, and you have absolutely no tolerance.

"So, to answer your question, whatever it was. I never knew my father. He died before we could ever meet. And it's a regret that hasn't changed.

"I wouldn't have minded had we met, say, ten years later, and then decided we didn't like each other. There comes a time with parents where they are just relations, or you are friends. We never got to choose. Or even had the opportunity to do so."

Simon raised his head and looked across at Belinda. She watched him as he refilled her glass, and then his own. He did it slowly, and put the bottle back on the table with a quiet determination.

She could think of nothing adequate to say.

"I don't think I will have any more after this," he said. He turned his head back to the window. It still hadn't rained.

"You bury the truth of your childhood in fantasy. You glance back, and it never rained, always sunny. And, as you did with childhood, so you do with life. It's called survival. Or existence. But always, there's got to be something. A hope, a surprise, something unpredicted for the next day. A reason to get up. An inquisitiveness, a curiosity, a challenge. A looking forward, not a staring back."

Simon slowly shook his head.

"Larkin had it right. 'They fuck you up, your parents do.' It left a legacy, and it's lasted. It drove me inwards. I don't embrace, I observe. Somehow not part of things. Distanced, peripheral, parallel. Unengaged. Cold. It's been a useful tool. When others have asked how, I have asked why."

He stared down at his hands, resting on the table, his voice no more than a whisper. "But it leaves you lonely. I'm used to being alone, I always have been to some extent. We all are. But sometimes, very lonely. Too lonely. Breaks your heart. Totally.

"I was formed, the attitudes entrenched, long before I ever heard this. But, at the time, she put it better than I could."

Simon stood up, a brief grim smile as he steadied himself, an arm on the edge of the table. "It's in the other room."

She followed his unsteady progress, concerned, not having seen him drunk before, unsure of what to expect.

A shelf of vinyl albums, eight or nine feet, stretched along one wall, beneath the books, behind a sofa. He hauled out the chair and perched unsteadily on the back of it as he ran his fingers along the spines. It took a while, and she watched as he pulled things out, forgotten treasures. She could not help him. Eventually, he found it, a double album.

He put the record on the turntable and, with elaborate care, found the track.

"Joni Mitchell," he said. "It's thirty years old now. 'Ludwig's Tune'."

When it was over he switched off the stereo and stood unsteadily, leaning sideways.

"I suppose, in the end, my father was never a hero to his son." Simon's expression was dreadfully sad, wistful. "Pity. Boys need that. Everybody does. I don't remember anyone at all."

twenty-six

Belinda lay, her eyes closed, her head resting on an outstretched arm. To Simon, she looked utterly beautiful. He examined her face as if for the first time, but it was impossible, for now he knew it almost better than his own. Knew its contours and its shape, its regularities and its asymmetries. The fine scar running through the right eyebrow, tilting the outer edge upward. A riding accident at eight. The slightest lump on one side of her nose, broken at twelve.

He sat looking at her, then gently stroked the back of her hand. Slowly, the eyelids opened. Her eyes showed a brilliant blue. He smiled at her. With her eyes opened, her face was transformed from beauty into something wondrous.

Simon leant over and kissed her lightly on the tip of the nose, whispered good morning, and slid off the bed.

She slept on, in storybook pose. Hands together as if in prayer, her head resting upon them. Simon glanced at her again in the half-light, reluctant to leave. She looked so peaceful, childlike.

As he walked back down the stairs, he was conscious of another change in his feelings. Slowly, despite his best intentions, his defences were being eroded.

He stopped on the landing. Something had caught his eye as he left the bedroom. His 'Next Customer Please' sign had been replaced. Instead, there was another. 'Till Closed'. He picked it up and took it with him.

He measured carefully, cut a piece of card to size and then wrote on it in marker pen. He then glued the card to her sign. 'Till Closed' now read 'Till When?'

Simon moved quietly, an exaggerated creeping around the house, suiting the remains of his hangover while Belinda slept on. With the radio low, he made a solitary browse through the newspapers, waiting for their day to begin. It was not the same without her, however so close.

They met on the stairs, Belinda coming up barefoot and naked, her handbag hanging from a shoulder; Simon, partially dressed, carrying the cups and glasses from the night before. Each trailed a hand on the other as they passed. Simon stopped and watched her climbing the stairs until she disappeared into the bathroom. Pondering muscle tone he continued into the kitchen to find the kettle already switched on. He took the beans from the refrigerator and began the coffee, the sound of the grinder competing with that of the shower running above him.

Belinda reappeared beside him dressed in two towels, one for her hair, another for her body. They sat either side of the kitchen table and between snatches of morning conversation, Simon continued his inspection.

"You must exercise," he said finally, after a suitable compliment.

She thanked him for the observation. "It's not unknown."

"What do you do?"

She put down her cup. "It varies. I belong to the local gym to use their pool and I swim there in the mornings a couple of times a week – between the businessmen and the pensioners. Otherwise, I've been known to run, a little yoga and lately I've been trying pilates. And there are the stairs of course. Major contribution my stairs."

Simon smiled and glanced upward.

She smiled back and nodded. "Of all I prefer the running or the swimming. It gives me space to think. You can think through a lot doing that." She smiled again. "Lately, I've been thinking about you."

"And?"

"Nothing substantial – though nothing threatening either."

"That's reassuring." Simon's tone was anything but reassured.

Belinda touched him lightly on the shoulder. "Be so."

Years of living mostly alone had given Simon a fairly relaxed dress sense when within the house. Knickers and T-shirt was normal, variations with prevailing temperature. But always the knickers. Running downstairs naked could produce the most excruciating pain; a slapped testicle was agony like no other.

Belinda, unencumbered, had no such inhibitions. Fresh from the shower, the bath; morning, late evening – he found her naked. He had almost become accustomed to the shock – almost. Her insouciant attitude was rare, and he commented on it.

"Well, so do you."

"But with knickers, and I've got less to show, as it were."

She gave him a slightly quizzical expression. "I don't parade if that's what you mean. I wouldn't were there anyone else here."

He didn't, and said so. "Neither am I complaining. No, it's just unusual."

"Perhaps." She paused. "I suppose it's Germany as a child. The Germans have this propensity to throw their clothes off at the slightest opportunity. At least they did where we were stationed. I sort of grew up with it. And at school, of course. Open showers."

"And your parents?"

She laughed. "Somewhat more restrained, though not as much as you might think. But never in front of the locals."

"No sports then?"

"No." She laughed again, an image of tennis in her mind. "If it bothers you, I can dress."

"Oh no," he said, just a little too quickly. "I enjoy it."

"You don't have to look of course."

An old scar, round, irregular, an inch across, showed stark white on the outside of Belinda's left thigh. From its shape it resembled an old bullet wound, but there was no corresponding exit scar. At that calibre a contained round might be expected to require an amputation. Simon ran a fingertip over it and enquired.

She stared at him, laughed dismissively and then gave him a rather more generous smile.

"Nothing so dramatic I'm afraid. It's an old vaccination scar. It was on my left buttock, but it migrated as I grew." She glanced down at it. "I've grown rather fond of it."

He found it on the stairs, a bra, in the inevitable black. He carried it into the bedroom and delivered it. As he passed it to her, Simon examined what there was of it. Peculiar garments. There was no underwiring. He'd noticed this before, when she'd been wearing them, and asked why.

"My tits are not so big that they need the support, and wires are uncomfortable, restrictive. They cut across the ribs." She laughed and looked at him. "I'm not a radial tyre."

Simon was impressed with the knowledge.

She looked suitably coy. "You're not the only engineer I've known."

"Fascinating conversations you must have had."

She smiled sweetly, ignored his comment and folded the bra in two, one cup inside the other.

Later, she stood at a sitting room window, coffee in hand, watching the birds squabbling around the freshly filled food trays. It had rained overnight, the leaves on the bushes by the wall still glistening.

"Something smells odd in here."

"What does?" replied Simon, sitting on the far side of the room. He sniffed to confirm. "I can't smell anything."

Belinda was unconvinced. "Perhaps it's me. My sense of smell always gets more acute when I'm pre-menstrual."

Simon smiled. "I had noticed."

"Noticed what?"

"Your hormones." He paused. "Every twenty-five days." His tone was weary. "I'm tuning into your cycle." He laughed. "The irritability, irrationality quotient."

"What deep joy for you. Not." Her tone verged on dismissive, vaguely threatening, hostile.

Simon smiled at her. Discretion, he decided. This was not a time to argue.

*

The sun appeared, heralding another day of pick, spade and buckets. A ton shifted before a late, very late, lunch.

Simon sat on the terrace, regaining the energy to eat, browsing through a paper. The silly season in full spate, though some stories of substance. Global warming, climate change, accelerated rates of extinction; animals and countries.

The sedentary strata exposed by his labours showed dark against their immediate surroundings. A hundred and fifty million years before, the whole area had been under hundreds of feet of water. In another few, from what he'd read, it might be again. The planet, forever dynamic; only the timescales varied.

Belinda lay supine on a sun bed as Simon worked.

"It's really quite primeval this."

Simon buried the pick in the earth wall and levered out another slue of clay, stepping back as it fell into the bucket at his feet. He picked up a spade and shovelled in the rest.

"What is?"

"Watching your man work with primitive tools."

"Glad you're enjoying it."

He carried the spoil to the top of the garden and returned, breathing heavily. Sitting beside her, he wiped the sweat from his face and reached for the water jug.

"Primeval! Later I'll kill a mammoth and while you cook, get on with my wall paintings!"

"What makes you think they were painted by men?"

She looked at him sympathetically. "By the way, you should know that I've never lived with a doctor before, medical or otherwise." She leant up on an elbow. "What was it in, or is that on?"

"Random association."

Belinda looked puzzled. "Isn't that somehow contradictory?"

"Oxymoronic." Simon laughed. "Not entirely, you'd be surprised. The dissertation's in an attic should you wish to read it."

She smiled back. "The summary sometime, perhaps. Always willing to learn." She laughed. "You can read my master's papers in return!"

*

It was a dangerous combination, alcohol and music. Missing his footing, Simon bounced off a wall, stumbled and fell into a sofa. There was a drink somewhere, his pipe, lighter and tobacco somewhere else. He found one and looked for the others. Belinda passed him, disappearing on a long slide past the chimney breast.

They danced differently. Simon, dropping into practised habits, years of performing; Belinda, more emotionally driven, just moving, legs and arms and body, fully engaged.

He watched her, the exuberance, the vitality; lost within. Simon knew he would love her for life, whatever might become of them. The feelings wouldn't change. Inviolate.

The track changed, slower, and she came to find him.

The day was still hot. Simon lay in bed, his hair still damp from the shower. The bedroom windows were open, the curtains pulled back. Moonlight met the light burning beside him. On the window sill, the wood gleamed from recent attention. The air was still, nothing seemed to disturb it. It was as if the heat of the day had drained the energy.

It was very quiet; he heard a car but it was a long way off. Further away still, he thought he heard a train disappearing into the distance. The smoke from his pipe lay on the air, vaporous layers, undulating away from him. Trails of exhalation.

He heard the muffled sound of water draining away, the bathroom door opening, and gentle footfalls on the carpet. Belinda, her body glistening from the bath, pulled back the sheet and slid alongside him. Her warmth, and her smell, engulfed him.

She leant up and there was a sloshing sound that he had not heard before. Water was poured into glasses. She rolled over and leant against him, a glass, crushed ice on top, in her hand. She rested the base of the glass on his stomach. It was damp and very cold, and he gave a start at the shock.

"What are you going to do with that?"

Belinda turned the glass against his skin.

"Wait and see."

twenty-seven

The bedside radio continued its polite burble of Radio 4. Belinda glanced at the display as she sat on the side of the bed beside the prone, inert figure of Simon. The clock read 7:47. She carefully placed the cup of coffee beside the radio and leant across the bed. She stroked his arm, and his head disappeared further into the pillows. Leaning further, she found an ear and blew into it. A small groan drifted out from somewhere near its vicinity.

"Coffee's beside you," she said. "I'll be back after six. Try and be up." She kissed the top of his shoulder and levered herself up.

He lay, partially aware; he was floating, somewhere between consciousness and deep sleep. Curled around within the duvet he felt secure within a private warmth, directing dreams. Complicated dreams.

Simon had been to London the previous day to see his solicitor. There was much to discuss and it had been a long and tiring day. He had returned very late. Belinda had chosen not to come, deciding instead to spend the day in the house to herself, organising.

Vaguely, he swung his legs from the bed and touched the floor. There was a cup of cold coffee beside him. He drank some, swallowing carefully. He wandered into the bathroom for a sleepy pee, concentrating on his aim. He washed his face and cleaned his teeth, his movements automatic, gentle, minimising disturbance.

He returned to the bedroom and looking at the clock, watched morning turn into afternoon. He dressed, picked up the remains of the coffee, collected his watch, pipe and lighter and carefully balancing the load, drifted off down the stairs.

He entered the kitchen behind a spider, crossing the floor ahead of him. Simon accelerated and, responding to the vibration from his feet, so did the spider. Simon lunged and landing on his knees, managed to scoop it up in his left hand. The sensation of the spider under his fingers, scratching at his palm, was not pleasing.

Simon carried it to the back garden and released it. The tingling sensation was still on his palm as he ran his hands under the tap. As he dried his hands on a length of kitchen roll, he smiled to himself. As she had said, it was the small things that made the difference. A few weeks before he would have left the spider, glad almost of the company. Not now. Belinda's cleanliness regime forbade multi-legged occupations.

Simon switched on the kettle and scanned the floor while he waited for it to boil. There did not appear to be any more banned species about. Small things, big differences.

Something had happened to the kitchen. Automatically, his eyes elsewhere, he reached up for the storage jar where the coffee lived. His fingers found a space. They traversed slightly and found a pepper mill. He put on a light, and located the coffee on another shelf.

Thoughtful, he pulled the curtains back and sat down at the far end of the living room to survey the kitchen; it sparkled under the lights. The clutter that for months had gradually accumulated had been cleared, the room returned to its place as efficient centre of operations for the household. The warm familiarity of the ancient cobwebs above the wall units had gone. Tiles gleamed, unaccustomedly. The cupboards, should he have chosen to open one, would have greeted him with a stark, surprising freshness; the lining paper crisp, the contents neatly arranged, uncrowded, in logical order.

He stood again in the kitchen and opened cupboard doors at random. The contents he recalled were gone. Instead, similar but unfamiliar packets and boxes stared back at him. They were all new. He freshened his coffee, and sat down again.

It was an odd experience. Old familiarity, replaced by a curious, alien regularity. He was beginning to feel like a guest in his own house. A tolerated disruption.

A short walk indicated that a similar transformation was going on all over the house. A line of black plastic rubbish sacks, marching down the driveway, seemed nearly to reach the road. And furniture was being subtly moved. No longer could he walk around the house as if blind; now he had to look where he was going.

It was strange and he was unsure of quite what attitude to adopt. He was, he recognised, in for a period of considerable and continuous adjustment, that while not unwelcome, would require an application of what he had grown unused to.

He read the note she had left him. The paper was purple, propped up on the kitchen table. His name was at the top, her name was at the bottom. There were three words in between. 'I Love You.' It was not a declaration that he could misinterpret.

He made more coffee, closing his ears to the sound of the grinding beans. Another two cups and he would begin to feel more like a human being. Another hour, and he would begin to look like one.

He walked into the sitting room, negotiated his way past a chair, and sat down at a table he did not recognise. Likewise the chair. He was surprised to notice that the curtains were missing. Instead, there was a yellow Post-it note stuck on the wall. 'We have gone to the cleaners,' it said. Another was stuck underneath. 'Not before time.'

Simon put Belinda's note on the table in front of him. The texture of the paper reflected in the sunlight. He read each one of her words, slowly, several times. He was mostly easy to be with, but difficult to live with; and he was easy to love, and he loved too easily.

He looked out of the window and considered the weather, a warm day, becoming hotter.

He stared at the view, and while he was grateful for the solitude, he was equally conscious of feeling lonely. It was a particular loneliness. The house felt empty, and curiously quiet. So did he, and the solution would not be appearing until after six o'clock. But, the relationship between them had now changed, or at least, its description had. The purple paper bore testimony to that. To answer it he would have to confront his feelings, consider what for the most part he had consistently managed to avoid.

He walked back to the living room and turned on the radio, retuning from Radio 3 to 4, and collected the post and the morning papers. Advertising leaflets fell from the papers as he carried them through. He picked them up and looked for the recycling waste bin, finding it in the side room. He stood over it, sorting through the mail, dropping each piece in after a cursory glance. There was a gas bill mixed in with it that he greeted with almost relief. For years, the appearance of these regular quarterly bills had been anticipated with dread. Now, with so little real post, and greater means, he almost welcomed the statements.

He made more coffee and retreated back to the sitting room. Avoiding Belinda's note, still sitting on the table, he sat on the repositioned sofa and opened the papers. He was aware of indulging in diversionary activities, and equally aware of their eventual failure.

As predicted, the contents of the newspapers did not capture his interest. He more scanned than read the text, and only glanced at the pictures. Even the crop of lifestyle advertisements failed to bring about the usual rise of bile.

He glanced up and was disconcerted to see an unfamiliar wall. He remembered the time when staring at walls had counted as a leisure activity. He had grown to know his walls well.

A smell of furniture polish and ammonia cleaners lingered on the air, oppressing him. He abandoned the papers and wandered back in the general direction of the kitchen. He vaguely considered his options, but there were no pressing tasks he could remember.

The radio continued playing. Simon stood and stared out of the window over the patio to the terrace and the wilderness beyond. The undisturbed view had a familiarity that he found almost poignant.

His life had undergone a step change, and while he welcomed most, if not all, of it, the sudden speed of the change bewildered him. It felt all too quick. The excitement of a new involvement, that almost instantaneous recognition and redirection of life's purpose to accommodate and all the simple happiness to enjoy, seemed now to have been passed through with an almost indecent haste. He felt left behind by the sudden acceleration. Instead, he was in the consequences zone. Consequences: where idle fantasies, conceived in isolation, unfettered by practical considerations, confronted a new reality, compared their compatibility and measured out the compromise. It could be a chastening experience, and he felt unsure, unable to predict an outcome. On the face of it, theirs was an unlikely coupling.

Love, when occasionally he'd considered it in abstract, might be seen as a journey; as a series of steps, either spiral or directly rising, measured by quantum leaps or continuous graduation. Either way, he had never achieved a sensible, easy gradient, only lurching starts and sudden falls. And then the choice. The struggle to catch up, slow down, or choosing neither; caring tripping over selfishness.

Sunlight felt its way into the kitchen and disturbed what was passing as thought. Simon's throat, encouraged by the tobacco smoke, began to react to the ammonia again. He coughed, his eyes threatened to water. He considered opening a window, but rejected the thought. He would take himself out instead, have a late lunch somewhere, give himself some external space. He collected his things together and automatically reached out for the old suede jacket hanging on the back of a chair. The chair had moved, the jacket gone.

Entering into the spirit of the new arrangements he found his jacket hanging on a hanger, suspended from the rail positioned for the purpose in the cupboard under the stairs. It seemed unaffected by its recent cosseted treatment. With a final check on the contents of his pockets, Simon stepped from the front door and closed it purposefully behind him.

He walked down the stone steps leading from the front door, ignoring the recently dispossessed spiders picketing the house, towards where his car was normally parked. There was a brief panic as he contemplated the empty space. He struggled to remember some fragments of conversation from the early morning. Gerald, confirming the recollection, stood brooding at the side of the drive, his doors sensibly locked. There would be keys somewhere in the house, but he couldn't remember where.

The day had turned from hot to very hot. Simon took off his jacket and swung it over a shoulder. Revising his choice of pub to the nearest, he began to walk. He reached the end of the drive and looked at the road, unimpeded by a windscreen.

There were new ruts in the gravel of the drive when Simon returned. His car stood parked adjacent to the garage and Gerald had gone. He put his hand on the bonnet as he passed; it was still warm. Simon hurried on, his thoughts focused on urination. He ran up the steps to the front door, opened it, dropped his keys, retrieved them and then unlocked the inner door, all the while hopping from foot to foot.

He had a choice of lavatories: the one beyond the utility room, and the bathrooms. From where he stood, to reach the utility room he would have to pass through the kitchen. The temptation to pee in the sink, as had been his solitary habit, now forbidden, would be too great. As a concession he ran up the stairs.

With nature temporarily subdued, he descended the stairs at a less frantic pace. Three plants stood on a working surface in the kitchen. They were very large and green. There was a note beside them, most of which was crossed through. 'See answerphone' was the only part to survive. Simon looked in the required direction to see the machine's red light flashing. He switched on the kettle and made coffee before pressing the replay button.

Belinda sounded in an awful hurry. He listened to himself being congratulated for getting up, and instructions on what to do with the plants. Finally, she remarked on the purple note and repeated its message. He replayed the recording three times.

Following her instructions to the letter, he carried each of the pots out to the utility room and, filling the sink with tepid water, plunged in each to soak until the evening.

He returned to the kitchen and, not looking where he was going, promptly fell over a pair of shoes. Shoes had started to appear in the most unlikely of places, though mostly constrained to the floor.

He glanced at the clock and wondered what to do with the hour or so before Belinda returned. Not for the first time he felt a helpless guilt begin to descend. So much was changing, while he seemed to contribute very little towards it. He gathered up the newspapers and carried them out to the veranda.

Simon sat, watching his pipe smoke curl lazily over the garden. He sat for a long time, his mind returning to the subject it had been considering for most of the afternoon.

When someone tells you they love you, there is only one answer. 'I know,' does not suffice.

He sat for a while longer and then stood up, a little stiffly. He collected Belinda's purple note from where he'd left it and, taking several sheets of paper, wrote two short messages in return. On one was written, 'Please consult the answerphone.' On the other, he wrote her name at the top, his own at the bottom. There were three words in between. He looked at them: such little words, so much significance.

Having recorded the message, he returned to the veranda and immediately engrossed himself in an article from one of the papers. Simon felt very happy, both with the news he had received, and with the feelings he had imparted. He had made the final admission to himself.

It was always the little things. The seemingly inconsequential, the small sharings, the ephemeral; the reassuring glue that held the whole thing together. The casual glance, the knowing look. The simply being one of a greater two. The whole of life was love; the rest was merely waiting.

It was the evening and they were sitting on the terrace. Simon was staring out over the garden, watching the branches of the trees that swayed slowly in time with the rhythm of the breeze. Belinda looked at his expression. Surprisingly, he seemed strangely distant.

"Is there anything wrong? You look somehow disconnected."

He turned to face her and smiled.

"I'm sorry," he said. "I was thinking."

He picked up his coffee cup, and then put it down again without drinking any. He looked across the table at her, and was disconcerted to find that she'd been watching him. She shifted her head and raised an eyebrow.

"I'm sorry," he said again.

He paused, lit his pipe and reached for his wine glass. Belinda watched these diversions, but chose not to interrupt.

He looked at her again. "I don't want to offend you, but I have to ask you this. It's important for me to know." Simon paused again and looked down at his hands, appearing to examine his fingertips.

"When you say you love me, are in love with me, is it an expression of feeling, or are you trying to convince yourself by familiarity?"

He stopped looking at his hands and looked up at her.

"You see, I'm not sure that I know what love is, at least, not well enough to explain it. Love is very subjective – my concept might be very different to yours. I need to know what you think you mean."

Belinda was surprised by the question. She had loved before, as she knew Simon had. No one had ever asked her what she meant by it before. She stood up and walked behind him, putting her arms around him. She kissed his cheek and rested her chin on his shoulder.

"I love you, and I'm in love with you," she said. "It's the truest description of the feelings I have for you. I'm not trying to convince myself, I don't have to. I'm not trying to convince you either. I just want to share it. Love's like that."

She kissed his neck and traced the outline of the kiss with her finger. "Don't worry."

He kissed her in return and squeezed her hand. "Thank you," he said. "I'll try not to."

The breeze turned to a sudden gust, disturbing the contents of the table.

"Would you like to go for a walk?" she asked.

Simon glanced up at the sky. Dark clouds threatened.

"How far are you going?"

"I don't know yet."

He smiled at her and stood up. "I'll bring along your mint cake and the water bottle!"

As they walked down the drive she turned and looked at him. Her expression was serious, though her tone was light.

"I'm hard to get. All you have to do is ask me."

Later, it sounded familiar. Later still, he remembered. But it didn't matter where it came from. What mattered now was from whom it had come.

twenty-eight

Simon emerged from the bathroom looking bewildered. "I think I'd better stop eating crusts, my hair is starting to curl."

Belinda was sitting at the dressing table, leaning forward towards the mirror, applying a fresh layer of mascara. Simon leant on the door frame and watched her, the quick practical motion of the brush.

"Try combing after you've washed it," she said without looking up.

"But I do comb it."

"How often?"

"Sometimes every day."

"Quite," she said, and moved to the other eye.

While he was doing his best to ignore it, this visit to her parents was making him nervous. Preoccupied, he wandered back into the bathroom.

His right eye felt as if it had grit in it. He switched on the light above the wash basin and peered into the mirror. He compared it with the other eye; both looked bleary, an equal amount of redness. He convinced himself that it was not the onset of conjunctivitis. Returning to the bedroom he made another inspection under natural light. Both eyes still closely resembled each other.

He had woken early. They were expected for Sunday lunch at 'Barnfather Towers', Belinda's parents' home, at around one o'clock. It was about forty miles, so he had suggested that they leave at eleven.

She laughed and glanced at him over the top of a newspaper. "No. A little before twelve." She smiled at him. "Nervous are we?"

"Very."

"Whatever for?"

"It's a long time since I played 'meet the parents'."

"There's no need. If I'm happy, they're happy. And besides, they will like you." She chuckled. "If all else fails, you and Daddy can talk about aeroplanes and defence, and all those other manly things."

He ignored her patronising and muttered something non-committal. "If it were me it would be straight under the lights for the interrogation."

She laughed at the expression on his face. "Don't be silly – that comes after lunch. And nothing so crude. Daddy has a way with electrodes."

"Most reassuring."

With Simon still fretting, they left well before twelve, Simon driving, and to Belinda's faint amusement, copious supplies of wine and flowers belted into the back seats.

Despite her attempts to jolly him along, his nervousness did not improve.

"Don't you think you're a little old for all this angst?"

"My own thoughts entirely. And it makes not the slightest difference."

They travelled a few miles in silence, Belinda working stoically through one of the Sunday papers, while giving road directions. Simon's agitation continued.

"Look, I know it's irrational, no excuse, but could you run me through it again?"

"Through what?"

"Your parents, and you. You and your parents."

"Which part?"

"All of it."

Belinda giggled. "Must I?" she asked, teasingly.

"You must, you must!"

"OK. From the top. Potted version. Eunice and Douglas, Mummy and Daddy."

She folded up the paper and put it at her feet, marshalling her thoughts. She didn't entirely understand Simon's trepidation;

nervousness perhaps, but not to this extent.

"Douglas, born London 1924. Joined the RAF at seventeen, trained Canada, pilot, returned UK early '44. Met Eunice on first operational station, she a junior officer in the WAAFs. He flew Spitfires. They married immediately after the war, Eunice twenty, Douglas twenty-one. Douglas stayed in the service, postings UK and Germany where, eventually in early '54, they had me. Gutersloh."

"You took a while."

"They had problems conceiving."

"Why?"

"Well it wasn't lack of trying, they tell me. Mummy's fault, according to Daddy, only firing on one side. It's quite a saga. If you want the full story, ask them."

Simon scoffed in alarm. "Oh yes. Bound to. Sure to be an early topic of conversation. 'And how are your ovaries and fallopian tubes these days?' I'd wire myself up after that." He laughed. "Please go on with the story."

"We oscillated between Germany and UK, though when they went to Hong Kong in '65, when I was eleven, I stayed here and boarded."

She paused, thinking back. "Odd that – it was the last time we lived together full time. I went to university straight from school, no gap year then, and then stayed on for the masters. I was in the flat with James by the time they finally came back to the UK for the final posting. Daddy retired at fifty-five, James died soon after. 1980. With my insurance money and the remains of Daddy's gratuity, we set up The Gallery. I'm the MD, Mummy's company secretary and Daddy is chairman. We have a board meeting late every summer, over a long lunch in the garden usually. Civilised, if not entirely professional. We celebrated twenty years last year."

She gave him another road instruction. "So there you are. Will that do?"

Simon thanked her. There was much more that he would have liked to know, but he sensed her indulgence was wearing thin.

"You have an enviable relationship."

"They're my best friends. I suppose it helped that we didn't see all that much of each other for, well, fifteen years, while I was at school and college. Holidays mostly. So we avoided most of the traditional confrontations. When we met as adults, we liked each other." She shrugged. "I'm very lucky."

Simon nodded. "So are they."

She smiled. "Kind of you to say so."

They reached a roundabout and Simon took the third exit as directed. It was a dual carriageway and he accelerated.

"Well," Belinda asked, "did the potted history help?"

"A bit."

"So why are you so nervous?"

Another roundabout. "Which way?"

"First exit." She waited until he had made the turn, and then continued. "Come on, it's not like you. I'm interested."

He thought back to find other disasters to cite, found none and thought again.

"I think it's me – or rather how I'd feel if the roles were reversed. The probable disappointment. The discovery that you knew less, much less of who your daughter was than you thought. So, this is the guy who's sleeping with my daughter. Oh, the worry," he added, almost seriously.

Belinda's laughter broke his thoughts.

"Why is this funny?"

She shook her head, apologised, and started laughing again.

Simon shrugged, faintly hurt. "You did ask."

She nodded. "I've brought people home before, obviously. You're not the first."

"But it's the first time you've brought me."

She looked at him. "You shouldn't worry." She laughed again, louder. "And, as regards the sex…" More laughter. "Mummy was more worried about the quality than the act."

Simon replayed her words. "What do you mean, 'was'?"

"She asked me a couple of weeks ago."

"Asked you what?"

"How it was."

"And?"

"And what?"

Simon blustered.

Belinda patted his thigh reassuringly. "She's intrigued to meet you," she replied, with cod conspiracy.

Simon changed down as they approached a junction and an increase in traffic. He turned right onto another dual carriageway. Belinda was still laughing.

"Are there any other conversations I should know about?"

"Probably."

"Great."

As predicted, they arrived with time to hand. He followed her final instructions and they turned into a fair-sized cobbled driveway. Beyond lay a comfortably positioned detached house, brick towards the front, stone to the side, wide.

Simon stared at it as they climbed from the car.

"This is the Victorian side," she explained, noticing his interest. "The original farmhouse is behind."

Guessing that her parents would be in the garden, she let them in and he followed her, carrying the offerings. The house seemed as deep as it was wide.

They were seated at a large wooden garden table, chairs to match. Belinda was opposite him, Douglas to his right, Eunice to his left. Simon listened to the easy flow of the conversation, and was happy to. They were each making appropriate asides to him continually and he felt relaxed, included. They were engaging to watch, this family. Simon knew precious little about families, beyond the peculiarities of his own; his only real experience had been temporary and peripheral. What understanding he had of the internal dynamics was gleaned from anecdote or fiction.

He glanced between them, noting facial features, mannerisms. Physically, Belinda favoured neither her mother nor her father specifically, rather she appeared as an amalgam of the two. They were both tall and fair and – he searched for the appropriate word

– distinguished. Belinda's colouring, however, the coarse white-blonde hair, rain straight, faintly olive complexion and ice-blue eyes, unusual enough in itself, resembled neither of them.

There was one commonality though: all three were left-handed, Eunice particularly so. For Simon, it was an intriguing thing to witness, rather like looking into a mirror image, and at one point he commented on it.

Eunice replied, "Yes, it is peculiar. More so since, as you can see, apart from being tall, it's the only obvious similarity between us."

"Daddy always said I was a changeling."

There was general laughter which Simon joined, though not entirely comfortably. Like a lot of the conversation that afternoon, prior knowledge contingent, the continuation of many others.

Simon had helped to carry the debris from the lunch into the kitchen. Eunice smiled and thanked him.

"Belinda tells me you met at a gallery."

Before he had time to reply, Belinda's voice answered from somewhere behind him: "I picked him up in the exhibition centre!"

Simon turned. "You did? I thought it was me."

"You would." She deposited the last of the used glasses on the worktop beside him and with a grin to her mother, went back out to the garden.

Eunice laughed. "You'd better get your stories straight."

Simon, now perplexed, agreed.

Eunice glanced up as Belinda passed the window and walked down to the far end of the garden to find her father. She watched her go. Her daughter was happier than she'd been for a long time and for that she was grateful. Simon was standing beside her, watching too. They exchanged smiles.

"My mother once told me," he said, "that she could recognise my back, the back of my head, in any crowd. Years of overseeing."

Eunice nodded. "It's true. It comes with motherhood."

Ushered from the kitchen, Simon strolled with more casualness than he felt, down towards Belinda and her father. She winked at him, and then left them to it.

"Thank you," he muttered as she passed him.

Douglas looked at him, seriously. It struck Simon as quite a ferocious stare.

"I believe this is the moment when I enquire of your intentions towards my daughter."

Before he could answer, Douglas's face broke into a mischievous grin. "You know, I've always wanted to say that."

Simon ignored the expression and answered, "I can assure you, sir, that my intentions are entirely laudable." He corrected himself. "Honourable."

They looked at each other.

"Laudable, certainly. Honourable, I trust."

There followed another pause which again reminded Simon of a Victorian novel. Not a very good one.

Douglas, meantime, seemed to nod. "Come," he said. "Let me show you the garden."

As he led the way, Douglas recalled a conversation with an old service friend several weeks before. Calling in a favour he'd had a check run on Simon's history, whose erstwhile profession had made it a straightforward task. Meeting him confirmed the report. Entirely sound, but something of a maverick.

Belinda had rejoined her mother in the kitchen.

"I see Douglas is giving Simon the grand tour. That should keep them busy for a while."

Belinda passed her mother some more plates for the dishwasher and looked over her shoulder in time to see them disappear behind the bean canes at the foot of the garden. She smiled to herself. The garden had become her father's passion since he'd retired. As she watched, her father reappeared, went into his shed, and returned pushing a wheelbarrow. They would leave with more vegetables than they knew what to do with.

With the dishwasher filled, Eunice closed the door with a flourish and turned to her daughter.

"Coffee," she said decisively. "In or out?"

"Out," replied her daughter, and began to load a tray.

They sat on the patio, watching the progress of the men around the vegetable garden. Simon waved a bunch of onions at them and Belinda waved back.

"What does Simon do?"

Belinda had been waiting for that question. The usual English casual enquiry, the answer to which determined, to an extent, a subsequent attitude. Though it wouldn't be so true of her mother.

She gave her a brief resumé. "Now, he's sort of retired. Having an extended pause is how he describes it."

"Really!" said her mother. "What a fortunate position to be in. It must be lovely to just stop and take stock."

Belinda gave a non-committal reply.

"He can afford to do that can he? I mean, there aren't any money worries or anything?"

Her mother looked concerned and embarrassed for having mentioned it.

"No, nothing like that."

Eunice was relieved. "He's very fortunate then, being…" She searched for the appropriate expression. "Financially independent."

Belinda topped up their coffee and lit a cheroot.

"I think it's become more of a problem than a solution. The trouble is that he never needs to work again, but he hasn't found anything to replace it. And he's not very good at being idle. Lazy, yes, but not idle." She laughed. "He's attempting to be a house-frau at the moment. It's a valiant attempt, but it doesn't suit him."

"I expect he'll think of something."

"Oh, I'm sure he will, eventually. And, if all else fails, I can always find him something in the business."

Her mother didn't reply immediately.

"That could lead to complications later on, couldn't it?"

"Possibly. Though it wouldn't be for a while yet. And I've had complications before." She smiled at her mother, recognising her concern. "Don't worry. I'm not."

"Oh, I shan't worry."

It was not a very convincing lie. Belinda looked around for her cigarettes, and went to retrieve them from the house.

It was a long time since Eunice and Douglas had entertained a new boyfriend of their daughter's. She smiled at the description; it hardly seemed appropriate at their age. What she'd seen of Simon she'd liked, but there were many more questions, and answers she needed to know. But not yet, and she would talk to Douglas later. She'd always found the division between the maternal concern and obtrusiveness difficult. It did not get any easier.

She caught sight of Belinda through the window. She was waving down to the garden again, and laughing. She seemed happy and relaxed. Eunice reminded herself that as long as their daughter was happy, and secure, everything else was of secondary importance.

She returned to the patio and leant over a chair, watching as the wheelbarrow was pushed across the lawn towards them. It was well laden. She looked at her husband reproachfully.

"Are you sure you've got enough in there?"

Douglas ignored his wife's jibe. "Can't send them back without provisions."

Simon pulled out a chair and sat next to Belinda.

"Are you going to become a vegetarian?" she asked, staring into the barrow.

He followed her gaze and grinned. There was enough to keep them going for a month. "I think I may have to."

Later, Simon cleared the back of the car and then watched as Belinda and her father loaded things in. In addition to the vegetables, a bewildering array of plants were included.

"You'll be gardening tomorrow," predicted Eunice, amusement in her voice.

"So it would seem," replied Simon. "I'm wondering where it's all going to go."

"Oh, I expect you'll find that our daughter has a plan."

Simon laughed. "Yes, I'm learning that. She usually has."

It was sunset. They stood on the drive, gathered around the

car, the doors open. Simon was standing with Eunice, Belinda was talking with her father. They were laughing, the pink sky behind them.

"So, we'll see you again?"

Simon agreed. "Soon, I hope."

"Come on a Saturday next time, stay over." Eunice laughed. "Douglas can take you off to his golfing chums on Sunday morning." She laughed more at the expression on his face. "You don't have to play."

"Oh yes I would. Ritual humiliation." He laughed in return. "A Saturday night, after The Gallery closes. I'd like that," he said.

Final goodbyes and departure. He took directions until they reached the main road.

"We've been invited back," he said.

Belinda smiled. "I know."

He negotiated a weaving caravan, thinking.

"Perhaps, before we go again, we should have them back to The Villa for the day. It's how these things are supposed to work isn't it, at the beginning? I mean, the reciprocal visits."

"That would be nice, thank you. Though it isn't strictly necessary."

"No, I'd like to." He laughed. "Fulfil their worst expectations."

Belinda smiled, but did not immediately reply. Her parents regularly called in at The Gallery and stayed the night as they required. It had been a while, some years indeed, since they had visited a new domicile. She wondered.

"Yes, if you're sure. I'll check the diary when we get back. But you will have to invite them, and draw a map."

"Just give me a date." He gave a resigned laugh. "Then I can start to worry all over again."

twenty-nine

From his position deep within the folds of the duvet, Simon heard Belinda's mournful sigh. He reached for her as she slid across the bed and squeezed her hand, receiving a squeeze in return. Neither of them spoke. She was having a disturbed night, patches of sleep disturbed by frequent visits to the bathroom. He lay analysing, trying to remember, counting days.

He was used to her peculiarities by now. Her bladder capacity was small. Several nocturnal pees most nights and what he now referred to as trampoline moments: her habit of appearing to levitate momentarily before falling into bed. This night though, her departures were more frequent. Menstruating, he remembered. He would make a note in his diary. He drifted back to sleep wondering which ovary it was. It seemed to be different, more difficult, every second month.

A sudden thought woke him. The menopause. He'd not lived through one of those. He thought on, recalling something read. Average age fifty-one. A while to go then, probably. No need to worry yet. A complacent thought, disturbed by yet another excursion.

Sitting on the lavatory, Belinda glanced over her shoulder at the day. It seemed limp; clouds seemingly hung on the air, unsure. She wondered whether it would rain. Waiting, her gaze turned back to the room. It seemed unlikely she would be able to sleep and she considered alternatives: none were remotely exciting, but all had to be done.

She looked in on him before heading down the stairs. Sleeping peacefully, gently dribbling into her pillow. Quietly, she kissed the exposed shoulder and with a final glance, closed the bedroom door. The man she loved slept on.

She made coffee, drank it and listened to the early morning news. The weather forecast predicted a hot afternoon. Feeling restless she walked quietly around the house, applying a critical eye. Should she and Simon stay together, this would be her home. She thought of the prospect dispassionately. There would have to be a lot of changes. She moved from room to room, considering.

The house, at least, the areas in use, were moderately tidy, but there were oddities. Most people, in her experience, moved their clutter with them. Simon, it appeared, had little nests all over the house, and, if there was a horizontal surface, it invariably accommodated an opened box of tissues.

Later, she asked him.

"Do you cry a lot?"

Simon, momentarily confused, groped for an answer. "It's not unknown, though not particularly. Though I do have overactive sinuses, and I sneeze a lot. Why do you ask?"

"The tissue boxes, they're everywhere."

"Convenience. Saves walking about looking for one. Same as the ashtrays, the notebooks and the rest of it."

Simon's furniture could not be called smart. Comfortable and lived-in might be a charitable description; distressed in its purest sense. As she looked around her, the immediate impression was of an extended Oxbridge study: shabby, functional. There were books everywhere, shelves now full supplemented by chairs, others piled on the floor under tables, a pine dresser sagging under the sheer weight. And dust, there was a lot of dust.

Simon found Belinda in the sitting room, looking out over the veranda. She turned and began to laugh. It was not the greeting he had expected. He looked hurt and she laughed the more.

"Quackers," she said. "To the life."

"Quackers?" A remembered cartoon duck.

"Go and look in a mirror."

Fresh from the pillow his hair had swept itself into a peak on the top of his head. "It could be worse – it could be bright yellow."

He joined her at the window. The bird food seemed to be low; a water bowl, pitched over by a squirrel, lay on the drive. Simon pulled on the jeans he'd carried down with him and went to see to the provisions.

It didn't take long: a few minutes and the mayhem had started.

Robins darted, bossy, bold and bitchy; tits bounced, blackbirds and thrushes ran, finches popped. Jackdaws, with lazy, deceptive aerodynamic ease, descended in tight turns. Magpies swooped. A pair of elusive sparrows were joined by another dozen species. High above, a pair of buzzards described large arcing circles. A heron, its daft legs trailing, the neck hunched, passed down the road on pond patrol. The first of the squirrels sprinted along branches.

She glanced at him as they both stared from the window. "You love this don't you." It was not a question.

"Yes, I do." He smiled. "It's so simple. Throw out a little food and the reward is immediate. The best free show you'll ever see."

Belinda chortled. "A little food!" She made a quick inventory. "There are six nut feeders and four feed bowls. Two water bowls. And, in the last week, say, the equivalent of two loaves." She paused; it was a comprehensive list. "Pasta, cooked. Three varieties of cheese. A box of time-expired cereal. Bacon rinds, chopped."

"I try to supply a balanced diet," he replied, only partially in jest.

"You should build a hide out there and sell tickets. I wouldn't be surprised if this isn't a scheduled stopover for migratory flights." Starlings began their bath routine. "How many peanuts do you get through in a year?"

"Ground nuts," corrected Simon, absently. "They're ground nuts."

Belinda looked at him, thought to comment on his pedantry, and thought again.

"I vaguely remember something about ground nuts," he said, frowning. "Scheme to grow them, West Africa I think, post-'45 Labour government. Famous debacle."

Belinda's eyes began to glaze over. "Rather before my time."

"And mine, effectively." He looked at her, remembering there was a question. "About a hundred kilos, hundred and fifty of the bird food. Hundred and twenty quid a year."

"Cheap entertainment."

"And benign." He smiled at her. "As I've said, I didn't get out much before I met you."

"You will now."

A shaft of sunlight bore through the window, highlighting the dust. Belinda announced a morning of housework. Her tone did not suggest negotiation.

She found the vacuum cleaner and carried it out into the light.

"I remember these, I had one twenty years ago. Can you still get the bags for them?"

As she spoke she released the hinged front of the cylinder to reveal the collecting bag. On the cardboard front was written the date of first use – the year before – and the number of times it had been emptied and reused: three.

He looked over her shoulder. "New bag," he suggested, helpfully.

With Simon despatched to the top floor, she began on the ground. He dutifully dusted the office, cleaned the table and chairs on the roof terrace and stood for a while, looking at nothing in particular. It seemed a waste of a fine morning. Gardening was promised for the afternoon.

He found Belinda washing the kitchen floor, sweating, obliviously naked.

"You don't really appreciate how big this house is until you come to clean it," she said, over a shoulder.

He offered to help, but was politely refused.

"I'm enjoying it," she said, catching her breath. "Can't you see the difference?"

Simon could. He watched her, a bead of perspiration slowly trailing down her back. *Don't interrupt,* he told himself. *She's only on the ground floor.*

After lunch, they began on the front garden and again a universal truth was confirmed. Turn over a little soil, leave a spade stuck in the ground, and a robin will perch on the handle within ten seconds.

Simon dug while Belinda planted the donations from her parents' garden. It was well into the evening before they finished.

Later, sitting on the veranda, handiwork admired, their conversation was punctuated by the occasional groan. It would be worse in the morning.

Suddenly, Belinda laughed. "This is not the sort of synchronised groaning popularly associated with a joint activity!"

Belinda had employed the same little cleaning firm for years. The Gallery on Monday and Thursday mornings, her flat on an afternoon. Two archetypal Irish women, with continual chat, great efficiency and a seemingly inexhaustible predisposition for tea. Simon had met them several times and had been suitably, amusingly, belittled. Formidable women with an easy charm. On a sunny Tuesday morning he had not expected to find them standing at his front door.

"It's Simon, isn't it."

He confirmed it was. He strained his memory. "Dervla and Siobhan."

"Our very selves."

He stood back as they walked in, homed inexorably on the kitchen and found the kettle.

"Belinda sent us; we have an arrangement for the next six months. Every Tuesday morning, four hours." Siobhan, or possibly Dervla, laughed. "She said you were not to argue."

"Wouldn't dream of it. Would you like any help?"

"Absolutely not."

thirty

The card arrived by the morning post.

"You've had your first mail," he said that evening, handing her the envelope.

Belinda looked surprised. "This is my mother's writing."

She opened the card and read it, smiled, and without comment handed it to Simon. The front showed an illustration of two bears hugging each other. Inside was written, 'Welcome to your Seventeenth Home.'

"Seventeenth."

Belinda took the card and propped it up against the cookery books.

"I think my mother is trying to tell me something."

Belinda was hand-washing sweaters, alternating between the kitchen sinks, Radio 3 playing in the background, Strauss. Feeling expansive, Simon swung his right arm around her waist and began to waltz her around. At least, she was waltzing, his attempt more an imitation.

"Ooh, you are romantic," she said, in a broad Lancashire accent, struggling to remove her rubber gloves. He had the remote control in his hand and was gradually increasing the volume. Strauss began to thunder around the house and he guided her out onto the patio.

"Thank you, kind sir," she said in the approved manner as the music ended.

Simon gave a little bow, lifted her right hand in his left, and conducted her back to the kitchen sink.

"Oh well," she said, pulling the rubber gloves back on. "Tea break over – time to get back on your heads!"

Simon laughed. "I didn't know you knew that joke."

"Simon, everyone knows that joke."

Several minutes later he stood behind her, his hands at her waist, his chin resting lightly on a shoulder.

"Aren't you supposed to lift a leg when I kiss you? They do it in all the old movies."

She turned to face him. "Kiss me again, and I'll see what I can do."

Simon kissed her again, and gently, she kneed him in the groin. He stepped back in shock.

"Sorry. Did I do it wrong?"

Belinda was emptying the drier and Simon, ever helpful, was standing in his habitual position leaning on the door frame, watching her. She pulled out a bath towel and looked at him.

"How do you like your towels folded?"

He stared at her.

"Well?" she said, attempting to be patient.

"Towels folded?"

"Yes, towels folded." She sighed, and asked with a heavy accent, "How you like?"

"Oh, I don't know. Please yourself, it really doesn't matter."

It seemed an odd question, and he said so.

"No, not really. It might not matter now, but someday it might. I've lived by myself too remember. One gets used to doing things in a certain way. And it's especially true of men. Someone else does it differently, and eventually it gets to be really irritating."

He laughed at her.

"Laugh if you like, but believe me, it happens."

Simon took the towel, folded it by his preferred method, and handed it back to her.

"Thank you," she said. "That was easy wasn't it." She paused. "I once had an argument that went on for days over something equally as trivial."

"Towels?"

"No, socks. You'd be amazed."

He was sitting in the living room waiting for her when she returned from the bathroom. She smiled at him as she came in. Her hair, lifted by the breeze as she opened the door, resettled around her face.

"How do you find the layout of this kitchen, where things are, and…" His voice tailed off. It seemed a ludicrous question.

"Tolerable. It has a certain logic. Why do you ask?"

"I wondered if you might want to change things around?"

"Not particularly. I've not given it any thought. I might when I next clean out the cupboards." She looked at him enquiringly, an eyebrow raised.

"Just wondered."

Belinda gave him a final glance and crossed the room. She refilled the kettle and switched it on, then leant back on a working surface and looked at him.

"I know it sounds pathetic, Simon, and it is. But it's always the little things that start to go wrong first."

She turned to make the coffee and brought him a cup. Collecting her own, she sat beside him.

"If you want me to go ahead and totally reorganise this house to my own satisfaction, then fine. But don't say I didn't warn you."

Simon checked the sign daily. It remained the same. He wondered if she'd noticed his modification but decided not to ask and, having resisted the initial impulse, stubbornness prevailed. The dressing table, for so long bare and dusty, now sported a variety of pots and bottles. It was in daily use; she could not have failed to notice.

As he dressed, he glanced again at the sign, unchanged. Irritated, he picked it up and turned it over.

There was another piece of paper, stuck over the original message. His question answered, he repositioned the sign, the new message facing outward. 'Till Whenever', it said.

thirty-one

Sunday morning, eight thirty, an unusual time for him to be up. Not unique, but unusual. The night had been warm and Belinda had risen early. Simon, returning from an enforced pee, found the bed had been stripped in his absence.

He sat on a sofa in the sitting room, absently flicking through the Sunday papers, a half-consumed cup of cold coffee within reach. He felt odd, as if something should be disturbing him, but wasn't.

Belinda appeared. "Have we any plans for today?"

She was wearing one of his old denim shirts, the tails pulled round and knotted under her breasts. He found it strangely erotic; it was also curiously familiar and he cast his mind back to remember. Mitzi Gaynor in *South Pacific*. He must have been about eight. The film had made no impression, but the knotted shirt had. One of his earliest erotic experiences, an image remembered thereafter.

There were others, private importances, and he thought of them. A picture by Dali, the civil war one, the thigh becoming arm becoming breast, striking the landscape. A little stream leading into the sea at Budleigh Salterton, losing his sun hat, and at five, powerless to retrieve it. An illustration from a book of Grimm's fairy tales that still made him shudder when he thought of it. And always those evocative, never-to-be-forgotten smells. Bird's custard powder, calamine lotion, the old Boots baby powder. And taste. He sat, smiling, remembering Gerber orange juice.

"Simon?" Belinda was standing over him. "Where are you?"

He smiled up at her. It was a childlike, sheepish smile.

"Do you remember Gerber baby orange, those little glass bottles?" He almost cooed at the thought of it. "I wonder if you can still buy it?"

She repeated her question.

"Nothing planned. Why, did you have something in mind?"

He glanced out of the window. It promised to be another sunny day. Her eyes followed his gaze.

"I thought we might have a picnic again. Down by the river."

They resembled one of those tranquil illustrations drawn to accompany an advertisement for something perfectly unnecessary but ridiculously expensive.

They lay under a tree at the water's edge where there was a slight bend in the river. All that was needed to complete the picture was a punt tied up alongside, a parasol left open at the stern. What the picture never showed was the unforgiving texture of the ground and the myriad of insects that inhabited it. He swatted again at a particularly irritating fly that kept settling on his hand, and again missed.

Simon sat up and reached for his glass. Belinda was lying on her side reading a newspaper, her back towards him. He reached across, and moving her hair to one side, kissed the nape of her neck. Still holding the glass, he lay down again, wriggling to find a more comfortable position.

"Who was it who said that the season for alfresco sex starts at Whitsun?"

She laughed. "I wasn't aware it had any particular season."

They skirted the edge of the field, not wishing to disturb the animals. It was a picturesque scene, the sort that Constable might have sketched. Belinda, who was leading, perched herself on a stile, claiming the most convenient position. Simon stood to the side of her, leaning on the fence. They watched a lamb, suckling from a ewe.

"Isn't it a little late for lambs?" asked Belinda.

Simon thought for a moment, dredging up another piece of information trawled from the radio, partially remembered.

"There's some sort of experimental programme going on. A hormone treatment to bring the ewes into season twice a year."

"Must be popular with the rams."

The lamb finished feeding and another immediately took its place.

"Twins," she said.

Simon watched the lamb feeding. "I wish someone had told me about that when I was younger."

Belinda raised an eyebrow and looked at him. "About what?"

"Breastfeeding."

"Why? Were you deprived?"

"No, not that." He smiled. "It was at junior school, I must have been about ten. There was a Scottish kid, Charlie Ottaway. A character was Charlie. Anyway, one day he comes into school with a hell of a story. Caught his sister feeding her baby with her chest! Of course, none of us believed him. A liar was Charlie. And besides, it sounded a bit rude. Children can be very prudish, at least, we were."

Simon laughed at his recollection of it.

"So, I get nominated to check it out. 'Ask your mother,' they say, she being known as a woman of knowledge and used to questions. 'She'll know.' So, I do. I don't remember the circumstances, but it must have surprised her. 'Extra muscles for women,' she said. I didn't mention the feeding you see, because it was rude. Just asked why did women have lumps on their chest.

"After lunch, newly informed, I go back to school. Other kids have asked their mothers. Mine was the only extra-muscles version – all the other kids supported Charlie. So I argue, lose, get into a fight about it, lose that. It was not a good afternoon."

Simon shook his head. "I can still feel the shame. Never really trusted anything she told me again."

He remembered something else and started laughing.

"I took her a used condom once that I found in the street. It must have been about the same time." He paused, trying to remember. "Something about being for men when they couldn't hold on."

Belinda laughed. "Now that, in its way, is true."

"Not the way I took it. It didn't look big enough. Funny what you remember," he said, thoughtfully. "I was a very trusting kid. It came as a shock to realise that she hadn't been telling the truth. It proved her fallibility, though that realisation didn't come until later. At the time, I just assumed she didn't know. So I told her. No doubt that was wrong as well."

"What did she say?"

"I don't remember. I vaguely remember telling her, but not what she said afterwards."

Belinda smiled. "Difficult things, parents. I sometimes think with mine that the roles are getting blurred, reversed. Who is the parent, and who is the child?"

Simon recalled his mother's later years. "It's normal," he said.

They continued to watch the sheep.

"They're not as stupid as is commonly believed."

"Parents?"

"No, sheep."

Belinda noted his change of subject. Losing a parent was the one thing she dreaded. She could only guess at what feelings the memories brought.

"Not one of God's more intelligent creatures though, surely."

"Agreed. But not entirely stupid either. There's a flock, somewhere in Wales, that invaded a village. Every morning they'd find them rooting through dustbins, grazing in their gardens, all sorts." He laughed. "How would you feel to see a sheep feeding from your bird table?"

"Amazed. It would be on the fourth floor."

Simon nodded. "Serves you right for living in the centre of town. See what you miss. It seems these sheep had learned to cross the cattle grids by rolling over them. They ended up having to put a fence around the entire village, and gates on the roads to keep them out."

Belinda swung her legs over the far side of the stile and jumped down. She looked at her watch.

"Come on," she said. "I think it's time we were getting back."

Simon took her hand. "You were right, thank you," he said. "This walk was a good idea."

They began to walk across the next field. "I wonder if children are so unknowing these days?" she said.

"I doubt it. There's so much more information about. It was the radio and books when I was a kid. Now, the whole of the world delivered daily to your living room. So much information, so little explanation."

They walked across another field towards a road. Simon was, by this time, completely lost, trusting to Belinda's sense of direction.

"It seems a pity though," he said finally. "Naivety is precious. Seems a shame to have it stolen so early."

They came to the road and he was relieved to recognise it, if only vaguely. The car was a couple of hundred yards to the left.

Simon complimented Belinda on her direction finding. She laughed at him, and then she kissed him. As he responded, she pulled back and placed a finger over his lips.

"I rarely get lost. Don't worry, darling, you're safe with me. I'll look after you."

"You must get really sick of always being right," he said.

She gave his hand a squeeze.

"You should know!"

thirty-two

August Bank Holiday Monday, traditionally the last frantic dash to the sea; traffic warnings had begun early. For Simon, never a day to leave the house.

Inspired by the weather, he determined to continue with the back garden excavations. Belinda meanwhile, decided on a day in the sun, horizontal on a sun bed, naked. Refreshments to hand, she began to read him a selection from the papers.

"You're a cock," she said. "More politely, a rooster."

Simon thought immediately of connotations. "Any particular reason?"

"Your birth date. There's an article on the Chinese zodiac. Animal signs," she added, helpfully. "There's a description."

There was a pause and then a chuckle. "The cock. A pioneer in spirit, you are devoted to work and quest after knowledge. You are selfish and eccentric. Ideal partner, a snake."

Simon was non-committal. "And what are you, or can I guess?"

"You guessed. A snake – just." She quoted again. "Wise and intense with a tendency towards physical beauty. Vain and high-tempered. Marry a cock." She frowned. "I'm not so sure about the vanity and high temper."

Simon looked to the sky but failed to find any flying pigs.

He had struck another layer of soapstone and stood, leaning on the handle of the pick considering how best to attack it, looking for voids. From somewhere below a voice drifted up, calling. A body followed, climbing the steps up to the terrace.

"Belinda, this is Andrew." He was wearing a pair of the now prevalent but, to Simon's eye, deeply repellent, loose-fitting check cotton shorts.

At the first sound of company Belinda had thrown a towel strategically across her bottom. She leant up slightly on her elbows.

"Good afternoon," she said, conversationally. "You'll excuse me if I don't get up."

Her tone was pleasant enough, though her comment left a space in the air.

Andrew, flustered, tried to concentrate on looking at Simon, but failed.

"Of course, of course. Sorry to disturb you. I tried ringing the bell but I couldn't get any reply."

Simon nodded. "You wouldn't." He paused just a little. "What can we do for you?"

"We're having a barbecue later on and Jane and I were wondering if you'd like to come?"

Simon looked over at Belinda. Her expression seemed positive.

"Sure," he replied. "What time?"

"Eightish?"

"Fine. Thank you for the invitation."

"Good. Glad you can come. I'll tell Jane. See you later on."

They watched as Andrew disappeared down the steps. Belinda peeled off the towel and rolled over.

"So, who was that?"

"Neighbours," replied Simon. "A few houses up." The invitation had surprised him. "This is not an invitation for us, it's for you. They've met me before."

"Did they invite you back?"

Simon shook his head. "No, come to think of it, they didn't." He smiled at the vague recollection, perhaps two years before. "I think Jane was trying to pair me off with someone. A divorcée cousin maybe. It was not a success. And I think their friends found me a little too abrasive."

Belinda smiled, imagining. "So, nothing to live up to then."

Simon noted both her expression and tone. "Nothing at all."

He returned his attention to the graduations of the earth bank ahead of him and the layer of stone at its base.

"And no expectations, either."

Simon scanned the wine rack, pondered, and finally selected a reasonable red and a white. Belinda stood waiting for him in the living room. She was wearing something he had not seen before, a close-fitting raw cotton shift, floor-length, long arms, V neckline. It was starkly white, relieved by elaborate embroidery around the neckline, cuffs and hem. It looked Indian, and somehow familiar. He asked.

"Yes, seventies I think," she said in reply. "I had some. This I bought for a couple of quid in a charity shop last year."

Her hair, freshly washed, hung straight down her back. She wore hardly any make-up apart from a little round the eyes, and a pale lipstick. He glanced at the cavernous canvas handbag at her feet, one of the regulation straw hats poking from the top of it.

"I assume I'm carrying all your clutter."

Simon smiled. "I would be grateful."

He continued to look at her. She seemed, somehow, to glow.

"Will I do? Not that I care, you understand, but I don't want to frighten the horses." She laughed, brightly. "I may just have to meet these people again."

Simon caught her expression as she looked at him. It questioned.

"Maybe not en masse." He smiled. "But certainly some."

He continued to look at her, an odd expression on his face. "You look amazing," he said, finally. "So fresh."

"It must be love," Belinda replied, not entirely seriously. She scooped the bag from the floor. "Are we ready?"

After a brief delay while Simon rehung the nut holders scattered by the squirrels and Belinda inspected the previous week's plantings, they turned right from the drive and began to walk. It was an ambling stroll, hand in hand as usual. Simon had the canvas bag over his shoulder, now further loaded with the wine.

"So, should I know anything about these people?"
"Our hosts?"
"The same."
Simon didn't reply immediately and required a prompt.
"I'm trying to think of something positive, polite."
"A rare restraint."

Simon laughed. "In truth, I don't know that I care much for either of them. Supercilious, irrelevant, trivial. Should it come, I will applaud their downfall. Andrew is a chancer, something in financial services, the parasitic sector. Charmless, though not to himself. I don't know what Jane does, or it hasn't registered. Poor taste in men. Both in their early forties, relatively successful I suppose, but somehow superficial. No children." He paused. "Yes, that's the best description, superficial. A kind of gravitous vacuity. And with that particular type of self-obsessed selfishness that is quite repellent. Jack and Jacky the lad."

Simon had spoken the last words with real distaste, though there was no malice in his voice. She glanced at him and gave one of her more saccharine of smiles.

"This promises to be a fun evening."
"Who knows."

They had not been up towards the end of the lane together, though Belinda had driven it early on for a look. Simon, pointing something out, missed his footing in a pothole and tripped. She let go of his hand as he stumbled a few paces to right himself.

Belinda laughed at his expression as he straightened up, one of affronted dignity. He had not dropped the bag. He gave her a suitably derogatory expression, momentarily dazzled by the low sun. He moved until the light was directly behind her.

"What have you got on under that?"
"A body stocking." She grinned. "Should I need a pee, I may be gone for some time."

The noise and the smell guided them towards the back garden. There were fewer people than Simon had expected: including themselves, about twenty. He recognised a few. Andrew immediately pounced upon Belinda, taking her around, making introductions. Simon meantime, was left talking to Jane. They had little to talk about. The barbecue was new, apparently, so they talked about that.

He watched Belinda's progress and was conscious of rather too many surprised expressions.

For want of something to do, Simon inspected the food on offer. It appeared to come straight from the M&S Barbecues for Cretins range, Premier Selection. He looked, too, at the new cooking facilities. The knowledge that barbecues wrongly prepared could be both highly poisonous and carcinogenic did not help.

Belinda meanwhile had slipped effortlessly into work mode, conviviality, that ease and easy ability to engage. Irascible, it was more difficult for Simon. He had rarely seen any of his neighbours collected together. Though undoubtedly useful to Belinda, he didn't find it a particularly edifying spectacle. Beyond those close to The Villa, he recognised few of them. Fewer still, he thought, he would want to.

With a glass in one hand and a plate of dubious food in the other, he caught up with Belinda. They circulated, or more accurately, a succession of people passed by to say hello. Belinda did most of the talking, Simon only joining in as required.

The evening passed, somewhat to his surprise, pleasantly enough. Simon even met several people he liked. It helped that it all broke up relatively early.

Moonlit, the lane had fairytale dimensions. They walked, accompanied by pale shadows beside them.

"I suspect, after this evening, there's going to be rather a lot of this – invitations." He laughed. "My desirability amongst the local populace seems suddenly to have increased. Can't imagine why." He squeezed her hand.

"Only too glad to contribute to your integration into society."

Something crossed the lane ahead of them. Too large for a fox, possibly a badger. Crashing sounds from the undergrowth and then a returned silence. They watched for a while longer and then moved on.

"We could, of course, reciprocate," said Belinda. "Pre-empt the curiosity."

"Meaning?"

"Hold a party."

Simon thought. "We'd need an excuse. An obvious one. The rumour mill will be on the late shift as it is." He thought more. "An idea though, good idea. I'll think about it."

"Do that." She laughed. "You might surprise yourself."

thirty-three

Responding to a request from an old friend, Belinda was going north for a few days to help organise an exhibition opening. The plan was that she should travel by train and he would drive up for the event and spend the night. Depending on their mood, they were to break the return journey somewhere in between.

The taxi arrived and Simon swung her suitcase into the boot. The driver, not to be outdone, put her overnight bag on the back seat.

Simon smiled. "You seem to be travelling in the front."

She smiled back. "So I do."

He kissed her before she climbed in. "I'll be thinking of you."

She kissed him in return. "I'll be thinking of you too. See you on Saturday."

He watched the taxi clear the drive and gave a final wave. It was only a couple of days, but by the evening he was missing her.

Sleeping by himself, the solitary bed. The listening for her breath that didn't come. The simple intimacies of touch, of love, the sexual love, the giving and the taking, the afterglow. The pressing feeling of a nipple on his back, the hand that rested on his thigh. The being able, at any time, to express what he felt, and the immediate response.

Belinda wasn't only his lover, his partner; she had become his best friend. The lack of companionship, the easy understanding that separation denied, was the hardest. Their first night apart for weeks. A fitful sleep.

*

The morning was miserable: grey clouds, fine drizzle. It suited his mood.

He was lonely without her, that difference from merely being alone. He had surrendered part of himself, diminished without her. The best of what he was, suspended.

They'd come a long way in a few weeks. That he loved her, he knew. How much he loved her he did not know. He could estimate, but not with any certainty. That knowledge would come with more time or, as had always been the pattern, retrospectively.

The investment: the hope, the joy, the rest of it, all of it. And then the withdrawal. The grieving process: pain, anger, denial, rage, acceptance. And all the rest of that. The escalation, always faster than the ever increasing trail of debris.

The news summary reached its hurried conclusion. The contents, like that of the newspapers, had done little to cheer him. Somehow, decades started poorly, a pattern repeated for the last hundred years. He made a cursory review, his mind taking each in turn.

1900: death of a queen, imperial upheaval, Boer War. 1910: the end of the elegant age and then the Great War. 1920: perhaps the exception. 1930: slump, fascism. 1940: World War II. 1950: drabness unrelieved, Korean War, Cold War beginnings. 1960: employment without prosperity, Vietnam War escalation. 1970: death of the dream, followed by the oil crisis. 1980: massive social change and unemployment, Falklands War. 1990: Gulf War, recession. 2000: bubbles bursting, reality squared.

That this new decade, century, had begun to so much hope and excitement yet had soured so quickly, saddened him. That it appeared inevitable only heightened the melancholy.

It began to rain heavily, ruining any thoughts of excavations. Feeling his mood descending he walked slowly up the stairs to his office, wondering what to do. He sat at his desk, watching the rain, staring aimlessly, his mind drifting without destination. It was like looking at walls again.

People passed through one's life in phases, or so it seemed. The natural span of friendship appeared to be about four years. After that, time, the individual happening, began the drift.

Some friendships lasted beyond the average span – ignoring those of geography, neighbours, colleagues – and he had a few, and those were maintained by regular if infrequent contact. Simon had three pairs of old friends. Occasionally he wrote them all letters, updates and solicitations for news.

When abroad, he had made it a rule never to send postcards. He'd always found the practice somewhat confusing, like Christmas cards: a ritual without a real, or even imagined, meaning. He didn't send those either. Letters were different, in part a rope thrown towards a shore, hoping for a responsive tug.

He began to write letters.

Night-time is the right time; afternoon delight: old song lyrics it didn't help to remember. Simon felt to the extremities of the bed, rolled onto his side and resigned himself to another fitful sleep.

The room was dark but they could see each other perfectly. As Belinda put her arms around his shoulders, Simon's hands slipped around her waist. She leant back against the wall and pulled him onto her. Their lips, open, began to creep around each other's faces, slowly at first, their tongues exploring. She found an ear, opened her mouth to engulf it, and breathed heavily within. The skin on Simon's neck tingled and he bit softly into her shoulder. He slid his hand under her top to the edge of the bra beneath. The first touch of her skin speeded his fingers and he raised his hands further until his palms enclosed each breast.

She ran the tip of her tongue across his face and down towards his mouth. Simon reached around her back and released the catch and pushed the bra upwards until he held each breast in his hands, a nipple under each thumb. Belinda undid the buttons of his shirt and pulled them together. Skin on skin. Intent replaced recreation, need became urgency.

Simon reached down a hand and hung his shoulder until he reached the edge of her skirt. He lifted the hem and ran his hand, slowly, up the inside of her thigh until he reached the moistness at the top. He could smell her, the wetness and the heat.

Belinda groaned and pushed her tongue further between his teeth, deep, flicking from side to side. She reached down and undid his jeans, sucking on his mouth as she reached within.

Simon woke up. He sat upright in the bed, staring down into the darkness. The night, apart from his breathing, was still.

He was confused, unsure of where he was. Gradually, the dream faded.

He felt the wetness along his thigh and reached down to confirm it. A smell of starch on his fingers.

I love you.

As he drove, he turned the phrase over in his mind. So many meanings, so many emotions and feelings. Those three words could induce the most wonderful warmth and profound relief, the glow of reciprocation. And they could chill; panic towards a rapid flight.

Love: such a small word, singular of syllable. A weak word, a strong word; the strongest word. The most noble acts, the most bestial of betrayals. Reasons and excuses.

What remains of us is our art, in the widest sense, and love. Love remains.

Simon knew something of hotels: many rooms, many beds, several continents. Years of travel, checking in and checking out. The overwhelming similarity, the strangely familiar furniture, fittings, carpets. He'd spent – an estimate before retiring – something like five years in hotel rooms. Anonymous spaces in which to exist, sleep, a temporary transit. Part of him delighted in that anonymity, other parts despaired. He had mixed memories. Occasional euphoria of jobs well done, tasks achieved. Crushing loneliness, the early hours of mornings, desperate; and that pervading distance, the anaesthetic from any real events. That hotel rooms were one of the favoured locations for suicide seemed entirely appropriate.

Following Belinda's directions he found the hotel with little difficulty, negotiated the barrier at the car par, parked the car appropriately and presented himself at reception. Instructions had been left. He swiped the plastic card through the lock of her room and gained entry at only the second attempt. He found the light switch, dumped his bag with hers on the raised plinth and heard the door close behind him. The room smelt reassuringly familiar. Her perfume hung on the air, her toiletries in the bathroom, her clothes in the wardrobe, an envelope on the table addressed to him.

He slit it open and read her note. Expect her after six. He looked at his watch: three hours. Afternoon tea, an exploration, a shower. A wait. He could occupy the time.

It was a while since he'd driven four hundred miles at a stretch and it showed. Occasionally, as his mind drifted, he twitched. Perhaps a nap, post-tea, pre-shower. He lay on the bed, the first bed they would share not one of their own. Smaller than they were used to, but adequate.

He remembered a thought he'd had while driving up. He was, in these circumstances, an addition to her, not an entire representation of himself. A sublimation. Should they meet anyone she knew, he should remember. It was a notable difference.

Simon took off his boots and rolled over. He would skip the tea. Awoken by a kiss when Belinda returned, he had difficulty in remembering where he was.

Since their destination was within walking distance of the hotel, they chose to eat in the restaurant before commencing the evening's entertainment, a shared bottle of red as fortification. A final pee before leaving.

An old observation, but somehow a curious and somewhat rigid code of ethics applied to behaviour within men's urinals. For example, conversations over wash basins were almost mandatory, while in contrast, during the act itself, silence beyond the sound of passing water reigned supreme. And of course, sideways glances were not to be recommended.

Simon had always been very conscious of his surroundings when in public lavatories. Several childhood experiences, confusing at the time, terrifying in retrospect, had taught him to be wary. It was a practice kept, the use of wide vision and an awareness of movement.

From his observations, men divided into one of two categories. To extricate the last dregs from the bladder, they were either shakers or pullers, with pullers being in the majority on a ratio of three to two. Pullers also tended to look downwards during this activity, while shakers preferred to continue their examination of the tiling or the upper reaches of the wall. Simon was a shaker himself; pulling had always seemed inappropriate in such circumstances.

Spitting also seemed to feature highly, and this was common to both groups. As to why, Simon had never found a satisfactory explanation. The experiments of boyhood, continued as adult habit? Male urinals were overdue some anthropological research.

He knew her well enough now to recognise it. Not with him any longer, in private, but with strangers, in public, constantly. Almost like a portcullis falling, a barrier erected. That faintly glazed professional face, impenetrable. Entirely charming, but chilled, controlled, detached.

Simon had noticed it before: women subjected to the media, public gaze, but never from the inside out. It fascinated him. The deployment was immediate, automatic, instantly effective.

Eventually, tiring of being polite to unfortunate strangers, he wandered off by himself.

Belinda leant gently on a pillar in the centre of the room, glass in hand. The opening was going well enough, though not as well as the sponsors might have hoped. She watched the owner of the gallery glad-handing some recent arrivals and felt sympathy. Her conscious choice never to hold one of these types of functions at The Gallery may have cost her money, but success was relative and she was relatively happy with her lack of compromise.

Someone she knew, but preferred not to, saw her. She watched him as he approached her; he looked hopeful. After polite greetings, they spoke pleasantly of nothing in particular while Belinda continued her inspection. The unwanted companion followed her lead.

"Who's that?" he asked suddenly. "I don't recognise him."

She followed his gaze. Simon was attempting to give a picture his serious consideration; his head was tilted to one side, and he was frowning.

"His name is Simon Kendal," she said. "We came together."

"A friend?"

She nodded.

"As in 'just good friends'?"

"Oh no. Not 'just good friends'." She looked him in the eye and smiled sweetly. "We're living together."

She paused, allowing the statement to register, and straightened up from the pillar.

"Please don't think me rude, but I think it's time I went back to join him."

"Oh super!" cried out a female voice from a distance away.

"Califragilistic," muttered Simon.

"Expialidocious," continued Belinda as she joined him.

They smiled at each other, knowing smiles, mutual understanding.

They were standing alongside a long canvas. Simon looked at it. He stared at it for several minutes. It stared back. He saw what was there; what he didn't see was why. The soles of his shoes squeaked on the floor as he changed position. The noise irked him and destroyed what was left of his concentration. He straightened up and smiled at her.

"When I'm with you, and we're doing something like this, I'm very conscious of my…" He searched for the phrase. "Visual illiteracy."

Belinda frowned. "I'm not entirely sure what that phrase is supposed to mean."

"Neither am I. But whatever it is, I haven't got it. I can't make any sense of these at all."

On the walk back to the hotel they found a pub, welcoming, real people and a good local beer.

Simon's mistake was obvious as soon as he stepped through the door. The fragrant smell, the flowers and the absence of urinals.

The Durex and Tampax machines mounted on the wall dispelled any lingering doubts. This was the ladies' lavatory.

It was too late. Simon, his mind having decided, his body anticipating, was now desperate. He quickly checked the cubicles. None were occupied. He nipped into the nearest and relieved himself.

Belinda had realised his mistake, but he had disappeared before she could call a warning. She kept a wary eye on the door and its approaches. A middle-aged woman bustled in its direction.

Belinda rose swiftly from her seat to cut her off. She put out a hand and smiled.

"I'm sorry, madam, but my husband's just gone in there!"

The woman stared at her incredulously. "But, it's the ladies?"

"I know."

"But I've got cystitis!"

Belinda looked concerned. "I'm sorry – but I'm sure he won't be very long."

Simon slipped out of the door and the woman turned on him.

"What's wrong with you? Can't you read?"

Simon apologised. "I'm dyslexic."

"Well, you should get it seen to."

He stood aside as the woman pushed past him. He shrugged to a group who were laughing nearby and followed Belinda back to their table.

"Thank you for rescuing me," he said, sitting down. "What did you say to her?"

Belinda told him, cutting him off before he could reply. "It seemed the easiest explanation. I thought it unlikely she'd ask for proof." She smiled. "And she looked the sort of woman who considers all husbands fools."

thirty-four

Worry, once a hobby, became preoccupation. He thought about them, the two of them. Already they had a history, days drawn into weeks, becoming months. It was measurable, and he measured it. They had even begun to speak to each other in a private shorthand. Everything was there – a child could not mistake it.

His emotions were confused. While the optimistic soared, the other half, the side that remembered, began to lay up provisions for the fall; the siege to follow failure. Hope, when thought about, did turn to apprehension.

That morning, as he'd reflected, all the excitement of their affair had left him. When would he cease to be the solution and become the problem? All the promise to come, the excitements and experiences to share, would instead be dreaded. Not something to enjoy, rather to endure. The memory of so many past failures haunted him, distressed, inhibited.

He wondered, of those who remained, the friends, the long acquaintances, how many if met afresh would he respond to, or they to him? People changed, some trivially, others fundamentally. A continuous process. But circumstance, and acquaintance, moved in quantum steps. How many marriages, friendships, were a reflection of who one was and not a measure of who one had now become? Frustrated apathy and weariness. The new become trapped within the what had been.

Accepting who one was, and had become, was the hardest. The recognition, stripped of ego and false aspiration, the most difficult. And, as the self did deconstruct, the others heaped upon with disappointment. The acknowledgement of what one's friends, ex-lovers, wives became, did not encourage. The promise and potential seen but not delivered. The compromises made, the principles betrayed. There was a natural span to anything, and so there was with friendship.

He had begun to worry about them. What was the future for Belinda and himself? Would they reach a plateau, coast a while, and then slowly disintegrate? It was the established pattern. Romance suffered when the living intervened.

He had no talent for long-term relationships, none at all. The life, littered with departures and premature endings.

Failure wrote large.

It was his one consistency.

Belinda sat leaning forward, elbows on the table, forearms upward supporting the inclined head. In her right hand she held a wine glass, in her left, resting lightly between her fingers, drooped an unlit cheroot.

They had finished eating and were talking. The conversation had begun easily enough, but Simon's recent days of renewed solitude had steered the direction. Again he felt the need to test the commitment, to force the pace. Belinda was evasive, resistant.

It was a reflection of their individual characters; his need to know, her apparent acceptance without the fraught analysis. Enjoyment without the confessional guilt.

Simon had been describing her from the position of a casual, uninvolved observer. What had begun as detached abstractions had rapidly dissolved.

She leant back slightly and put her unlit cheroot on the table, sipping from the wine before she spoke.

"Thank you," she said. "It's very kind of you. But to me, it's very simple and not at all special. Put at its most basic, it doesn't amount to very much. An educated, above average intelligence, no more. A variable personality, curious and critical, that's mostly calm, at least from the outside. Controlled might be a better description. And physically, five foot nine, size ten, with thin arms and legs. A regulation coat hanger. Blue eyes, blonde hair, passable bone structure. Left-handed. It's nothing special." She snorted. "Every boy's dream, tall, blonde and slender. But only because it's fashionable. I'm not particularly beautiful, or even especially attractive." She laughed, though without much humour. "I present well. The rest is in the head."

Simon thought her comments disingenuous and said so.

"They might be to you, but they're not to me. It's how I am, what and whom I'm used to seeing in the morning." Belinda paused and gave an ironic smile. "Oh yes. And a talent for personal failure."

She picked up the cheroot from the table. "All told, if someone was trying to sell me, to me, it's not what I would describe as a faultless recommendation. The provenance is flawed. But thank you for the compliments."

Belinda lit the cheroot and looked across the table at Simon.

"Accept me for what I am, Simon, don't build worlds around me. Other people's structures turn into walls. Stop pressurising it. Just let it go its own way for a while."

A moth flew in through the open window, heading for the light behind them. They watched as it beat itself senseless on the bulb and then fell to the floor. Simon rescued it and put it back out the window. Then he closed it.

"Male. It's the infrared from the light they're attracted to," he said. "It's sexual."

She smiled. "It would be."

Sarah, Belinda's assistant, had taken the afternoon off. Belinda sat at the reception desk, idly watching two perspective customers walking around the floor space. Simon had rung earlier, suggesting lunch. She checked her watch: twenty minutes. She continued to look over her customers.

One, brisk, thirty seconds at each picture, checking on the price labels before viewing. The other, the least well dressed, viewing for minutes at a time, barely a glance at the labels. A viewer with taste, a buyer without. It was, she thought, typical of the last few weeks.

She was doing some business, easily sufficient to meet her limited overheads, but the figures were well down on the year before. The whole of the local area was reporting the same, and there was a general consensus that there was worse to come. That The Gallery would survive she had no doubt, her particular cosseted circumstance would see to that. But she worried for some of her immediate neighbours.

Predictably, the phone rang the moment she switched on the answerphone. Belinda stood at the desk, telephone in her right hand, rapidly making notes on a pad with her left.

Left-handers wrote in one of two ways. Crab-handed, the left wrist hooked, the pen pointed back towards the body, the text in full view. The writing was long and spiky, and while effective the method was awkward and inelegant. The other way was conventional, the pen away from the body, but with the head offset to the right in order to see the text. Belinda used this second method. She wrote quickly across the pad, pauses followed by rapid flurries.

Simon arrived and watching her thought that Hebrew and Arabic, their convention running from right to left, must come more naturally for left-handers.

Belinda put down the phone, underlined several phrases of her notes, and putting down the pen, looked across at him.

"Storm in an eggcup," she said.

"Shouldn't that be teacup?"

Belinda smiled at him.

"It was a very small storm!"

Simon was late; not entirely unexpected. A restaurant in the middle of town, an early meal before an evening's theatrical entertainment. The plan was that he would park behind The Gallery and walk in to join her. He'd rung before leaving but she'd heard nothing since. Traffic indeterminate. Simon did not possess a mobile and she made a mental note to get him one. Irrespective of his protests, they could be a useful tool, like now.

The table, booked as required, was towards the back of the room, Simon to sit facing the door. For all his easy acceptance of the ritual and pantomime of eating out in England, the need to face the door was always paramount.

He joined her, sat in the appointed chair, apologised for his enforced lateness, and looked around. Comfortable with his position, he relaxed. Not completely, but sufficiently. Belinda watched, recognised, accepted, but did not entirely understand. Simon's residue from incidents long passed, years of eating mostly alone in societies not his own.

thirty-five

It was becoming a week of outings. Tonight was film. There was some while to go before the performance started and they had repaired to a pub close by to wait. As he sat down, Simon caught Belinda's eye.

"I'm sorry," he said, remembering how he had earlier rushed her from The Gallery. "I should have double-checked the times."

She accepted his apology with a shrug. "No matter." She smiled at him. "It is the right cinema, I suppose?"

"Depends on what film we decide to see."

Picking up his glass, he glanced up to find her looking at something over his shoulder.

"I think we're being gawked at." Simon put down his glass. "No, Simon, don't turn round."

"Who by?" he asked, resisting the urge to turn.

"I don't know. I don't recognise him. He's not one of mine."

Simon started to make a slow half-turn.

"He's recognised you," she said, keeping up the commentary. "He's coming over."

"Hello, Simon, I thought it was you!"

Simon groaned as he recognised the voice and it was with effort that he greeted the owner with a smile.

"Hello, John," he said. "I've not seen you for a while. Have you been away, or have I just been lucky?"

John laughed, just a little too heartily. "Always the ready insult, as ever." He introduced himself to Belinda and shook her hand. "He won't introduce me. Never does. Always have to do it myself."

"We're trying to restrict ourselves to interesting people this week," replied Simon, not entirely unkindly.

Simon watched him as he blustered over Belinda. Simon interrupted to enquire how things were, and answered that things were fine in return.

"Anyway," said John, following another meaningless exchange. "Must get back. Only popped out for a pint and a sandwich."

Belinda watched him go.

"Do I ask who that was?" she asked lightly.

"He works in my old office."

"I gathered that."

"And that's where he's gone back to. He always works long hours. Twelve, sometimes fourteen-hour days. Pity it isn't to more effect."

"He seemed a mite breathless, or is that just his style?"

Simon shook his head. "He has a heart condition, physically and mentally." Simon paused. "He tries too hard," he said. "He's the sort to be cremated and have his ashes scattered over the office carpet. The work is his life unfortunately."

Simon's tone was sad. Unless checked early, Belinda had learned, he was likely to decline further.

"It seems a rather extreme form of shake and vac," she said.

Simon laughed, and then looked at his watch.

"We have time for another drink."

Simon stood at the bar, waiting to be served, sensing that he may have become temporarily invisible. Getting served in pubs, the art and artifice thereof, could be the basis of another half-decent sociological research project. That, and the optimal selection of supermarket checkout queues. He pondered which research council, local university department, even the OU, to call with the suggestion. 'Sod's Law in everyday retail transactions' could serve as the working title.

The barman looked straight through him and immediately served Belinda's request coming from behind his left ear. He carried the drinks back to their table.

She laughed at his expression. "I did point to you before I spoke."

"I wondered why I paid. Most impressive though," he added, it a little sourly.

"What, ordering the drinks?"

"No, the service," he replied thoughtfully. "Physiologists call it the halo effect. Beautiful people are consistently chosen, and are assumed to have all sorts of desirable attributes. Works for tall as well apparently."

"So I fail on both counts then?"

"Afraid so – you just can't win."

Although it was only midweek, the place was packed, the clientele averaging about eighteen. The atmosphere was heavy with hormones and popcorn.

Belinda sighed, and headed towards a kiosk. An overpriced array of inessentials, available in frighteningly large portions, demanded purchase. Simon commented as much and was accused of being a killjoy. Even so, she resisted.

"Memories of illicit trips into town from school," she said, as they walked on. "The pictures, Sunkisk popcorn and Kiora. Forbidden fruit."

Simon vaguely remembered the names. "And Poppets," he said. "Peculiar cardboard-tasting chocolates in a box."

She laughed. "Yes. I'd forgotten those. And all of them only ever found in cinemas."

Belinda handed him another pile of tissues and squeezed his hand. Simon cried at the most extraordinary things, and she loved him for it. Though it was not the only reason.

With the film over, they joined the outward flow from the cinema. Car parks for the moment were best avoided.

They were deciding what to drink when another erstwhile colleague of Simon's joined them. They seemed to be collecting like buses. Simon couldn't remember his name, but it didn't seem to matter. After he'd introduced Belinda, he exchanged sarcastic pleasantries and enquired after another mutual acquaintance and whether he was still shaving his forehead.

Simon finally remembered his name as Tim, just in time to thank him for offering a round.

"It's your fault," said Simon, after Tim had gone to the bar. "If I wasn't with you, it would be a nod, a quick word, and goodbye."

"Sorry," said Belinda, without apology.

Tim returned, glasses in hand, and sat between them, a fraction closer to Belinda. She produced a cheroot and asked him for a light. The expression on his face made Simon laugh.

Tim's conversation, gushing at first, began to dry up. He turned to Simon.

"I heard this great joke the other day."

"Well, come on then," replied Simon encouragingly.

"It's a little rude," he said, glancing at Belinda.

"Don't worry," she said demurely. "I have a filthy mind."

He drank a little from his pint while they waited for him to start.

"You're not Catholic are you?" he asked, looking at Belinda.

She smiled reassuringly. "I won't be offended."

"Well, it's about this guy who's a church warden in a Catholic church. Its Monday, lunchtime, and he's in the church, doing what church wardens do, and the queue for the confessional's stretching out the door onto the street. It's been a busy weekend.

"Anyway, he keeps hearing this hissing noise. He looks up and sees the priest. His curtain's pulled back, and he's calling him over.

'Can you do me a favour,' asks the priest.

'Sure, what is it?'

'Can you take some of these on? I want to go and put a bet on before two.'

'What, take the confession?'

'Not all of them, just a few. It's easy. Just listen to what they say, hand out a few penances, and you're away. There's nothing to it.'

The priest is very persuasive.

'You'll be doing me an awful favour. I'll see you all right afterwards.'

He's only the assistant church warden, but ambitious. Perhaps he'll get a promotion.

He's been at it for about twenty minutes. By this time he's assumed the appropriate authoritarian tone and the power's gone to his head, Hail Marys increasing with every one. Another sinner is despatched in fear for his mortal soul, and is replaced by a young girl.

'Bless me, Father, for I have sinned.'

'And what is it you have done, my daughter?'

'I can't tell you, Father.'

'Yes you can. And yes you must.'

There's a pause.

'I have indulged in oral sex, Father!'

The church warden leans forward and bangs his head on the grill.

'How many times?'

'All night, Father. I can't remember.'

His face is now pressed up against the grill, trying to see what she looks like. Perhaps he can meet her later.

'And did you enjoy it?'

'Very much, Father.'

'That's very wrong.'

'I know, Father. I know. That's why I'm ready to repent.'

'Good. Let me think here for a minute.'

He doesn't know what to do. This is outside his job experience. He needs advice. He opens the curtain. The priest is gone. Then he sees the choir master walking by. He waves him over.

'What are you doing in there?'

'It's a long story, never mind. Now quick, I need advice. What do I give for oral sex?'

The choir master thinks for a moment.

'Well, I usually give them a Coke and a Mars Bar!'"

thirty-six

The coffee, untouched, had cooled beside the bed. Belinda eased him over and sat alongside the still sleeping body. Since they agreed it was unnecessary for him to get up every time she had an early start, this was becoming a ritual. The telephone had not woken him, neither had the radio. She spoke, but he did not hear.

She cocked her head to one side and aligned her face with his. Simon was dreaming; she could see his eye movement beneath the lids. It was an animated dream. Occasionally he spoke, incoherent muffles into the pillow. He laughed suddenly and she leant back. Then he frowned, almost a scowl, the eyes screwed up, the forehead lowered. An arm moved and he relaxed again. She wondered what he was dreaming about. She drank some of his coffee, an eye on the clock.

She leant over him, allowing her hair to fall across his face. She let it drape over his eyes, moving it like a curtain across him. As it drifted over his nose, he snorted, and turned his head.

She smiled to herself at his reaction and flicked her hair back as she leant down further. She kissed him on the side of his cheek.

"Good morning, darling. Time to begin the day."

'Once a king, always a king. But once a night is enough!' As Belinda was fond of saying, the old ones were the best. He pondered the irony, how age reversed the roles.

Simon was lying on his back, looking at the ceiling. Bright sunlight, reflected from the curtain lining, glowed at the edges. He remembered the day. Belinda's parents were arriving at three, their first visit. He sat up and groaned. There was a lot to do. There was a list somewhere.

Belinda sat in the bath considering an earlier telephone call. Years before she'd been involved with a barrister; the relationship hadn't lasted long, but some of the stock legal phrases had. As she thought of Simon, one consistently came to mind: previous. Simon had a lot of previous. It was not that she minded; the events, women in his life that had occurred before they met were, to an extent, an accident of history. And nothing that had happened since had given her any cause for alarm.

Mostly it was she who answered the telephone, took the calls from the previous and passed on the messages. Simon never lost touch, or rather, they never lost touch with him. But, benign as it might be, Simon's previous had other, moderately threatening dimensions.

Jennifer, the ex-wife, she could understand, but it was the others: the ex-lovers stretching back over years. The previous, checking out the current incumbent; the substitutes waiting for the opportunity to run on the pitch.

Simon, of course, was blissfully unaware and she let him be so. He was unlikely to understand. She answered the questions as to his health and welfare, was strictly polite, whilst disclosing as little as possible. A secretarial task. On good days it even amused her. Simon's previous, poised on the periphery, awaiting developments.

Whereas in her experience men tended to rely on their partners for emotional support, women sensibly made use of their friends. Simon's friends, being almost exclusively female, shared the burden. It was unusual, and although it did not worry her unduly, she was conscious of it. Should it come to it, she would not be able to rely on sisterly solidarity.

And he'd had far too many women. And he talked about them often. Too often. Lacking family, the memories, they were the substitute. He remembered dates, events, by whom he'd been with at the time.

Initially, she had found it irritating, threatening; herself viewed as merely the latest of a continuing series. She felt more secure now, and as she understood the process, she accepted it, however grudgingly. It was how his mind worked. Men did that, remembering. Simon was no different, just more extreme.

They were reaching the end of the first floor, Simon giving his well-rehearsed house tour, Douglas as audience.

"You've done a lot."

"I've been here a fair time, though I did more, oddly, when I was working. At least, when the funding and the enthusiasm coincided. The last couple of years or so I've spent mostly in the garden. It may be untidy, but at least it's underfoot."

"The front looks fine."

"It does now. It's the back that needs the attention. You'll see better from the top." Simon thought of Douglas's particular interest. "I've found I enjoy gardening, more than I expected – now I have no excuse."

Douglas laughed. "It's normal. So did I. The trouble starts after that." He glanced at Simon. "With the garden and the house in order, you sit down and think, well, that's done, what shall I do now for the next twenty years?"

Simon nodded. "At this rate of progress it will take me another twenty years."

They completed the first-floor tour and Simon led the way to the top. Douglas listened attentively as Simon indicated the various features and explained the history. They ended, as usual, on the roof terrace.

Douglas looked around, asking questions, admiring the view. Belinda and Eunice were at the top of the garden, amongst the trees, looking back. Waves were exchanged.

"As you say, you have a lot left to do," commented Douglas, as they made their way down.

Simon agreed, and then laughed. "And, I suspect, encouraged by your daughter, I'll be getting on with it quite soon."

Douglas laughed in return. "That would not surprise me."

*

Douglas had, inadvertently, spoiled Belinda for other men. Too good, too caring, too clever. Eunice watched them together as she had countless times before. Fathers and daughters. It was not a thought she could share with either of them; they would be horrified. She continued to reflect. So far, Simon was holding his own. The sex would help, the quality and the quantity, always a high priority. Belinda had told her, as usual.

Showing off, Simon had cooked a goose. Belinda had noticed he was nervous, or maybe it was tense, it was difficult to tell. Either way, he'd drunk the best part of a bottle of red before they began eating. The meal itself went well; apart from the goose, the three varieties of potatoes were thoroughly enjoyed, those roasted in the goose fat being particularly favoured.

Simon continued to drink, albeit at a slower pace, though he ate little, but was apparently happy, entertaining them with the saga of his conception. She had, of course, heard it before, but her parents hadn't and he told it well.

His nervousness had been infectious; she had drunk far more than intended and so, she thought, had her father. Eunice meantime, the nominated driver, stuck resolutely to water, watching the three of them.

As the night progressed, Simon told more stories, some she hadn't even heard before. And, as men do, Douglas had told some of his. Each triggering a memory from the other. It reminded her of drunken mess nights when younger. From her mother's reaction, her too.

thirty-seven

Rising early, Simon caught 'Thought for the day'. It had been a Muslim that morning. All religions; common guilts with different holidays.

Belinda was rifling through the pages of her diary, making notes. As Simon joined her she gave him a date for a month ahead, a Friday.

"And?"

"It's a dinner dance, formal, black tie."

Simon groaned. He'd loathed this type of social occasion with a deep hatred since boyhood. The events, the people, the dress code; the enforced social ethics. In ways, they represented everything he most despised in society and he had always avoided them. And failing that, attempted to subvert them.

"Why?"

"It's the local retail association. They, we, raise money for Romanian orphans. This is the autumn fundraiser or, at least, that's the excuse."

"Can't you just send them a cheque?"

"No. Certainly not."

Simon's expression was one of acute distaste. She put down her reading glasses and looked at him.

"I have to go, and I would prefer, much prefer, to go with you."

He gave her his reservations. It was a reasoned argument, but general, not specific to the event.

"And besides, I have none of the clothes." A final, almost frantic gesture. "I have nothing to wear."

She dismissed it. "We hire. Your clothes, maybe even my frock."

Belinda paused and reached for the coffee Simon had brought in. She chose her words with care.

"Unlike you, Simon, I earn a living and, very occasionally, I have to compromise. This is one of those times. I have been to the last couple of these things by myself. I do not intend to make it a third time."

Simon listened to her and accepted the invitation with a grace he did not feel. He fetched his diary and wrote in the date.

'Sometimes I sit and think, and sometimes I just sit.' He'd forgotten the source but remembered the words.

No was a shorter word than yes. Required less effort to say, used no further thought beyond rejection. Yes was a harder word. It demanded a commitment to an unknown journey with sometime hazardous destinations. Places that may never make returned. If in doubt, so no, and be conscious of the loss, and of the consequences.

And, as it was with no, so it was with contempt. Approval or contempt, no shades between. Like trusting people; best not, and avoid disappointment. Least of all the self.

Simon reserved his gross contempt for himself, the person he knew best, mostly thought the least of. He may be nothing if not critical, but he was harshest towards himself. He viewed this as a saving grace. It was poor justification, but it was the only one he had. Contemptuous; the little that he'd done did not afford a satisfaction. Like saying no.

It was yet to begin, that feeling, but he sensed its shadow ahead. That feeling of enclosure, containment, trapped. He hesitated to call it a loss of freedom, more beholden, that loss of independence. The options closing.

And with the alienation developed, he would withdraw. Not physically, but mentally. Part of him would leave, his mind elsewhere.

Then to engineer an ending. Perhaps. He always had and they had always left. Pride, he hoped, intact. Women, always practical.

To a certain extent, happiness is based on self-delusion; a benign deception. Truth and lies. Yes and no.

thirty-eight

The joys of menstruation. Beginning the day weary, events had not lifted Belinda's mood. She felt bloated, heavy and tired; too tired. Simon's obsessive discussion, analysis, had continued now through the previous weekend and beyond. The evening ahead promised no relaxation.

Belinda closed The Gallery, grabbed a couple of things from the flat and drove back towards The Villa. They had to reach a resolution, whatever it was going to be.

"We work on, from, fundamental differences," she said.

Simon refilled her glass.

"You assume rejection. You guard against it all the time. It determines everything you do. I don't. I assume acceptance. Okay. Women, pretty, blonde, tall – real easy. No, actually – real hard. What's that phrase? Beauty frightens, brains terrify. Beauty and brains drives you shitless."

Simon laughed. "I've not heard that one."

"Perhaps I made it up."

He refilled her glass again. It was her fourth and they were yet to eat. The effects were beginning to show.

"I'm getting pissed," she said, observationally.

Simon nodded.

"Who cares," she said, half emptying the glass. "It's been a hard day."

"Any particular reason?"

"No. Just you."

Belinda lit a cheroot and held it, watching the smoke rise.

"I assume I will succeed. You assume you will succeed. But you expect alienation while I do not. You ask nothing from anybody. I ask from mine and I give to mine, continuously, unquestioningly. You only give as you have received. And subsequently."

She emptied her glass again and raised it for a refill. Simon responded, watching her as he did so.

"I'm prepared to give you time, Simon. Let you work it out for yourself. But eventually, soon, you will have to decide. Let me know when you have."

She drained her glass in one, gathered her things and stood, walking slowly towards the door.

"I'm going to bed. The alarm is set for seven. I have meetings at nine."

They exchanged expressions, Simon seated, Belinda standing. They were unresolved, the atmosphere persisting.

"Do you remember, when you were a little girl, fantasising about your perfect boyfriend?" Belinda's expression was neutral, hostile. "Obviously not," he added.

"I never did then, though I have since." Belinda looked at him, seeming to make a decision. "And more so lately."

"Go on." Simon's tone matched her own.

"Women are not like men." She waved away his interruption. "Obviously. If I were to write a specification, even if I was able to, you wouldn't be the obvious candidate. But I take it as I find it. We get on, we have a similar sense of humour, the same life values, and you are supportive. We work in bed. You are neither violent nor abusive. And you can cook." Belinda laughed. "Wonderful in bed, and can cook. What else does a girl need?"

Simon didn't reply.

"And," she continued, hesitating. "Most importantly, I feel comfortable, natural, unpressurised. Well, at least, I did."

She looked at him. It was a long, hard look.

"It's not, I suspect – no, I *know* it's not the same for you.

Something there says you could do better. Maybe, maybe not. I can't tell you, no one can. But this frightens me. I can leave, and soon, and recover. Another experience to write off. If I stay, it gets harder. I know. But you have to decide by making your own decision."

She looked around for her handbag, but failed to find it.

"I have a busy couple of days so I'm going back to the flat. Don't ring. Don't visit. Think about it." She continued looking around. "Today is Thursday. Monday week. Let me know. You have to get there by yourself, Simon. I can't help. And when you do, I'll give you an opinion."

She threw up her hands in mock despair. "Now, I only need to find my handbag. Have you seen it?"

"I think it's in the kitchen," answered Simon automatically. He stood looking at her while she looked back.

"I think we ought to talk about this. You can't just leave."

"I can."

"Of course you can. I didn't mean that. I mean like this."

She walked out of the room towards the kitchen leaving Simon staring out of the window. He heard her on the telephone, ordering a taxi. Then he heard her go upstairs into the bedroom. Then into the bathroom. Then come down the stairs. He wondered what to say. He did not get the opportunity.

"There are parts of you I can never reach. I glimpse them, and then you shroud them. You always have. Ever since you were a little boy you learnt to do that. It kept you safe, it kept you sane. Hard-learnt. Now, its second nature, first. You always will. I can accept that – but you can't. I can live with you as you are. You remember how, but you can't do it."

Belinda laughed, brittle, dismissive. "I can't heal you. But I can live with the symptoms. I'm prepared to make the effort, commitment if you like. But are you? Settle for this, us. Or is it still the great expectation. Waiting until it finally comes. Whatever it is. Real world or fantasy expectation."

She gathered up her bag and began to look for her shoes.

"You choose. I'm getting tired. And, Simon, really tired. I love you, I'm in love with you. The best that I can do. I can't promise anything. Just that. So you choose. From this point we either go forward, or we go nowhere. We cannot stay as we are."

Belinda walked from the room and let herself out of the house. The taxi had not come. She couldn't wait. She kept moving, walking down the drive and out of the gate. As she turned down the lane, it started to rain. So bloody typical.

She reached the trees at the end of the lane and stood under them. Her hair was soaked and there was still no sign of the taxi. She kicked at the ground in frustration and began to cry.

It was there he found her.

"I love you," he said.

"I know," she said. "I love you too. That's the problem."

As Belinda showered, Simon sat on the side of the bed, staring at the carpet. He sat for what felt a long time before she joined him.

"I'll tell you what love is," she said. "Love is missing someone immediately when they leave the room. That they've only gone a few feet away, that they'll be coming straight back, doesn't make any difference. You still have that feeling of loss." Belinda's expression showed feelings of disappointment as she looked at him. "That's love."

Simon nodded. He waited a few seconds and then reached for her hand, reassured to feel her fingers wrap around his.

She leant forward, her hair falling around his face like a shroud. She held his neck tightly between her hands, their eyes level, without focus. The air warmed from their breathing. He could sense shafts of light, peripheries, but within only vague outlines. Neither of them spoke, just long even breaths, shared rhythms.

Slowly, she released her hands and leant back. Her hair slid down his face as she withdrew and he could see her again. She was crying.

Simon reached out a hand but before he could touch her she slid into the bed. He lay beside her, an arm around her shoulders, grateful as he felt her pull his hand in tighter.

He dare not ask, and she did not tell. Eventually, they slept.

thirty-nine

Belinda was away. A buying opportunity in Scotland, convenient and hastily arranged, that he could neither enhance nor contribute to. She had been gone four days, due back within another five.

To begin with, secure in the knowledge that she was indeed coming back, he had enjoyed the respite. The return to what he still remembered; the silence, the indulgence of time. But now, it had begun to oppress him. The line of perfume, thoughtfully left in the bed to remind him, was wearing off. He missed her company, the casual conviviality, the sharing. He felt suddenly more alone, lonely, than he had in years.

An ominous warning. His future might only be this, unless— While resolution didn't guarantee success, or even a successful continuation, at least it was a start. Direction if not destination.

The following day, he awoke early. The sun was shining warmly, the birds were singing, everything a late summer's day should be. It promised much. His mood, as the morning progressed, lightened. It carried him out of the house and down towards the river. He walked and thought, thought and ambled. An hour found him on the far bank and he sat for a while, overlooking the lock with its adjoining weir. He watched the quiet water, his mind describing what it saw.

First it was the colour: green, blue, shoals of brown changing as the sun reflected and his mind, reflective, registered.

It had been three years, three years of continuous upheaval. His mother's death, retirement and recently, the advent of Belinda.

Three years. Change upon trauma, recently perturbed.

He refocused his eyes on the water. Texture. Ducks landed, bickered; fish rose. An active surface drifting with the current and the breeze. Never still; the individual within the whole.

All the while, that gentle drift towards the weir. The all-consuming fall.

His investment of hopes and dreams, joy and pain, life and love; the ever closer desperation. He had to be sure. Perhaps thirty good years left, and now, approaching, conscious of them. It was his own dilemma, conundrum, the ultimate irony. Until he did, he could not know, and until he knew, he could not do.

Simon found a likely stick and threw it into the midstream. The ducks ignored it, so did the fish. It moved slowly towards the weir, accelerated and then disappeared.

And then it re-emerged, not where he was watching but further downstream, like a conversation temporarily interrupted.

Events reminded, confirmed, the fragility of life. The one you had was the only one you knew. Better to live it, and better that you could. 'If only' – the phrase that unless acted upon would come to haunt him. Belinda was not the 'all' he wanted, as he was not to her, but his life was much enriched by her. And now, it would be impoverished without her. He remembered.

Three years now since that before. Now an after. He had recovered his own identity and found it changed. Calmer, older, partially adult. Healed, the mind quieter.

Contentment implied other than he felt. He'd never be that, but there was a certain recognition.

He recognised he had decided. Not so very difficult. There were only two promises he would ask.

Eventually, and perhaps soon, he would need something more to do. House, garden, even Belinda would not be sufficient. Simon watched as a heron landed on a rock overlooking the weir. Motionless, it watched the water.

So would he. Something would suggest itself.

*

Realisations were gradual, glacial and occasional, rarely instantaneous. Gradual, he understood, could accommodate; instantaneous, frightened.

Simon had made a late entry to the day, surfacing soon after noon, addled. It was raining. With a distinct lack of imagination, he consulted the *Radio Times*. An old black and white movie on Channel 4. The advertisements: insurance, equity release, burial plans, accident claims, stairlifts and walk-in baths; forgotten actors eking out a living, appalling. The assumed audience and the presumptions equally so.

It was a film from the forties, when dialogue and the intricacies of plot assumed an intelligence. And, in its way, the story was moral, witty, not simplistic. He'd recorded the last hour to share.

He loved her. Belinda would be the love of his life, whatever happened.

It was not an understanding he'd had before the film had started, though it was by the end. And, curiously, the film had very little to do with the recognition; it was not a shared theme.

Just the realisation, sudden, obvious.

You said what you felt as you felt it, immediate. He always had. Not so much heart on sleeve, more the whole garment.

Expressions of pain, expressions of love. Expressions of contempt, disdain.

And then you thought about it; dispassionate. And mostly, berated the self, condemned the self; extricated. Always the room to rationalise, restore the self-respect.

Not now.

He did not recognise this. It was extraordinary, unique. There were doubts, but not knowing ones. Like times before.

Failure was not a viable option.

Not this time.

Simon was reminded that to love meant accepting that one would be casually hurt every single day.

Belinda had returned early, appearing late on the previous evening.

The radio alarms woke them at eight and Simon, showing solidarity, had risen immediately. As Belinda monopolised the bathroom, Simon walked slowly down to the kitchen to begin her breakfast.

With coffee made, bread from the freezer under the grill, he collected the morning papers and, accompanied as ever by Radio 4, began consuming the overnight cricket reports. Within twenty minutes, Belinda had joined him.

"An interesting day?"

Belinda paused between coffee and toast. She frowned and then gave a brilliant smile.

"I'm having lunch with Graham."

"Graham?"

"An old friend. He has a gallery in Manchester and he's down for a few days. I like Graham, he's good company. I've been looking forward to it."

Simon smiled, nodding, choosing not to question her further.

She glanced at the clock. "I've got to go, I've a client coming in at ten."

She kissed him goodbye, gathered up her bag and disappeared from the kitchen. He heard the front door close, her car start and the sound of distant crunching from the drive. Simon stared at the remains of his coffee and reached for the cafetière.

He was surprised at his feelings. He felt jealous, irrational but recognisable. Perhaps not so much jealousy as exclusion. It was a part of her life he had no part of, could not participate in. It made him feel vulnerable, unsure, in need of reassurance.

He stood up, walked into the sitting room and stared at the sky. It was clear and blue. He would take out his irritation with some pick-wielding.

Simon cooked and they chose to eat on the veranda while the weather held. They were polite, considerate to each other; exchanging news, sharing jokes. Waiting.

Simon opened another bottle of wine.

"I have two promises to ask," he said.

Belinda looked at him.

"They're not negotiable," he added, seriously.

"Go on."

"Don't die on me. Don't ever leave me."

Belinda smiled. It was a quiet smile.

"Is that all?"

Simon's expression did not change. She smiled at him more brightly.

"I have no intention of dying, at least just yet. And likewise, I have no intention of leaving." She looked at him without smiling. "I promise."

"Thank you," said Simon, after a pause.

She continued to look at him and he looked back.

"No thanks required."

As they sat, the sun slowly disappeared. A gloaming rose from the garden and the surrounding trees, while the hill ahead rose up, the grass a golden green.

Belinda continued to watch the effect of the changing light on the trees and the grass beyond. Constant shifts of colour, imperceptible when observed, obvious if not. Her mood was mellow and she felt strangely peaceful. Old questions came to mind.

"What do you want to do when you grow up? Who do you want to be?"

Simon looked at her. The light had given her face a peculiar aura, like some medieval religious painting.

"You don't grow up – you just get older," he said. "So much older. Much, much older."

forty

Somehow, through a process not entirely comprehended, he'd come to an accommodation, a settlement. No longer alone. Not the wondrous perfection sought, but a tangible reality. Someone to touch, be touched, have respond. To love, and be loved. As Belinda reminded him, often: perfect they were not. But good they were. Very good. And much preferred to how they were. Separate.

It was not an area Belinda knew particularly well. Having taken one wrong turning, she cruised the village high street looking for the post office. The cottage she was looking for should be a few yards further on. She found it and parked close to the kerb. There was little other traffic.

An artist, previously unknown to her, had made an approach; an introductory letter and then a telephone call requesting a meeting to present a portfolio. Those fresh from the art schools were so much more professional now, their curriculum including the dubious delights of self-promotion. Starving in garrets was no longer cool.

She had listened to what he had to say, asked the usual questions and a few not so usual. Refusing his request to come to The Gallery, she had suggested instead she visit him. Though the prospects of new talent were always exciting, the risks were considerable. Talent, however outstanding, was never enough. It had to be supported by application. Visiting the place of work, rather than just viewing it, would give her a better assessment of intent and reliability.

Belinda climbed from the car, hung her bag from a shoulder,

put on the day's obligatory hat – large, black straw – and approached the door. A large bell push with PRESS embossed upon it was set into the wall. She did as requested.

Simon had a weakness for make-up departments. The pots and the potions, the almost religious zeal applied to the essentially frivolous, and the intoxicating smells. And, of course, there were the women. Full slap at nine in the morning, the attitude of charm and condescension; an allure suspending reality. It was a small, entirely self-contained world, and on occasion he had enjoyed himself within it.

He consulted the note Belinda had given him and headed for the appropriate counter. There was not an assistant to be seen so he amused himself with the testers while he waited. Using the inside of his wrist in the time-honoured fashion, an area extending up the inside of his left forearm had become a palette of lipstick stripes by the time she appeared. His immediate request for a cleansing wipe was satisfied with a frosty stare.

The assistant was wearing a long-skirted suit in powder blue. It was an attractive colour and the suit had been well cut. Alas, it was several sizes too small. The three buttons on the jacket strained to retain; the material pulled, dividing the upper torso into distinct quarters like a tightly trussed joint of meat. She spoke and Simon concentrated on the upper half of the face, avoiding the complicated motion of her chins.

He made his request and she turned towards the furthest end of the counter, reaching down towards a lower shelf. The view from behind was simply appalling. Simon's gaze wandered around the rest of the area while he waited, desperate to find something more tolerable. No amount of artifice could disguise that: the years of food that fattens but does not feed. His sympathies were mixed.

Eventually, a small pot, beautifully packaged, was presented for his inspection. He checked the description against Belinda's note and asked for an additional one which, with poor grace, duly appeared. In turn he presented his credit card, signed a receipt for a ridiculous quantity, dismissed his thought of a surprise lipstick and, with his purchase secured in a glossy cardboard carrier bag with cord handles, made his way from the store. The price of beauty was rising. Thank God he wasn't a woman.

It was not an original thought. He moved down the high street, consulting his list.

All of the staff, all women, in the building society were wearing little pink bows on their uniforms. Simon enquired as to why.

"Breast cancer awareness," came the bright reply.

He looked grave. "I hope that doesn't mean that I have to go round feeling them all…?"

As usual, he was accused of being smutty. It had become the custom, expected in their exchanges, ever since he'd remarked that their new customer service desk, whilst obliging, looked bloody uncomfortable.

Simon heard the front door close as he came down the stairs. He followed Belinda into the kitchen as she dropped her bag and keys into a chair, kicked off her shoes, kissed him and, collecting two glasses, opened the refrigerator door. She took an opened bottle and half filled each glass.

Simon glanced at the clock and she followed his gaze.

"It is a little early."

He nodded.

"But it is October!"

Something on the evening news prompted the conversation. Belinda waited while Simon paused. It was a disconcerting habit until one got used to it. His practice of stopping suddenly in mid-sentence to consider. Rather as if he'd stopped breathing.

"But men lie. They lie to women automatically, to other men most of the time, and to themselves constantly." Simon shook his head uncomprehendingly. "I've only just understood this. It's a shock."

Belinda stared at him. "I'm amazed."

"That men lie?"

"No, of course not. I'm a woman – that knowledge comes with

the gender." She paused. "No, not amazed, surprised." She paused again. "No, not even that."

Simon looked at her quizzically. He was losing her train of thought and said so.

She smiled; it was an indulgent, kind smile. Almost maternal.

"It was an early thing I noticed about you. Well, there were a lot of things, of course, but one especially. You don't lie, at least, not intentionally. Not that you couldn't, but it never occurs to you."

Simon interjected. "But why should it?"

She laughed. "Quite."

Later.

"It gets worse," he said.

"Meaning?"

"I'm consistent."

"I'd noticed that as well."

Later still.

"And I don't have any secrets. Only erstwhile professional ones – and other people's."

Vermilion leaves, an almost unnatural red, stretched down the length of the garden wall from house to road.

As Simon went to fetch another bottle, Belinda walked down from the veranda to examine them more closely.

"Virginia Creeper," said Simon, when she returned. "Defiant in death."

She looked at him and smiled. "Speaking of death, I ordered your clothes today. They'll be delivered next week, Wednesday."

Simon remembered why, the dreaded dinner dance, and forced a smile. "Thank you. And yours?"

"Yes, mine." She glanced at him. "I've been thinking about that. We'll be sitting down for most of the evening."

"That's a relief."

Belinda ignored the comment. "If I wear what I have in mind, I'll be taller than you."

"That's not unusual."

"Much taller – from tip to toe, about five inches." She thought for a moment. "No, perhaps not as much as that. It depends on the hair."

"I'll bring a box to stand on." He laughed. "Better still, one with castors, so when we dance you can twirl me around."

She gave him a half-smile. "That's all right then. The dress is at home. I'll get Mummy to courier it over."

Simon thought that excessive, and said so. "Why don't I go and collect it?"

She smiled at him. "That's kind of you."

He shrugged. "As we know, I have less call on my time than you."

She nodded. "Can you remember the way?" She answered her own question. "I'll draw you a map."

Later in the evening, Belinda looked at him and raised an eyebrow.

"I wish I could do that," he said, with genuine admiration. "I tried for years but never mastered it."

She stared at him.

"The eyebrow."

"I can do both sides." A demonstration.

"Aren't you wonderful."

"Aren't I just."

She laughed and tried to remember what she'd been saying. Simon was very good at distracting her, intentionally or otherwise. Better than most. Then she remembered.

"Oh yes. I have a puzzle for you, Doctor. A mathematical one."

Simon frowned. His maths was dreadful these days. Apart from normal arithmetic via a calculator and a little basic algebra, anything higher had reverted to the mystery it was before he was taught it. And he loathed puzzles, always had.

Reaching into her handbag, Belinda handed him a sheet of paper. "One of my clients gave it to me to give to you this morning. Apparently, it's been doing the rounds of the university's maths department for days."

"Thank you," said Simon, with heavy irony. "I feel another ritual humiliation coming on."

He looked at what she had given him with deep suspicion. It was typed.

'Considering the numbers 1 to 20, what singular peculiarity do the numbers 7 and 12 share?'

Simon took a pad and wrote a column of figures to twenty, stepping out seven and twelve. Then he wrote the numbers horizontally. Nothing immediately suggested itself.

"Do you know the answer – there is one presumably?"

Belinda laughed. "No, and yes, in that order."

"And who gave this to you?"

"You met him at that opening we went to. The one in the pub." She raised an eyebrow. "He thinks you have an interesting mind!"

Simon ignored the mocking tone.

"He thought you might be able to solve it."

"Did he," replied Simon, without conviction.

He worked on the numbers. He added pairs, subtracted thirds, multiplied and cross-divided. Ten minutes and several sheets of paper produced nothing beyond an increasing irritation.

He read the question again, carefully, considering the sentence and particularly the alphanumeric construction.

"How are you getting on?" Belinda appeared, freshly showered, at his elbow.

"I'm not," he said, and cast the pad aside. "You smell very clean."

They were due to eat in the village, walking via the pub. She reminded him of the time.

Simon stood in the shower. As ever, a well-practised mechanical procedure encouraged his mind to drift. Between shampoos of his hair he recited the numbers one to twenty, slowly. Then again, then again, quickly. The solution was childishly simple, and nothing to do with mathematics. Belinda could hear his laughter as she came up the stairs.

"You solved it then?" she asked, as they set out.

"Yes, I think so." Simon paused to pick up a fallen conker, still half buried in its prickly shell. "Say the numbers one to twenty in sequence."

She did as he asked.

"Notice anything?"

"No."

"Do it again, quicker."

She did. "This is getting boring."

"Syllables," said Simon. "Seven has two syllables, the remainder, one to ten, have one. Similarly, twelve has one syllable, the others, eleven to twenty, have two. So the singular peculiarity of seven and twelve is their number of syllables."

"Is that it?"

"I think so."

Belinda laughed. "He's right. You do have an interesting mind, if a little peculiar."

Simon snorted. "Simple, more like."

forty-one

Simon was invited for lunch. Eunice opened the door, greeted him with mild surprise, and led the way into the sitting room.

"Good journey?"

"Fine. Surprisingly, I didn't get lost. I'm sorry if I'm early."

She smiled, dismissively. "Please don't concern yourself."

The windows along one side of the sitting room were open and he could smell the flowers from the garden. Eunice bade Simon to sit and he sat on the sofa, alongside a pile of cardboard boxes.

Eunice positioned herself in a chair opposite him.

"I'll make coffee in a moment but firstly, apologies from Douglas – he's had to go to some meeting or other."

As Simon replied the boxes moved, disturbing a sheet of paper resting on top. Eunice retrieved it.

"This is the dress," she said.

Simon counted. "Five boxes!"

Eunice laughed at his reaction. "Yes, five." She indicated as she spoke. "Dress, underdress, bag, shoes and headdresses, three, and a choker."

Simon looked faintly alarmed. "Serious dressing."

Eunice laughed again at his expression. "Oh yes, very. And I've sealed the boxes as Belinda requested so you can't peep."

"I wouldn't dream of it."

She gave him a disbelieving glance. "I'll make that coffee. Do smoke if you wish."

Simon stood up in search of an ashtray and found one on a side table. He paused and looked at the family photographs, displayed in the approved manner across the closed lid of what he took to be a baby grand piano. Silver frames, polished. The subjects were the three of them, together, separate. Aircraft featured, the family group with Daddy's aeroplane, the child Belinda sitting on wings, in cockpits and in one case, crouching in an air intake. Simon looked at them with care, noting different locations, the passing of years, the change from monochrome to colour.

A colour portrait of Belinda was particularly striking and he picked it up. The date and location were written on the backing of the frame. She would have been twenty-five. He put it back in place as he heard Eunice enter the room behind him. He turned as she spoke.

"Douglas once said that our daughter was one of the most beautiful women he had ever seen." She smiled. "Perhaps all fathers do that."

Simon nodded. "Though only if they have cause. Natalie Wood," he said, thoughtfully, "would be one of mine. Pity she drowned. These days, Michelle Pfeiffer's not bad."

He looked again at the portrait. "Eyes and beholders," he said and turning to Eunice, smiled. The expression he received in return reminded him. That same close examination. They stared at each other for a few seconds more before he spoke again. An unspoken question, given an answer.

"I can't make promises, only statements of intent."

They sat again in their respective positions, the coffee arrayed on the table before them. Simon sensed that there were more questions to come, but perhaps not quite yet. He sifted questions of his own by way of diversion.

"Why Belinda? The name I mean. I asked, but Belinda said to ask you."

Eunice put down her cup. "There's no big mystery, though Douglas and I did have, shall we say, some discussion over it. Douglas wanted Bettina – he had a German secretary at the time. Lovely girl Bettina, she taught Belinda German." Eunice smiled. "Douglas rather fancied Bettina, though he always denies it. She's one of her godmothers and Belinda has Bettina as her middle name. No, Belinda comes from an actress. We saw her in a play while I was pregnant. A very pretty girl and when we came to choose, I remembered the name."

Simon's mind struggled to remember. The recent years of old television movies, late into the night.

"Belinda Lee?"

"Yes, that's right."

"She committed suicide."

Eunice paused. "Yes, I think I remember that. Unfortunate."

She said nothing more and Simon waited before he spoke again.

"Belinda Bettina Barnfather." He smiled. "It's quite a mouthful."

"Yes it is, isn't it. B cubed. She still signs herself like that to us." Eunice laughed suddenly. "Like Mister Cube. Do you remember him?"

Simon said he did. "Tate and Lyle. The sugar cube with the sticky-out arms and legs." He thought, fleetingly, of the similarities, but chose not to mention it.

A timer sounded from the kitchen. "Lunch," announced Eunice.

It was starting to rain, a fierce, short-lived shower. Eunice and Simon sat on opposite sides of the kitchen table, tea between them. Leaf, pot, cups, milk jug, sugar, saucers and spoons.

The pleasantries had been exhausted, the packages were piled on a table near to the front door, the box with the dress surprisingly heavy. Real conversation about to begin.

Simon watched as Eunice served the tea. He recognised elements of her movements.

"You have no family, I understand."

"None whatsoever." He shrugged. "A long line of non-producers. And an only child."

"And no children."

"None." He chose to get ahead of the questions. "Never any born at least. I never wanted any."

"May I ask why?"

"Sure." Simon paused, framing his answer, selecting the shorter version. "No real big reason, just lots of little ones. My generation were the first who had the luxury of being able to choose to have children, rather than just accepting them as inevitable. I chose not to." He shrugged again. "I never had that sort of courage."

"One finds it."

"Only if it's there." He reached for his tea. "And yourselves, you had only the one. And grandchildren?"

Eunice smiled, noting the change of tack. "We would have liked another. There was, at the time, something of a duty to breed. Memories of the war were still fresh, in Germany particularly, which was where we were for most of the time. But there were difficulties." She glanced at Simon. "Belinda may have told you."

Simon nodded but chose not to interrupt.

"Though I don't know that I ever felt particularly maternal." She smiled. "You could say that we have all our eggs," she laughed, "or rather, my egg, in the one basket."

"And grandchildren?" repeated Simon, after a suitable pause.

"Ah yes, different story. I don't really know. After Belinda had the abortion," she glanced quickly at Simon. "We have no secrets in this family."

"I know. Neither do I."

"So I understand. I was gratified to hear that."

"It can make life very difficult," commented Simon, with more feeling than he'd intended.

"In the short term. But the alternative is decidedly worse."

She paused, then offered to refill Simon's cup which he accepted.

"Anyway, after that, and then the demise of James, I rather concluded we wouldn't be getting any grandchildren. Any lingering doubt went when Belinda decided to have herself sterilised after reaching forty."

She smiled at Simon. It was an enigmatic expression, impossible to read.

"Grandchildren are not in one's own gift."

She stirred her tea. "Belinda tells me you're retired."

"More or less. I've done some consultancy, a couple of contracts for MoD and the like, but nothing spectacular lately." He thought for a moment. "I was very grateful for those, it allowed me a valedictory."

"From what Belinda tells me, deservedly."

"I'd like to think so. These days my involvement's limited to long telephone conversations on a promise. It's rather expected in that business – you never really get away."

Eunice concurred. "I remember."

Simon smiled, pre-empting her next question. "As for now, I'm in danger of turning sloth into an art form." It was a self-dismissive statement, as he had intended it to be.

The rain was easing. Simon's eye was distracted by movement in the garden. He looked out of the window and followed the movement of a blackbird, listening to the lawn.

They sat in silence for a while, watching the wildlife. Eunice, standing, opened a kitchen drawer and produced another ashtray, a packet of cigarettes and a lighter. Smoke rose from either side of the table.

Simon, suffering from an increasing state of perplexity from almost his arrival, suddenly guessed what this conversation was about.

"There's a phrase," he said, finally. "One, I think, of my mother's. If you have sons, you worry. If you have daughters, you pray."

Eunice smiled, an expression of recognition. "It's true."

"And you still worry?"

"Of course. It comes with motherhood. Genetically programmed."

"And now, not unreasonably, you're wondering about me."

Eunice smiled again, momentarily taken aback by his directness. She thought for a moment.

"Douglas has always been happy to take his cues from Belinda. If she's happy, he's happy. For myself, I tend to be more suspicious. Overprotective if you wish."

"And it doesn't get any easier."

"No. It does not."

She smiled, and Simon smiled in return.

"If it's any consolation, it doesn't get any easier for Belinda and me." Simon picked up his pipe and appeared to be making a close examination of its contents. "It's very Victorian, this. I assume what you wish to know is what they would have referred to as my intentions."

"I think perhaps I am."

Simon leant back slightly, his hands on the table, and looked directly at Eunice. "It's very simple," he said formally, and without any embarrassment. "I love your daughter. My declared wish is to spend the rest of my life with her. We've come a long way together in the last four months, and recently, a lot further. Belinda, I think, feels the same. We have, as you might suppose, talked about this at some length. But I wouldn't say I know – one never does. One thing, however, I do know. Whatever she decides, it will be her own choice."

Eunice's expression puzzled him. He picked up his pipe again.

"Does that help? In the old language, my intentions are entirely honourable. The meaning and the words are clear."

Eunice smiled at him. It was an open, warm expression.

"I think the rain is finally beginning to stop," she said.

forty-two

It was the day of the dinner dance. Doing his best to ignore it, Simon had spent the morning reading, reducing the accumulating pile of newsprint. The news itself was bad enough, but it was the comment pages that really angered him.

Some things he loathed with a deep and passionate hatred. Bigotry, prejudice and wilful ignorance. It was an unholy trinity. But recently he had added another: certainty. While you couldn't change the past, you could change the way you remembered it. And the trouble with the past is that you forgot what you should remember, and remembered things best forgotten. He gave up with papers and turned to the magazines. Several articles of biased histories did not help.

Memory was selective, seductive, convenient. It remembered the past in fragments, then reinvented it.

In the end, the only things that mattered were art, love, and the pursuit of knowledge. It was not a fresh thought, or even original, but its truth did not diminish. Simon smiled to himself, more rueful than amused.

He made a light lunch and wondered what to do for the remainder of the afternoon. Belinda would be back early, too soon to begin anything substantial. There was nothing on the television.

The array of bookshelves lining the inner wall of the sitting room were twelve feet high, built from 18mm ply, formidably strong. The book he wanted was near the top. He began to climb.

As pitches went for bookshelves they would rate only two. Even so, he was careful to retain a three-point contact. Finding what he wanted, he lobbed it onto the sofa below. As ever, the descent was harder than the climb.

Simon, distracted by his own thoughts, wandered into the bedroom. Belinda, naked, was silhouetted against the window, her arms outstretched, trying to see her back in the mirror. Her skin tone appeared darker than an hour before. She turned to face him.

"Fake tan," she said. "All over – at least it should be. Now you're here, could you check?"

Simon found his reading glasses and made a thorough inspection. Indeed, all over.

Cleanse, tone and moisturise: the mantra taught young and practised ever since. She sat in front of the dressing table mirror, others to either side, and turned up the lights, the artifice kit deployed. She examined her face critically, detached. Whatever Simon might say, it was starting to crumble. So too was the body. She reminded herself not to obsess.

Belinda was neither fond nor disdainful of her looks – neutral. As a child it was not the body or the face she expected to have. A female friend had once remarked on how she treated her beauty as a casual, everyday thing. That was the point, because to her, it was. But, like anything, it could be improved. She began applying a gel.

She had thought to put her hair up but she would tower over Simon. Instead, she decided on the snood, and it required considerably less effort.

Simon, sitting on the bed, watched as she turned slowly in front of the full-length mirror, her expression critical. It reminded him, knowing women were only too aware of the faults with their own bodies. A distinction not shared by men.

"You look fine to me," he said lamely, rather pointlessly.

She took another half-turn. "Time you started getting ready."

Of the two, Simon much preferred women. Men were invariably so much less than they considered themselves to be. Women, the opposite. So much better than they supposed. And, within the company of women, one could always learn, grow. From men, beyond the narrow boundaries of specific knowledge and information, pure conversation tended towards that of minimal content, tedious and boorish. Women were always so much more interesting.

Simon owed his whole life to women; from conception, through education, to opportunity. Every single influence. He would never understand them as a gender, but he glorified the race.

Fresh from the shower, Simon walked into the bedroom. He was supplying his own socks, knickers and shoes; the rest was provided. Belinda had unpacked, laying the contents of the two boxes on the bed.

"Cufflinks?"

Simon shrugged.

"Do you have any?"

"Not that I remember – at least any I could find." He stared at the double cuffs of the dress shirt. "Not as such." He grinned at her. "Though I have an idea."

He wandered off into one of the storage bedrooms, returning minutes later with two chromed 10mm bolts and a pair of thick hexagonal nuts for each.

He held them out for inspection. "You tighten the nuts against each other so they don't come undone."

She laughed. "The engineer's solution."

Simon put on the shirt and trial-fitted the bolts. "Nuts inbound or outbound would you say?"

"Outbound I would think." She smiled at him sweetly. "It is, after all, nature's way."

Simon had been dressed and ready to leave for the best part of half an hour. With the radio for company, he sat on a sofa in the sitting room to wait. The phone was beside him, another call from the taxi driver, still looking for the road, expected. He could hear Belinda moving around above him.

The driveway lit up as the phone rang.

"Am I here?"

Simon confirmed he was.

As he leant forward to stand Belinda swept in behind him. Simon turned and met the full swing of her skirt across the side of his face. It was like being slapped with chain mail. His eyes watered; it was a wonder that his nose didn't bleed as well.

His discomfort was short-lived. As his eyes focused, they did so on Belinda. He looked at her for some time. The dress was silver, beaded, a tight-fitting bodice above a full skirt that trailed close to the floor. A thirties original.

"You look amazing," he said finally, unable to decide on any other suitable description. She really did.

"Thank you," she replied, and beamed. "So I should after all this effort. I'd forgotten how long it all takes." She glanced from the window. "Our pumpkin's arrived then."

They travelled on opposite sides of the cab, Belinda and her skirt monopolising the main seat. Simon shifted on the other, trying to find a more comfortable position. His clothes fitted well enough, but they lacked the comfortable familiarity of his own. He moved again, without success, and commented something of the sort to Belinda.

"It's part of the ritual, Simon."

"Oh good," he said, without enthusiasm.

She gave him a tolerant smile and received one in return.

"No one, well hardly any, attends this sort of thing simply to enjoy themselves. It's much more subtle than that. You make every appearance of enjoyment while really just enduring it."

"Like Christmas."

She laughed, remembering a previous conversation. "Yes, if you like. It's a social evening, not a party. Proprieties will be observed. No one gets entirely drunk, insults each other, fights, throws up, gropes at anyone's partner, their own!"

Belinda laughed again, trying to cheer him up.

"You survive with your integrity more or less intact, and then, in a few weeks' time, someone remarks how successful it all was and another follows the next year."

The taxi deposited them before the old university's banqueting house. Forty steps to the entrance and Simon wondered if it was some form of natural selection process for the guest list.

Following a rather too ostentatious greeting they were directed towards the bar. A large, though difficult to read, seating plan was neatly placed to obstruct their progress. Drinks in hand, Simon looked for his name, failing to find it.

"I can always go home," he said, hopefully.

Belinda directed his gaze. "Miss Barnfather's guest," she read.

"Bugger," replied Simon.

They were tables apart but, he judged, within eye contact. There were three tables in all, long; what he presumed was the head and two others, arranged in a horseshoe formation around some central refuge. He estimated about two hundred people in total. They had been positioned diametrically opposed to each other about halfway up the two limbs, facing inwards.

Belinda scanned the plan, assessing as to who was around her immediate vicinity. Simon, oblivious to the names, looked at the people arriving.

"Tolerable," she said at last. "Do you want to know who you're sitting with?"

Simon smiled. "Would it help?"

Belinda looked at him and said, with moderate solemnity, "Business."

"I have not forgotten." He smiled again and nodded. "Message received and understood."

The event was even more appalling than he had predicted. Simon was delighted.

The food, last-century catering; the obligatory guest speaker's after-dinner address, too long and irrelevant to the point of farce – going for a pee he'd found a queue. And the toasts and the speeches, stupefying in their inanity. He'd loved it, clapping enthusiastically at every escalating stupidity. Contrary to his expectations, he'd stayed entirely sober.

When the formal proceedings of the evening had died a painful and dishonourable death, dancing began. Simon stared in stupefaction as a small combination – he could think of no other description –

appeared on the stage ahead of them. He watched as it settled down to murder innocent music for a two-hour engagement.

Standing with Belinda, he listened to the band. Their interest in popular music had ceased sometime during the 1950s.

"Which museum or institution did they escape from?"

"Don't be cruel. I think they're rather quaint. We have them every year."

"It must be their only gig."

"They don't charge."

"They should pay you." Another tune began, Simon struggling to recognise it through the rendition. "Tommy Croker lives!"

They heard a German accent. "Don't mention the war."

"Which one?"

He lifted an arm, encouraging her to spin. She swung out and then, rather like a yo-yo, wound back in. They collided with some force.

"I've just remembered my first ever dirty joke," he said, breathless.

"And?"

He spun her again, more expertly this time, their reconnection less forceful.

"A definition of a close dance. A naval encounter with no seamen."

"That's a joke? How old were you?"

"About twelve. I didn't understand it then either!"

The evening progressed, as did their alcohol consumption. They were both, by now, a little pissed. And so they danced. Simon, attempting stylish, defying the music; Belinda, with increasing extravagance. Towards the end he found it easier to mostly trail her off his left hand as she spun, cleaving the floor like a scythe, the weight of the beaded skirt increasing her inertia.

Simon shortened his arm and she spun in like a magnet. He reeled with the blow and straightened up.

Belinda was giggling. "I'm usually so restrained at these things. Behaved. We may not be invited next year."

Her skirt unravelled from around his legs, allowing him to stand unaided. He spoke, his voice, to his surprise, regretful.

"That would be a pity. I don't know, but I've enjoyed this evening."

She spun away from his raised hand and spiralled in again. She kissed him.

"I said you would. It's just a question of effort, Simon."

She looked at him before she moved away. The look was deep, needing nothing more to say.

forty-three

Simon had settled on a date in early November and a convenient, if obvious, excuse: Guy Fawkes.

Belinda's response was encouraging. "Have you ever had a party here before?"

Simon thought. "No, not as such. Many drunken, very noisy dinner parties, but no party parties." He smiled grimly. "Not if you mean the sort where you greet some of the arrivals wishing they would leave."

"So, not for over twenty years."

"No, I suppose not."

"About time then." Belinda chortled. "I might even meet someone who knew you when you were young – well, younger."

Simon's expected response did not follow. Afraid for his feelings, she put an arm around his neck and kissed him softly on the cheek.

"Never mind. If it all gets too much for you, I can always wheel you around at the end to say goodbye."

She fell back on the sofa, laughing, as he pushed her over and landed heavily alongside.

"Now, now. Remember your age."

"I am," he said, gruffly. "It might be the last time."

She kissed him again, more seriously this time.

"I'd better make an effort then!"

She smothered his reply with her mouth.

Simon kissed her and then leant back, opening his eyes. Something in Belinda's gaze startled him. Then he remembered her convention: use of tongues indicates sex to follow. He smiled and nodded, deliberating between the nearer sofa or the further bed. Belinda had already decided upon the sofa.

Her eyes had a malicious sparkle.

"I've always thought that the ultimate insult to a man would be, 'Are you in yet?'"

Simon grimaced. "That would work." Pausing, he gave a pained smile. "I'll bear it in mind."

Belinda grinned at him, a sweet innocent smile, but made no further comment.

"Thank you," he said.

Eventually he thought of a retort.

"Say the morning after a first night. Smitten. Can't remember the name. 'I love you…thingy!'"

Belinda smiled. "Nowhere near as cruel."

Sex needed selfishness. A taking. Love complicated sex. A caring, a giving, a sharing; the physical expression of an emotional state. More fulfilling, certainly, but viewed as a purely physical animalistic act, less satisfying. And familiarity removed the sometime excitement of strangers. The unpredictability.

Simon much preferred the love. But he recognised the change. Belinda too. Sex beyond the obvious, the widening of reasons. The reassurance, communication, companionship, confirmation, connection. So many functions now.

And making love far exceeded simple sexual responses. One made love with the body and the mind. Copulation only required the body, while the mind, unoccupied, looked on and criticised.

And more, not only multi-functional, somehow multi-dimensional. Reasons and planes.

Simon lay on his side, his eyes open, scanning the sky. His back rested against Belinda's and he could feel her breathing. His mood was curiously contented, a feeling peculiar to him, fulfilment. He followed the transit of a passing aircraft, its navigation lights flashing, a green light on the starboard wingtip, red to port. Hours before he had lost himself within Belinda, almost a suspension.

It was not unique, but it too was rare. In bed, invariably, always the observer. Monitoring, counting orgasms like waves, judging the intensity. It had made him a good mechanic, however clinical. But rarely the surrender.

Sex was about surrender, unconditional giving, the yielding of suspicion, the giving in and the giving to; an ultimate in physical trust, generous and complete. Sex without love was pleasurable, enjoyable, the moment in them all. Sex, with love, transcended, became the ultimate expression that no words could describe.

Simon awoke suddenly. Their arms were still entwined. Belinda lay sleeping to the side of him, her head on his shoulder. The tears ran hotly down his face and dripped from his cheek into her hair. He tried to move but her arm restrained him, and then he realised that she too was awake.

She kissed his shoulder and gently stroked the side of his face. She too began to weep. He felt her tears on the side of his chest and he eased her closer to him, the arms enwound, the legs enwrapped.

Neither of them spoke. They lay together, each with their own thoughts. The grief, the joy, the pain surrounded by the hope.

Belinda lay, a curious smile, utterly relaxed, sliding into sleep. Her back was tucked into Simon's, his left hand stretched back and resting beneath her bottom, his middle finger gently stroking her vulva. Such a delicious feeling. She tried to think of a comparison, but sleep intervened.

Belinda had taken control of breakfast. Simon sat near the table, quietly contemplating the state of his hands, and in particular the middle finger of his right hand. It was stiff, the joints refusing to crack when pulled. It appeared to be faintly swollen.

Belinda enquired and received a reply. She remembered, could still feel the residues of their night before. She began to giggle.

"RSI," she said by way of explanation.

Simon stared at her.

"Repetitive Strain Injury."

"I know what it means."

She laughed more. "RSI from continual clitoral stimulation. Oh joy!"

He laughed with her. "That would be a new one at the doctor's surgery."

She laughed again, sourly. "Alas. More likely, men go to ask where to find it."

forty-four

Simon was working his way through the invitations. He rang one of his pairs of friends, Jack and Jill, who lived, somewhat inevitably, on a hill. Simon and Jack had shared an office thirty years before, had worked on the same jobs, spent extended stays in hotels in the Midlands – their first experience of spending company money. Youthful exuberance. And also, not the least important, played a considerable amount of cricket together. Many an anecdote.

"You're spoiling us, Simon, we only saw you earlier this year," said Jack, answering the phone.

They talked; Jill came in on an extension and a confusing, though entertaining, three-way conversation ensued. During an exchange between Jill and Simon, Jack interrupted.

"Simon, do you remember Angus?"

Simon thought: a vague recollection. "Huge enthusiasm, no real direction, cavalier attitude. Yes, I remember."

"I think that's what he's doing now."

"Doing what?"

"Events."

"Really." From what Simon remembered, it could only be an improvement.

"I've got his number somewhere. I'll ring him if you like, and if he's interested, get him to ring you."

"Sure, it can't do any harm. And it would solve a problem."

November approached and the date for what, despite Belinda's continued reassurance, had in Simon's mind escalated to an alarming indulgence. He recalled the modest bonfire nights of his youth; the 1950s, all their childhoods.

As he understood it, for reasons of maritime distress rockets, and the memories of the war still close, it had been unlawful to discharge fireworks of any kind other than on the fifth of November. Any sailor foolish enough to be afloat in North West London that evening would have been imperilled. Community did not extend to social gatherings in his road. Thus, the individual bonfires in each back garden. The small box of fireworks costing around thirty shillings.

Thruppenny rockets, penny bangers; golden rains, boring. Catherine wheels sometimes spinning, mostly not. And jumping jacks, a zigzag mayhem. Others, old money, impervious.

Him and his mother standing respectfully back as his father, with sole responsibility for ignition, chain-smoked, bad-tempered; much cursing and complaint at the failures. One year, a chance spark had landed in the open box and ignited the lot. They had not been allowed to laugh. Another year, his grandfather, maternal, his favourite, suspected heart attack, left alone, setting off something every ten minutes just to show he was there.

When younger, tightly holding his mother's hand when near the fire. Wrapped in coat and scarf and gloves, and worse, a hat. Coming back into the house when it was over, leaving the fire to his father. Smelling of smoke, burning face, freezing back. His father's coughing in the morning. Avoiding.

Late teens and college when they made their own. Bangers, weed killer and sugar mixes in twists of brown paper with a Jetex fuse. Bombs, loaded with aluminium and magnesium powder, known as pipe bombs now. Casting and coring rocket propellant; unpredictable results. *The Anarchist Cookbook*, banned. A surprise that no one had died. The all-so-innocent sixties.

Simon looked through his list, as ever there was a list, and ticked things off. He thought again of his childhood. For what this was likely to cost, back then he could have bought the little terraced house and its back garden, and its yearly bonfire. Dangerous thing, memory.

To Simon's surprise, his invitations to those left of his old friends had, without exception, been accepted. With Belinda's parents to be installed in the best of the spare bedrooms and a pair of her friends taking the only other with a bed, his guests had the storage rooms: sun beds or otherwise. All were bringing their own kit. House as shed was to become house as tent.

He walked the unused rooms, making allocations, listing. In places the dust had become so thick, it could almost be classified as an archaeological deposit.

Simon seldom looked in mirrors. It was that old double vanity; however he looked, it would always be wonderful. Even when shaving he didn't look at himself, only at what he was doing.

They had been on an outing; Belinda retail therapy combined with exercise by climbing a nearby tor. Cameras had been taken, used. Romantic portraits against skylines lit by a descending sun. Having collected the processed film, Simon viewed the results.

Belinda looked, well, Belinda; as with anything visual, she projected, photographed well. He turned to the images of himself: appalling. The need to cultivate a range of less inane expressions was obvious. As he looked through the remainder of the prints he realised something else. Facially, he was beginning to resemble his mother.

forty-five

Simon sat, overlooking the drive from the French windows, telephone to hand. As expected, Angus had lost his way. Another call, another set of revised directions. Another five minutes and a large four-wheel drive tentatively crunched its way up the gravel.

Angus had changed. The personality was similar, the same almost tiresome enthusiasm, but physically he was very different; older, much less hair, considerably more body. Perhaps that's what four daughters did for you.

Simon greeted him on the steps.

Angus shook his hand warmly. "It must be twenty years," he said.

"I suppose it must be, at least," Simon agreed, leading him into the kitchen. He smiled. "Many changes."

"Hillary sends her regards. You remember Hills?"

"That's kind of her, and yes, I do remember." Hillary, Angus's wife, yes Simon remembered. Horsey, county and loud; somehow typical. Simon's memories were mixed.

After coffee and the inevitable reminiscences, Angus collected his bag from the car and they began to walk the back garden. Simon watched as Angus wandered around, an expensive-looking laser measure in his hand, making notes.

They stood on the rising ground ahead of the copse, looking back towards the house, Angus measuring the distance.

"Two hundred and eleven feet," he said, writing it down.

Simon was impressed. "I must get one of those," he said, more to himself. "It's about a hundred and fifty to the terrace from here," he added.

"A hundred and sixty-six, give or take," corrected Angus.

"Quite."

Simon could feel his patience evaporating.

"If you don't need me for a while, I'll be in the kitchen."

He made more coffee remembering how keen Angus had been to work for him all those years before and how he'd managed to dissuade him. Angus reappeared, setting out a laptop and a printer on the kitchen table. He started making entries.

"Aren't they wonderful, these modern machines." He plugged his phone in. "Instant upload to the PCs back in the office. I couldn't do without them now."

"Likewise," said Simon. He remembered a quote. "'Computers, able to calculate a complete irrelevance to hexadecimal accuracy.'"

Angus laughed. "I remember that. What was his name?"

Simon reminded him, an ex-boss.

"And that old mainframe we thought so powerful. Pathetic really."

"Progress," commented Simon. "You will be able to make exactly the same comment in another twenty years."

As the printer came to life, Simon carried over the fresh coffee. In return he received an annotated plan of the rear garden, full colour. Even to Simon's eye, Angus's spelling had improved.

Angus took the plan back from him and stared at it, making more notes.

"OK. Let's scope this out."

Simon tried not to groan. The phrase reminded him of too many management courses, jargon speak confused for real thought.

"Let's," he said.

"How much?"

Simon shrugged. "I've no feeling for how much these things cost."

"OK. How long? Under a quarter of an hour is hardly worth it, twenty minutes minimum. Thirty, better thirty-five, gives time for lots of variation."

"Thirty-five then."

"OK. Laser light show? Back projections? Music?"

"Music possibly."

"Nothing hung off the house I suppose?"

"Correct."

"Public liability insurance?"

"What about it?"

"Do you have any?"

"Not that I know of."

"No matter, I have one that will cover this."

"That's reassuring."

"Got to in this game. Catering?"

"Taken care of. Belinda is providing her usual company."

"Ah yes, Belinda. I'm looking forward to meeting her."

"People do."

Simon reminded himself of the effort that Angus would save him and weighed it against his growing irritation.

"Third of November?"

Simon nodded.

Angus reached for the laptop. "A Saturday."

"Indeed."

"Sunset's early, of course. So, say around eight o'clock?"

Simon smiled. "You're the expert." His tone did not even convince himself.

Angus looked up at him. It was an odd expression; a mixture of hurt with touches of defiance.

"Perhaps I should leave you in peace."

Angus nodded.

With instructions to call if needed, Simon took himself off to the sitting room. He stood and watched a group of jackdaws bitching over the food trays.

He was being too harsh, and he knew it. People did change; perhaps Angus had found his forte. It could be a disaster otherwise. His mind imagined large explosions, house as bonfire, many casualties. He must ask about extinguishers.

A squirrel appeared and hung upside-down on the nuts. Belinda's approach was to do all the preparation thoroughly, trust people to do their jobs, and then maximise the enjoyment. Simon resolved to be positive, or at least try.

He gave Angus a few more minutes before he rejoined him.

"More coffee, or perhaps you'd prefer something else?" His tone was placating.

Angus smiled at him. "A beer wouldn't go amiss."

Simon nodded. "Good idea. I'll join you." He found glasses, bottles and poured.

"How many people are coming to this extravaganza?"

Simon thought. "I'm not entirely sure, Belinda has the full list. Something over forty at the last count."

"Are you inviting the neighbours?"

Simon grimaced. "Yes, all of them. Though mostly from courtesy. Why do you ask?"

"Depending on the wind, there could be some fall of shot – cardboard, a little plastic."

Simon smiled at the old phrase, once much used. "I can't see them complaining, though I can always have it cleared if there are any problems."

He carried the beers across to the table. An A3 print had appeared and Angus indicated it.

"This is the plan, subject of course, to your approval."

"I'm entirely in your hands, Angus. This is your job after all."

Angus nodded. "For the last twelve years. We haven't killed anybody yet." He laughed. "Though there's always a first time," he added, looking rather directly at Simon.

Simon grinned. "Point taken. So, take me through it."

This time, Simon did not have to try. The ideas were imaginative and equally important, comprehensive. He was truly impressed. The plan showed the back garden from the terrace upwards. A broad matting walkway ran across the top of the terrace, and then headed up diagonally towards the copse, terminating in a broad Y at the top.

Angus indicated the salient features.

"It's basically in three parts. The fireworks, the fire and the food. I've copied the layout of your driveway to minimise the slope. The pyrotechnic pits will be here, back from the top of the terrace, one either side." He indicated the two rectangular blocks. "You will need to build the bonfire here." A circle drawn between the limbs of the Y. "And catering here. A couple of trestle tables and whatever else they need, set up amongst the trees, back from the fire and facing the house. Seating with tables either side of the fire to watch the show. We will set up our master fire control position about here." He indicated a point halfway down the garden, well back from the fireworks. "Low-level lighting all over and external heaters in amongst the seating. I've assumed it will rain. There'll be awning frames on either side of the fire, though we won't roll the coverings over unless we need them."

Simon studied the plan as Angus talked. The control position intrigued him.

"So the ignition is all electrical?"

"Yes, all the initiators are. There are timelines then assorted burn fuses." Angus smiled. "The days of light the blue touch paper and then retire are long gone."

"Do you need electrical power? There's a dedicated ring main out there. The points are on the back wall of the utility rooms."

"I'd noticed those. We may, depends on the lighting setup. We use solar recharge units as standard. Useful backup thought. Either way, three kilowatts will be more than ample."

"How big is your team?"

"For this job, small, just three. Alan, my assistant, Hillary and myself. We'll do the basic setup on Friday, the pyros on Saturday, and strip everything out on Sunday. You remind me. What's the local accommodation like?"

"Hotels and pubs, B&Bs, there's a good selection – though you can always stay here." Simon smiled. "Every other bugger seems to be. Rooms we're not short of, though beds we are. It would be a bit basic."

Angus was surprised. "That's very kind of you."

"Not at all. Seems the obvious suggestion."

"Well yes. Thank you. Hillary will be delighted. The sleeping kit's not a problem. We used to take the girls camping a lot when they were younger. Alan will probably prefer a country pub." Angus gave an embarrassed smile. "Cramps his style otherwise."

"So," said Simon, leaning back from the table holding the remains of his beer. "That only leaves the cost."

"Yes," replied Angus, carefully. "I've done an estimate." He made a few alterations to a sheet of paper and handed it across. "Considering all the circumstances, it's more or less at cost."

It was a four-figure number, less than Simon had feared, though more than he might have hoped. He nodded his acceptance. "Would you like a deposit?"

Angus shook his head. "Not from you, Simon."

They shook hands on the deal.

With Angus gone, Simon walked the back garden armed with the plan. He'd taken a few sheets of A4 with him and positioned them with stones to correspond with Angus's specifics.

He sat on the grass slope within the copse and looked down the garden towards the house. The unnatural white of the paper sheets was easily seen. He had another beer in one hand, his pipe and lighter to the other. He consulted the layout again, comparing. A full pack would arrive from Angus within the week, complete with running order.

Simon thought of Belinda, thought of himself and, more particularly, thought of them as a couple.

As their sort of official launch, this promised to be quite a party.

forty-six

The evening before with Angus and Hillary had been surprisingly entertaining, and more relaxed than Simon had expected. Belinda had enjoyed herself. Mercifully, they'd been left to themselves on the Saturday morning.

As Belinda prepared to leave for The Gallery, Simon re-engaged with the day. He felt slightly hungover, troubled. Something had happened during the night, a conversation with Belinda. It had left him feeling particularly happy, but he couldn't remember why.

He stood by the side of the car waiting to see her off. Belinda gave him a very odd expression, not the first that morning, then she smiled.

"Don't look so worried, Simon, it's going to be fine."

He did his best to look cheery.

"I'll be back soon after four. Remember the caterers are arriving at three."

He nodded. "I have the list."

The caterers duly arrived at the appointed time and began setting up under the trees. Alan meantime had reappeared, looking unnervingly fresh, joining Hillary and Angus on their charge laying.

There was little, or rather nothing, for Simon to do. Standing around making admiring noises somehow didn't seem to contribute. He retreated back to the house to wait.

Their guests began to arrive by mid-afternoon. He knew most of them. An hour of meeting and greeting, sorting out the rooms, reminded Simon never to run a hotel. The constant calls of 'Basil', amusing at first, had begun to grate.

Belinda returned, meeting Jack and Jill on the driveway.

"I found these people outside, Simon, do you know them?"

Her parents arrived, and were introduced to all and sundry. The sitting room was filling up. The caterers had thoughtfully provided mountains of sandwiches and soup for the afternoon. They now monopolised the kitchen. Simon found the sudden influx to The Villa peculiar, its character subtly changed. There was noise and activity quite unlike the normal, and from abnormal places, and he wandered around almost as a guest himself. It was not upsetting, just strange.

After dusk, the neighbours began to drift in. Simon gave up trying to make unnecessary introductions and stood watching for a while. Belinda, as hostess, calm, professional, capable. Clumps of people standing, sitting, noise and bursts of laughter from whichever direction he looked. It was like a good recipe. Just put the ingredients together and leave the rest to physics and chemistry.

He retreated to the roof terrace to take another look at the sky. Some high cloud but no sign of rain. It felt quite warm, considering. Guessing where he was, Belinda had joined him.

"It's organised mayhem down there though everyone seems to be enjoying themselves." She put an arm around him. "How about you?"

They saw Angus waving to them. He lit a match and held it high, pointing to the bonfire. They waved back. It was time to start.

The estimate of thirty-five minutes extended to over an hour. A lull midway for reprovisioning, drink and food, the chilli proving particularly popular. Throughout, Simon busied himself taking photographs. Beyond the obvious, it gave him something to do. And it was, he thought, something they would want mementos of. There was one shot of her parents that might even grace the piano.

The display reached its extravagant finale, Tchaikovsky valiantly accompanying the crackles, bangs and multicoloured patterns in a final defiance of night. The sudden silence brought applause. With the entertainment concluded, some of the neighbours drifted away. There was a gathering around the fire, smoke lingering around the trees, the smell of cordite evocative. More bottles being opened, more food being eaten.

One of Belinda's guests was the builder she used for The Gallery. They were standing to the edge of the garden, talking. Belinda was gesticulating with her arms and pointing, the builder nodding. There was a lot of laughter. Come the spring, the days of pick, spade and basket excavations would be numbered. Recalling his rather pathetic progress, perhaps just as well.

Arms continued to point, sideways and upwards. There would be the question of access; getting a digger up the side of the house would be complicated, though not impossible. Simon thought idly of a crane in the front garden, or failing that, a helicopter. Exciting, but impractical. Bulks of timber laid up the steps to the side of the garage would do.

Belinda's parents were standing back amongst the trees, holding hands. They beckoned Simon over, congratulating him on the display.

"It seemed to go well."

Douglas glanced down towards the fire and the throng.

"Still is."

His tone seemed suddenly to become stern. Had it not been for Eunice, rolling her eyes skyward, Simon would have felt real concern.

"So, young man. I understand from our daughter that you are to visit me within the next few days."

Simon stared at him. "Well yes, if you want me to."

"It is, I believe, the accepted protocol."

"Is it?" Simon blustered, totally confused.

He then realised that both were laughing. Douglas grabbed his hand and shook it, and Eunice gave him a fulsome kiss on the cheek.

"Welcome to the family."

Simon blushed, deeply, and thanked them.

"I think I'd better go and find your daughter."

He found her.

"I think your parents have just congratulated me on our engagement."

"Are you sure that it wasn't commiseration?"

Simon stared at her.

She stared at him back. "Well, you did ask me, and in a moment of weakness, I did say yes."

Suddenly, he remembered. "Last night. Middle of the night. In bed."

She nodded. "The very place."

He took her hands in his. "Will you marry me?"

"Of course."

forty-seven

The rain continued blowing against the window, the rivulets of water swirling momentarily sideways, then upwards. Simon put down the newspaper and looked out at the sky. The day had started sunny; now, what suggested as a passing shower had become a full-scale downpour. He didn't really care for they had nothing planned. It was the Monday afternoon; Belinda's parents, the last of their guests, had left that morning, it was Belinda's day off and they had the house to themselves again.

He repositioned himself at the end of the sofa and re-crossed his legs, disturbing Belinda, who was stretched along it, using him for support. It was their usual position; he at one end, usually at the right, she monopolising the rest, her head and back leaning against his side. Simon derived much comfort from this close proximity; feeling her breathe, conscious of her lightly perfumed smell, the slight movements of her shoulder blades as she turned the pages of the newspaper.

He picked up his paper again and returned to the article he'd been reading. Almost involuntarily, he began to stroke her head with his free hand. It was warm, the hair soft to his touch. She put up a hand and pulled his fingers around to her face, kissed them, and still holding his hand, rested it on her shoulder. They sat, contentedly, stroking each other's fingers.

People he'd grown up with, formed part of the backdrop to his life, had begun to die. The everyday, the obituaries. Rarely a name he did not recognise. Another one gone. War would be like this, only quicker, speeded up. Unlike the life, ageing, threatening to slow down.

Simon hoped for a natural span. Things done, completed; all appetites, desires, abilities depleted. Though ageing brought its own compensations, they were unlikely to be enough. Not enough done, or even yet begun.

Though still some weeks away, reviews of the past year had begun early. There were going to be many. Reassurance sought from any quarter, however unlikely. World-changing event, so often quoted, now become reality.

Even before, as the arbitrary euphoria of the new millennium dissipated into ashes, the country was found as not at peace with itself. There were serious problems, those fundamental, more serious than at any time he could remember. Recent events highlighted them. And, underlying all was the lack of any form of spirituality. Or even the recognition of it.

No one, beyond the transient, appeared happy, fulfilled or remotely content. Hedonism would not be the answer.

As Belinda went through her list for the following day, Simon watched *Newsnight*.

"Bollocks," he said suddenly, with a vehemence which surprised her. "There's no such thing as bad language. It's language. Inappropriate certainly, but not bad. The usage is bad, not the language. The same with bad weather. It's weather. Good or bad effects depending on the circumstances."

Belinda peered at him over the top of her reading glasses and then glanced at the television. Whatever had prompted the outburst had finished.

"Pompous, tiresome, ill-informed and just plain wrong. When I want a moral guardian, I'll ask for one. Meanwhile, piss off."

Before he had a chance to launch into another tirade she gently deflated him.

"Oh, I do love it when you come over all manly!"

He joined her laughter.

"Fuck it," he said, in conclusion.

Her list completed, she poured them a final glass of wine.

"So, what are you going to do tomorrow?"

Simon looked at her but didn't immediately reply.

"I've had this idea," he said, finally.

Belinda raised an eyebrow. "And?"

He smiled. "Not yet, I've got to think about it. Possibly it's a daft idea. I want to see if it works first."

forty-eight

Salvation through effort; it had always been his recurrent theme. This time, perhaps for once, he knew what he was doing. He was hesitant to be happy, but he was certainly happier.

It was a much overworked cliché, soul mate. Like meeting yourself, or rather, those parts of yourself that you liked, most admired, were better than you, had the best of you but somehow improved. How, on optimistic days, you thought yourself to be. Belinda had much of that.

Loving freed a part of his mind, so long unused, latent, now activated. He felt more whole, complete. That he was loved in return only enhanced it. He knew: no one wins, it depends on how you lose. Eventually, it would end in tears. It always did. Failure, most likely, and failing that, death. Tears. Deep, stricken, dreadful. And always, an end.

Simon smiled, oddly, a rueful, self-critical expression. But, the end would not be soon. There was a whole new life yet.

Christmas and New Year were going to be different this year, not the self-imposed festive house arrest. And their birthdays a month later. The new year – there was an expectation, an anticipation. They would marry, at a season and a month not previously used. A late spring perhaps.

Marriage: that needed public statement of a private commitment.

The phone rang as Simon was between floors. He reached one just as the answerphone switched in.

"Simon Kendal. Breathlessly."

"Belinda Barnfather. Breathily."

"Hello, future wife, wellspring of all future happiness, love of life."

She laughed. "You really know how to excite a girl." She paused. "At least, I think that's what I mean."

Simon sat in his office looking out of the window. He leant his elbows on the desk and watched leaves, browning seriously now, leaving trees. He was remembering.

Simon's memory was selective, impressions and moods in preference to actual events. Distillations and distortions, subjectively biased, objectivity inexact.

He did not want to forget the events of the past six months. The meeting, the loving, the commitment to Belinda. The inestimable gain. There would come, he was sure, another time when he would need to remember. And accurately, not through the prism of some future development.

Simon took some sheets of paper and selecting a soft pencil, he began to write.

'Doing nothing wasn't easy. Doing very little was even harder...'

Lightning Source UK Ltd.
Milton Keynes UK
UKHW01f0726030718
325148UK00001B/56/P